COUSINS

By Nancy Genung

Contents

Chapter 1

They stepped out of the ocean covered in droplets like rain on a newly waxed car, their bronze muscular bodies glistening in the hot sun. Chris had an athletic body, six feet two inches tall, and he was handsome, with thick brown hair and big brown eyes. Giuseppe was big, two inches taller than his cousin, with a chest that spanned fifty inches, chestnut hair streaked with blonde, and he somehow managed to maintain a five o'clock shadow. He was a personal trainer who worked at looking good and attracting women. His cousin was obsessed with his flourishing construction business and only went to the gym when he could fit it in.

Christopher grabbed a handful of water and ran past Giuseppe up the beach to his mom, who was reading a book, and let the water pour down her back.

"Christopher Michael Yacenda! Really?"

He grinned at her and sat in another sand chair.

As far back as he could remember, his father and Uncle Mike had rented a big three-story house on Silver Beach for the first two weeks in August. Chris promised his mom he'd keep the tradition going as long as he could. Now he rented the house himself, not allowing his father or uncle to pay for a thing. His father and Uncle Mike had a bunch of siblings—some they talked to, some they didn't. Some of their brothers had passed from unnatural causes. The brothers wanted to keep their immediate family as far away from that life as they could. If that meant John was hard on his son, then so be it. There was no question Chris was going to college. He got his degree in business at Montclair State.

His sister Susanne was sound asleep under one of the umbrellas. She had been driving everyone crazy with her wedding plans. They had a cooler filled with drinks and meatball, bologna, and cheese sandwiches. John reached in, grabbed a sandwich, and took a huge bite. Mike told him to toss him another beer. Annette shot Mike a dirty look. She told them both not to eat too much because she was grilling steak with hot peppers and potatoes later. Her son Giuseppe told her he wanted pasta instead of potatoes.

"If it were up to you, Giuseppe, you would eat pasta with every meal. Tonight, you are having potatoes."

"Come on, Ma, for me? Just a small bowl for your favorite son."

She waved her hand, dismissing him.

A couple of girls strolled past the family, eyeing Chris and Giuseppe. Chris did not notice, but Giuseppe planned to take action. "Nine o'clock," he whispered to his cousin, and nodded to the left. "Blonde, big tits, heading our direction for the fourth time in less than an hour."

As the girl got closer, Giuseppe stood up. He'd developed good timing. He stepped to the side, looked into her eyes, and said, "Oh, excuse me. I didn't see you there. I was just heading to the water. Would you like to join me?"

"Yeah, sure."

The tide was coming in, so the water was getting a little rough, but it was warm for South Jersey.

"I'm Giuseppe, what's your name?"

"Karen."

"Are you a 'bennie' or do you own down here?" Bennies were people who rented houses down the shore.

Karen laughed. "I'm a bennie. How 'bout you?"

"I'm a bennie too."

A wave hit them, and Karen stumbled backward. Giuseppe grabbed her. She landed on him, and he went down.

"Oh my God! Are you okay?"

"I'm fine," he said, smiling. "But now you owe me."

"Oh, really?"

"What'cha doin' tonight?" He dove under the next wave, and when it cleared, he was a few feet away, so he swam back to her.

"I think my friend and I are going to Karma tonight," she said.

"Cool. I'll meet you there around eleven."

"That sounds good."

"Great, see ya later. I gotta get back to the family." He gave her a wink and jogged back up the beach. He sat in a chair, put his sunglasses back on, and looked at Chris. "We're going to Karma tonight." Success and confidence were all over him. Chris laughed and shook his head.

After dinner, the folks were playing cards. Chris took a shower outside, wrapped the towel around his waist, and headed to his bedroom on the third floor. Susanne was blow drying her hair and applying her makeup. Giuseppe was already dressed in a tight pale-yellow Calvin Klein shirt and G-Star jeans, pouring himself a Jack Daniel's and Coke.

"Giuseppe, you look very handsome," Chris' mother said.

"Thanks, Aunt Marie."

"He's gonna kill the ladies down here," his father said. "Look at those fuckin' muscles!"

"Mike!" Annette scolded. "Why do you have to be such a pig?"

"I ain't no pig, Annette. Shut your mouth." He had been drinking Johnny Walker Black on the rocks most of the day. "Yo, Giuseppe, pour your dad another one, would you?" Mike yelled out. Giuseppe looked at his mother and rolled his eyes, then grabbed his father's glass and did as he was told.

Susanne's perfume entered the kitchen before she did. She was dressed to dance, singing the last song she had heard on the radio. "Tell me he's not ready," she said. The parents let out a snicker because Chris was always late. "Really, why isn't he ready? I took my freaking time knowing he takes FOREVER to get ready!" She went to the circular staircase and yelled, "Chris... Come on, for Christ's sake!"

Marie looked at her husband John. "That's your daughter! She's got your mouth." John smiled and winked. Susanne was a daddy's girl who could do no wrong in his eyes. Chris had to work a little harder for his father's approval and love, but he was his mother's baby boy.

He came into the kitchen wearing Rag and Bone jeans with a coral Ted Baker shirt unbuttoned to show off his baby-smooth chest, and his usual Tom Ford cologne.

"Finally," Susanne said.

"Shut up, I'm on vacation!" Chris answered. "Let's go. Who's driving?"

"You'd better drive because I'm hoping to Uber my way home tomorrow morning," Giuseppe said with a wink.

"I told you, Annette," Mike told his wife. "He's going to kill the ladies down here."

Chris grabbed his keys and kissed his mom's cheek. Susanne followed. "Lock the doors and we'll see you in the morning," she said.

Giuseppe just waved. "See ya later."

***

There was a half-hour wait to get in, and the club was jumping by the time they entered. Chris and Susanne pretended they were out together whenever their dates weren't with them. It made things a lot easier. They were both in serious relationships and didn't want to get hit on. Chris handed the bartender $150.00 and said, "Keep the rest. Just take care of the three of us all night."

The bartender smiled. "You got it!"

Giuseppe said, "I'll see you guys later. I gotta go find my big-titted lady." He gestured melon breasts with upturned palms. Chris and Susanne laughed. They were used to his no-respect-for-women attitude.

Susanne leaned into her brother as she sipped her Cosmo. "When is Nicole coming down?"

"I think tomorrow after she finishes in court." For about a year and a half, Chris had been dating a beautiful attorney with blonde hair and stunning brown eyes. She was working her way up the line at the Essex County prosecutor's office and took her job seriously. She wanted to put drug dealers, gang members, and murderers away.

They were both ridiculously diligent workers. Chris started his construction company at the age of twenty-two, right out of college, mostly building residential additions. His business had grown to include office complexes, multi-million-dollar homes, and upscale apartment buildings with a staff of construction workers, plumbers, electricians, attorneys, accountants, and secretaries. He'd come a long way fast, and recently moved into a six-bedroom Colonial-style home he'd built for himself on Ross Road. Until he built that house, he lived just around the corner on Luciana Drive with his parents and his sister. He had hired an interior designer to do the whole house. The first time Nicole saw his place, she thought he was out of her league, but the better she got to know him, the more she realized that he was a special guy.

Susanne yelled over the crowd, "This is Pitbull! I love Pitbull and I love this song! Let's go." She grabbed her brother's arm and pulled him out to the dance floor. He motioned to the bartender to watch their drinks.

Chris and Suzanne loved to dance. They were on their fourth straight song when a guy danced up to them. "You look thirsty," he shouted at Suzanne. "Can I buy you a drink?"

"No, I'm good," she said and moved closer to Chris.

"Okay, then how about dancing with a real man?"

Susanne stopped dead in her tracks and looked the guy square in the eyes. "Fuck off!"

And he did. Chris was ready to step in, but he knew his sister could handle herself. He nodded toward the bar and Susanne followed him. Their seats had been taken, but the bartender pointed to two seats on the other side where fresh drinks were waiting for them. "See what a good tip will do for you," Chris said. "It's always worth it in a place like this."

"Yes it is, yes it is," Susanne said, taking a gulp of her Cosmo.

Giuseppe, who had been dancing and feeding drinks to the big-breasted blonde, was leaning against a pillar locking lips with her, his hand lightly caressing her ass. She spread her legs slightly as he got closer to her pussy from behind. and he felt himself getting hard. She asked him if he wanted to go back to her place. He gulped his drink down and led her to the door.

Karen had rented a house for the week with a few friends. As they walked the three blocks from the bar, she rubbed Giuseppe's forearms, feeling the muscles he worked so hard for. Two of her housemates were watching TV in the living room. She whispered, "This is Giuseppe, and we'll see you in the morning." She grabbed a bottle of wine, and they went to her room. She lit a few candles while Giuseppe poured the wine. He handed her a glass, then gave her a long, lingering kiss. He drew a line of kisses from the side of her neck down to her big breasts. Her nipples were becoming hard and obvious through her bra. She cupped his face in her hands and gently brought his lips back to hers. She rubbed the fly of his tight-fitting jeans. He pulled her blouse over her head and kissed her shoulders as he slowly slid the bra straps down her arms, then unhooked the back, letting it fall to the floor. Finally, her breasts were revealed, and he was a happy man. He unbuttoned his shirt and threw it to the floor as Karen leaned back onto the bed. He kicked off his shoes, crawled onto the bed, took her breasts in his hands, and gently massaged them. She arched her back and reached for him, rubbing him up and down. He began to lick her hard nipples, then kissed her stomach down to her panties. She lifted her butt so he could slip off her shorts. He pulled off his jeans and underwear, then rubbed his hands over her breasts, down her thighs, and back. As he passed between her legs, he entered her with his fingers, a little deeper each time. He was ready. He reached behind him, ripped open his condom, and put it on like a pro. He wanted to feel her wetness, so he slid his finger into her, and she moaned with pleasure. He added a second finger with a little more pressure. Her hips began to rock toward his fingers, then away. He got up on his knees, spread her legs with his body, and slid into her. She grabbed him and moaned. He pulled out and reentered her with the same slow movement. She moved her hands up and down his back as her hips moved toward him. Giuseppe pulled out, but not completely, then pushed back. She rocked with his rhythm. He picked up speed. He was getting close and so was she. His hips were in full motion. Karen grabbed the bedpost, moaning as he pumped in and out, faster and faster. She begged him not to stop. They were covered in sweat. Karen climaxed. Giuseppe waited as long as he could, then let go.

***

Chris woke up to a noise by his door. He pulled the pillow over his head. "What? I'm on vacation."

"Chris, open the door, it's me." He opened one eye, threw off the sheet, and unlocked the door. Beautiful Nicole was standing there with a suitcase in one hand and her sunglasses in the other. "Sorry I woke you, honey, but I wanted to beat the traffic."

"No, no, that's alright. What time is it?"

"Eight-thirty."

"Okay, good, we can go back to sleep." He crawled back into bed and Nicole put her stuff down.

"Yes we can." She kicked off her shoes and jumped on him. "I missed you."

"I missed you too," he said and rolled away from her. She wasn't going to get much more out of him, so she snuggled up and they fell asleep.

A loud crash woke him up again. He jumped over Nicole and ran downstairs. Giuseppe was standing in the kitchen and there was glass all over the floor. "What the fuck happened, Gee?"

"The blender stopped working while I was making my protein shake, so I threw it against the wall."

"What the hell is wrong with you?" Chris headed back to his bedroom. Nicole asked what was going on. "It's just Gee acting like a goddamn baby. I swear, I do not know what the hell is wrong with him. He's had a really short fuse lately. He just threw the blender against the wall because it wasn't working."

"Oh my God! Really?"

"Yeah, he's a crazy man lately, and I have no idea why." Chris climbed over Nicole and lay face down. She rolled toward him. He loved it when she used her fingernails to lightly scratch his back. "Aaaaah, that feels great." He looked at her from the corner of his eye with a big smile on his face. "You better be careful. I haven't seen you for a few days."

"Yeah, I know." She moved her hands over his muscular back and butt.

There was a soft knock at the door.

"Christopher, are you awake?"

"Yeah, Ma, one sec." He turned toward Nicole and said, "Keep that thought," then kissed her as he jumped out of bed, readjusted his boxers, and opened the door.

"I'm sorry to bother you both." She was wringing her hands as she often did when she was nervous. "Annette is downstairs cleaning up the mess Giuseppe made, and she's crying. Yesterday, she told me she was worried about him. She said he hasn't been acting like himself. His mood changes like the wind. One minute he's fine and the next he's throwing things at the wall. She thinks he's on drugs. Do you know anything? Can you help him?"

"Wait, wait, wait, hold on a minute. He's not doing drugs, Ma, I would know. He's always had a temper. I haven't seen him do anything weird. Maybe you and Aunt Annette are blowing this out of proportion."

"I don't know, Christopher. I've never seen him act like this. He threw a blender across the room because it wasn't blending his protein shake quick enough."

Chris had a tough time thinking Gee was on drugs. They were like brothers. They did their share of drinking, but they never tried anything stronger than a joint. When they were kids, they'd made a pact that they'd never let each other get hooked on anything, alcohol included.

"Annette told me that Giuseppe and Uncle Mike recently got into it over something stupid at the dinner table," his mother said. "Giuseppe knocked the tray of pasta off the table and walked away. Uncle Mike went after him, and she had to break it up."

"Really? Wow! He didn't tell me anything about that! Listen, tell Aunt Annette I'll talk to him, but seriously, I don't think he's on drugs. Maybe he's got work problems."

"What work problems?" she asked. "He doesn't have a real job. He works at a gym! Aunt Annette and Uncle Mike give him money all the time. That's what the fight was about. Uncle Mike wants Giuseppe to get a better job. He's not like you, Christopher. Mike's tired of giving his son money all the time. I think he sees how hard you work and that it's paying off for you, and he wants the same for Giuseppe."

"Ma, I'll talk to him. Just tell everyone to calm down and leave him alone." Chris was trying to protect his cousin from more family eruptions. "And why is Aunt Annette cleaning up his mess? That's part of the problem. They don't make him clean up his messes."

Chris opened the door. His mom took the hint and waved to Nicole as she left. Chris leaned on the dresser and stared into the mirror, thinking. Nicole got up and wrapped her arms around his waist.

"I don't know, Nic, I just don't see him doing drugs. But I didn't know he had a fight with his father. We used to talk about everything. Lately, he seems to be moving away from me. He's been hanging with this big dude—I don't even know his name." He turned away from the mirror and held her.

"So, are we on vacation or what?" she asked. "Let's go to the beach!"

"Okay, but I'm starving." He kissed her like he'd really missed her. "You want to go to the diner down the street?"

"Perfect."

Chris went toward the dresser, then playfully pulled off his boxers, exposing his butt cheeks, and Nicole burst out laughing. "You're too much! But I love that ass of yours."

***

Chris' business was a family affair. Susanne managed it, and she'd met her fiancé, Dan, when Chris hired him as a site manager. They'd set a date for the wedding in October. When Dan was getting out of the car that afternoon, she'd jumped on him and wrapped her legs around his waist.

"Suze, you're hurting me."

"I'm so glad you made it," she said, kissing his face all over.

"Okay, okay, okay. I gotta put you down, honey." He gently lowered her to the ground.

John, who had been watching from the steps, said, "I hope you know what you're getting yourself into."

"Hi, Dad," Dan replied, waving. "I think I can manage her."

"Hello! I'm standing right here," Susanne said. "I've been down here for a week without Dan, and I missed him."

"I missed you too."

John laughed. He was glad his daughter had found someone who loved her. He went inside carrying a box of donuts he'd bought at the bakery up the street. One of the great things about renting a house at the beach was that everything was within walking distance.

John and Marie took walks every morning for exercise. John still called her his "bride." And they were still cuddled in front of the TV in the evenings. Chris and Susanne had grown up seeing their parents' loving relationship and joked about how many times a week they had sex.

Chris and Nicole decided to drive down to Atlantic City after dinner. Susanne and Dan wanted to join them, and so did Giuseppe. Chris said he was fine with that, but insisted they take separate cars. He led the way in his bright red Jaguar, and Dan and Susanne followed in their car.

During the hour-long drive, Nicole told Chris about the case she'd argued the day before. He half-listened, thinking about how much he'd missed her. They'd spoken every day on the phone, but it wasn't the same as having her close. He rubbed the soft skin on her thigh below her skirt, looked at her for a second, and said, "I really missed you, Nic."

"Am I talking too much?"

"No, no! I just wanted you to know that. I realized we haven't been apart this long since we started dating."

"I know! But I didn't think you would recognize that."

"Well, I did." Nicole unfastened her seat belt, wrapped her arms around his neck, and kissed his lips quickly, then kissed his neck, his ear, and back to his neck again.

"You'd better put that pretty little ass of yours back in that seat before I crash this car," he said, smiling.

"You're no fun."

"I'm just trying to keep you and me safe, my love! You just wait; I'll show you who's no fun. Craps table, here we come." Chris had taught her how to play, but she often forgot.

Nicole dutifully buckled her seat belt, but she noticed that Chris was getting excited and rubbed between his legs. "You'd better keep your eyes on the road," she teased.

"I *told* you," he said.

She reached over and unzipped his jeans. He popped out of his pants and took his foot off the gas pedal. Nicole pulled a towel from the beach bag in the back seat. This time, he didn't object. Slowly and gently, she began tracing little "O" shapes with her thumb on the tip of his penis while she slowly moved her other hand up and down, feeling him getting longer. Chris had a death grip on the steering wheel. He moved to the slow lane, then the shoulder of the road, and put his foot on the brake as he exploded into the towel. "I love you, Nic," he said.

"I love you too," she said, and they shared a long kiss. He reached into the back seat for a water bottle and took a long swig, then put the car in drive, noticing that Dan's car was no longer in sight anywhere.

Chapter 2

The cousins met at the bar on level one of the Borgata Hotel and Casino. "Where the hell have you two been?" Giuseppe asked. "We're on our second drinks."

"We had to make a pit stop," Chris said.

Nicole ordered a cosmopolitan and Chris a double shot of their best tequila. "Give them another one," he said, pointing at Dan and Susanne, then, pointing at Giuseppe, "He's paying for all of them!"

"Hey, yo," Giuseppe laughed. "I'm not the millionaire here."

Chris and Giuseppe busted each other, tit for tat, having a great time. When the server asked if they'd like anything else, Chris handed her his credit card.

"No, don't take that card," Dan said. "It's no good." He threw his credit card on her tray and handed Chris' back to him. "I got this," he said.

"Okay, thanks," Chris replied. "I appreciate that. Take this for the tip though," and he handed Dan a hundred-dollar bill.

The craps tables were all packed. Chris had Nicole stand by a table, waiting to get in. Giuseppe called to the pit boss, "Hey, chief, can't you get us in there? How much longer do we have to stand here with our thumbs up our asses?"

The pit boss ignored him, but a guy who looked a little drunk said, "Hey, bro, why don't you go find yourself another table to play on?"

Giuseppe stared at the guy. Chris grabbed Giuseppe's arm hard. "Let it go! Just let it go. I don't wanna get kicked out of here. I plan to play for a couple hours. Please, Gee, let it go."

Giuseppe shook him off and nodded. A passing waiter called, "Cocktails, anyone?"

Giuseppe said, "Yeah, right here. I'll have a Jack and Coke. Yo, Chris, you or Nic need another drink?"

A few aisles down, someone called, "SEVEN OUT," which meant all the money on the table was lost and the house won. People around the table were cursing, gathering their chips, and walking away. Chris motioned to Giuseppe, and he moved like a bouncer, spreading the crowd. They were finally at a table, which made Chris incredibly happy. He didn't gamble often, but when he did, he played with big money.

He threw $10,000 on the table along with his player's card. The controller called, "Cash of $10,000." The pit boss took Chris' card and asked for his driver's license. He entered the information in his computer and returned them to him, saying, "Good luck, Mr. Yacenda."

Chris gave Nicole some money, then placed his bet. She liked to watch until she got reacquainted with the game. Five people were placing their bets. The dice was on the table in front of an older gentleman. Nicole knew not to leave her hand dangling in front of her, so she rubbed Chris' back as she watched. The older gentleman rolled the dice, and the number eight came up, making the number each player needed to roll to win. Chris called out his bets and threw money on the table. The stickman collected the dice and handed them back to the old guy to throw. This time, the number nine came up.

The stickman pointed to Chris and told the controller, "Fifteen hundred over here."

Chris waved and said, "No, press it." The controller added chips to those Chris already had on the number nine. The stickman gathered the dice and gave them to the same guy, who threw them.

"Nine...nine...again, nine," the stickman called.

Nicole yelled, "Yes!" and jumped up and down.

The stickman said, "Thirty-six hundred over here," tapping his stick in front of Chris, who grabbed the chips and placed them on the table in front of him.

Nicole was ready to play now and asked Chris to help her.

He told her how to make a few bets. Giuseppe was holding his own. Sometimes he and Nicole sat it out for a while, but Chris was in his glory and kept on playing. The pit boss asked if he needed anything. He said, "Yeah, the cocktail waitress would be good." He turned to Giuseppe, "Have you seen my sister?"

"Want me to take a walk around and look for them?"

"Yeah, that would be great."

"Want me to go too?" Nicole asked.

"No, I don't want you to go anywhere," he said and kissed her hand.

Susanne and Dan came up behind them.

"Where have you been?" Chris asked.

"Gambling! Why, is everything alright?"

"Yeah, I guess. I just hadn't seen either of you, so I sent Giuseppe to do a circle around the casino."

"Eight...the number is eight...winner eight," the stickman called.

"Yes!" Chris shouted. Nicole had won $600, plus $1,750 for the hard eight. Chris won $4,000 plus $950 for the hard eight. Giuseppe won $1,250 and $2,450 for the hard eight. Nicole was yelling and jumping around, clapping her hands with joy.

Chris placed his bets again, but Nicole decided to cash in her chips. Chris looked around for Giuseppe and was horrified to make eye contact with his ex-girlfriend, Michele. After he broke up with her, she'd stalked and tormented him for months. He looked away just as the stickman called, "Seven out!" And all the money he had on the table was gone.

"Dan," he whispered. "Michele is here."

"Oh no! Crazy Michele?"

"Yes, and she just saw me."

"Oh shit. What do you want me to do, man?"

"I don't know."

"*Chris Yacenda*, is that you? What are you doing down here?" Michele screamed as she ran up to him.

"Hey, Michele, how are you?" He stepped back and held up a finger, then turned to the collector and said, "Cash me out. Dan, collect Gee's money for me." He threw a thousand-dollar chip on the table, tipping the stickman, the collector. and the pit boss.

"Thank you, sir," the collector said.

Chris turned around, hoping Michele would be gone, but she moved even closer to him.

"Oh shit!" Susanne said as she returned to the table with Nicole and saw Michele.

"What? What's the matter?" Nicole asked.

"Chris' ex. Crazy Michele has a hold on him."

"What? That crazy bitch is here?" She picked up her pace.

"Yup, that would be the one," Susanne said, but Nicole was already gone.

Nicole placed herself between them, a spike heel positioned carefully on Michele's foot. "Oh, excuse me, I didn't mean to step on you," she said.

"Ouch! You fucking bitch," Michele shouted, and pulled a fist back to swing at her. Dan grabbed Michele's arm and yanked her out of Nicole's face. Chris lifted Nicole off the ground.

"Let's go," he said, and led her away, followed by Dan and Susanne. He swung open the big glass door, and there was Giuseppe with a shady-looking character. "Gee, what the fuck is going on here?" Chris yelled, and the guy ran off.

Giuseppe shoved his hands into his pockets. "Nothing."

"Really? What the fuck is in your pocket?" Chris was all over him.

"Get off me!" Giuseppe yelled and pushed him so hard he landed on his back.

"You fuckin' son of a bitch!" Chris screamed as he got up and went back after Giuseppe. Dan grabbed him under his arms and walked him away. "Dan, let me go! Let me go!"

"No, calm down. The cops are right down the street, and they're heading in our direction."

When the police reached them, they looked at them, but said nothing.

"Where're Nicole and Suze?" Chris asked.

"First," Dan said, letting him go, "are you okay? What the hell was that all about?"

"Tell me you didn't see what I saw."

"I was sticking close to the girls to make sure Michele didn't go after Nicole again."

"When I opened the door, Gee was making a drug deal. The dealer ran when he knew I saw what was happening."

"Maybe he was just buying some weed."

"I don't think so. He's been acting strange lately."

They watched the cops run toward a group of people. Susanne yelled for them to hurry, and they took off running.

"Put the knife down. Put the knife down now!" One of the cops was pointing his gun at two women who were wrestling.

"Drop the weapon! Drop it!"

Michele had a knife to Nicole's throat and was pulling her hair back with the other hand. Dan grabbed Chris by the shoulder, but he broke free and ran. "Michele, let her go!"

"Sir, step back! We got this," the cop said. The other cop hit Michele's leg with his taser, and down she went, dropping the knife and hurling Nicole to the ground.

Chris ran to Nicole. "You okay?"

"Yah, I'm okay, just get me up." One of her heels had broken off her shoe, and blood ran down her knee.

The cops asked if she was okay, and she started to cry. Chris held her tightly, whispering, "I've got you, babe. I've got you now."

He pointed to Michele, who was still on the ground. "Arrest that woman. I have a restraining order against her."

The cops handcuffed her and led her to the police car.

"You guys need to come down to our headquarters," one of them told Chris. He gave him a business card with the address. "Are you sure you're okay, miss?"

"Yes, I'm just a little shook up."

Susanne asked, "Is there anything I can do for you, Nic?"

"No, I'm doing better," she said. "We have to head to the police station, and I'm sure we'll be there awhile."

"You want me to come, since I saw the whole thing?" Susanne asked.

"Yes, I think you'd better come too," Chris said.

After two hours at the police station, they were all too exhausted to drive back to the house, so they went back to the Borgata and Chris checked them into adjoining rooms.

When they were alone, Chris looked into Nicole's eyes. "It's just you and me now. Are you really okay?"

"No," she said and broke down crying.

"Okay, I got you. Let it out."

She cried in his arms until she fell asleep. He headed to the shower, and after a few minutes, she joined him. He felt as if it was his fault this whole event happened. He wanted to make her feel safe and loved, so he gently soaped her body, found the hotel shampoo, and washed her hair, massaged her neck and shoulders. She relaxed in his arms and loved how gentle he was. He stepped out and wrapped her in a big towel, then took another towel for himself.

In bed, he kissed the cut on her knee, pulled the blankets up to her neck, and crawled in beside her as they both fell asleep.

Nicole thought she heard something. She reached for Chris, but he was gone, then she realized his voice had awoken her. He was in the bathroom, talking softly on the phone. She looked at the clock. 10:45. She hadn't slept that late in years. She got out of bed, and her whole body screamed. Her knee was stiff. Her arms felt as though she'd been working out too hard, and her butt was sore. She opened the blinds and the sun streamed in. For a few minutes, she stood at the window, soaking in the sun and watching the waves crash onto the shore. Chris came out of the bathroom and caught her making the sign of the cross. He took her in his arms. "How are you doing?"

"So-so."

"I'm getting increasingly pissed off," he said. "I was just filling my dad in on what went down last night, from Giuseppe to crazy bitch Michele. He said to tell you he's glad you're okay. He also said Giuseppe's car is still in the driveway, and no one there has seen him."

"Didn't he say he was going to Uber back to the house?"

"He did! I have to tell you, he's on his own! I'm done with him!"

"No you're not. You're just mad right now. Give it time. You'll get the answers you're looking for."

"Well, I'm done with him for now anyway. It's all about you. You want to hang here for a few days or go back to the house?"

"Let's get the hell out of here," she said, and they both laughed.

Chapter 3

Giuseppe got out of the taxi looking like he'd been in several fights. His clothes were ripped, a bruise was forming on his cheek, and his eye was almost swollen closed. His father was sitting at the kitchen table when he walked in. "What the hell happened to you?"

"Bad night, Dad."

"I can see that. Are you okay?"

"Yeah, I'm fine. I just need a shower, and then I am getting the fuck out of here. I'm going home."

"Wait," Mike said. grabbing him by the shirt. "Tell me what happened."

"It's fine, I'm fine." He pulled away.

"I'm trying to help you."

"I don't need your help! I don't need anyone's help. I'm fine, I said."

He slammed the bathroom door and turned on the shower.

John and Marie came back from their walk in time to hear the door slam.

"Hey," John asked, "what's going on?"

Mike shook his head and told his brother what had just happened.

John told him about the phone conversation he'd had with Chris that morning.

"I just don't know what to do anymore," Mike said. "I gave that kid everything I have. I don't have anything left. Annette and I supported him in anything he wanted to do. We wanted him to go to college with Christopher. We thought that would be great for him. But no, all he wants to do is work out and screw women. I sat him down so many times, trying to set him on a better path, but he doesn't listen to me. He thinks I'm his endless money pit!"

Annette came in and saw the stricken look on her husband's face. "What is it? Did something happen to my Giuseppe?" She was already crying.

"Dear lord, woman, get a hold of yourself!" Mike shouted. "*Your* son is just fine. He's in the shower. He looks like he was in a fight, and for a change, he got his ass kicked. But that's not what we're talking about."

"What, what, what?" she said and pulled out a chair.

"Chris caught him in some sort of drug deal! Annette, I am *done*! I mean it this time. I'm throwing his ass out of our house. He needs to grow the fuck up and stop acting like a teenager."

"Oh, and who did he learn that from?" Annette snapped.

"Don't go there, lady. I'm warning you, don't fuckin' go there."

Annette caught him cheating on her ten years earlier, and never let him forget it.

"It's none of my business, Annette, but maybe Mike's right this time," John said. "Giuseppe's not a boy anymore. He's twenty-eight years old. We were married and having kids at his age."

"Damn right," Mike said.

"Try talking calmly to him when he comes out of the shower," John said. "And, Annette, you need to support your husband, not Giuseppe. That kid is heading down the wrong path."

When they heard Giuseppe's bedroom door open, John and Marie left to give them some privacy.

Giuseppe came into the kitchen carrying his suitcase.

"Please, have a seat for a second," Mike said. "I need to talk to you."

Annette screamed, "Oh my God! My son, look at my son. Giuseppe, what happened to you?"

"Ma, I'm fine. Relax! I just got into a fight last night."

"With who, a bunch of animals? Did you break your hand? Look at your hand, Giuseppe! Mike, look at his hand."

"Annette, he's fine. Relax! Giuseppe, we just want to talk to you for a second, then you can go," Mike said calmly.

"Can't this wait? This isn't a good day to talk to me."

"Not this time, Giuseppe. You gotta hear what we have to say."

Giuseppe dropped his suitcase. "What?"

"Giuseppe, do you have any idea how much your mom and I love you?"

"Oh geez, this must be serious. Yes, *Daddy*, I love you too."

Mike slammed his fist on the table, making Annette jump and catching Giuseppe off guard. Through clutched teeth, he said, "I was trying to stay calm and talk to you like a man, but since you want to be a fucking asshole, I'll talk to you like one. I am *done* supporting you, giving you money, paying for your car, and putting a roof over your head, I am *done!* I want you to get the fuck out of my house. Get all your shit out of there now. I don't know what's gotten into you or what drugs you're on, but you are not welcome in my house until you straighten your lazy ass out."

"This is Chris' fault," Giuseppe said. "Chris told you I'm doing drugs, right?"

"Shut your fucking mouth. I'm not done talking, and *no*, I haven't even spoken to Chris. You, you did this. This is your fault. Take responsibility for once. You pushed me to the point that I'm throwing my son out. Be out of the house by the time we get home on Saturday. I'm no longer paying for your shit! You have slowly sucked your mother and me dry, and we are done!"

"Ma, you okay with all this?"

"Giuseppe, we can't even talk to you anymore," she said. "You step all over us and just expect us to keep giving. We're truly running out of money. We're having a tough time paying our own bills." Tears were running down her face.

"Fine! Can I go now? I have some moving to do." He picked up his suitcase and left.

Mike went to his wife and held her. "It will be okay, Annette. It's for his own good."

Chris pulled into the driveway just as John and Marie were coming back from the bakery. Nicole stepped out of the car and they both hugged her tightly.

"We're so sorry to hear what happened to you," Marie said. "Are you sure you're okay?"

"I love you guys," she said smiling. "I'm doing much better. Your son took really good care of me."

"I taught him everything he knows," John said, winking at Chris. Susanne and Dan pulled in behind them.

When Susanne saw Annette crying, she asked why.

"Just a little tough love," Mike replied. "We decided to kick Giuseppe out. He has to grow up. We don't know what else to do for him and it's killing us."

Susanne took her aunt in her arms. "You're doing the right thing."

"It's just so hard. He'll always be my boy."

Chris said, "Well, it's about time! I'm sorry if that sounds harsh, but really, he needs to grow up. He's had it too easy."

In their bedroom, Chris asked Nicole, "How about we get the hell out of here and go home? We both have a couple more days off, and we could just hang out by the pool and relax without all these people around."

"Sounds like a great idea. I haven't even had a chance to tell my parents what happened last night. Getting away from everyone and all this Giuseppe drama sounds like a plan."

***

They both had their own cars, so Chris followed Nicole back to his house. She left her car there, and they drove together to visit her parents. Chris felt it was his fault she'd been assaulted, so he wanted to be there when she told them. They found them in their backyard pool. "Hey, Jim," Nicole's mom called, "look who's here! What a pleasant surprise! Thought you two were down the shore."

"We were, Mom, but we decided to come home a day early and hang out by Chris' pool."

"Well, feel free to jump in," she said, splashing water from her raft.

"Maybe later. Can you park that raft at this end of the pool? We need to tell you something." When Nicole finished telling them what had happened, her mother got out of the pool and hugged her, wet bathing suit and all. "Mom, I'm fine! Really! And you're making me wet." Her father hugged her too. "Okay, now I'm soaked," she said, and they all laughed with tears in their eyes.

They had a lot of questions, so Carol asked them to stay for lunch. She dealt with things from behind the stove. Nicole helped her and Chris found cold beer in their backyard fridge.

"Jim," Chris said, "I'm so sorry this happened. It's my fault. I can't tell you how bad I feel."

"It's not your fault," Jim said. "You can't control a crazy person." He patted Chris' back. "You're a good man. I know Nicole doesn't blame you. She's in good hands with you. We worry about her because of her job. She's dealing with some of the worst people. Even if she puts them away, they all have connections." Chris knew he was right; her job was dangerous. The gang members she puts away all have connections on the outside and could take revenge on her.

Since Chris was still in the process of moving in, his house was a mess—boxes and packing peanuts everywhere. Nic tried to help him get organized, but they both worked long hours, so it was taking a while. Although she had her own townhouse in nearby Madison, she stayed at his place a lot.

While she was in the kitchen, bending over to sweep a pile of packing peanuts, Chris came up behind her with a box full of them and couldn't resist dumping it on her. She screamed, then started to laugh. He dropped the box, wrapped her in his arms, and kissed her passionately. "I'd better take that shirt off you, so you can get those peanuts out of your bra," he said.

She smirked and raised her arms so he could pull the shirt over her head. He kissed her lips, her neck. He found a peanut in her bra, bit it, and spit it out. She giggled, and he lifted her onto the center island. He whispered that he loved her, kissing her breasts, gently sucking one nipple, then the other. He moved his hand into her pants, feeling her wetness through her underwear. He kissed her stomach while unbuttoning her shorts, and she helped him pull them off. She lifted her butt as he kissed her thigh.

The sun shining through the window reflected on her tanned skin. She bent her knees, and he pulled her toward him, spreading her legs and kissing her inner thighs. Then he put his hands under her butt and licked her up and down until he found her opening and put his tongue inside as far as he could, then out and in again. She played with his hair as he worked his magic between her legs. He slid a finger inside her, then moved it in and out with increased pressure while licking her. Her breathing was fast, and her moans were getting louder. She reached for him, and he moved up to her face. She held him tightly and climaxed. Catching her breath, she said, "God, you feel so good! I love you, Chris."

"I love you too," he said. He took off his pants and underwear and climbed onto the island. He entered her slowly. She rubbed his back and rocked her hips to his rhythm as he moved in and out of her. They were both breathing hard and moaning. They reached orgasm together.

Afterward, as she lay with her head on his chest, Chris looked around the kitchen. "Didn't you say you were going to help me clean some of this shit up?" She smacked his stomach playfully. "Ouch!" He kissed the top of her head.

***

As Giuseppe drove home in his leased Corvette, he became increasingly angry. How dare his parents throw him out? Who the hell were they to do that to him? Fuck them! He didn't need their shit anyway. Now he could do whatever he liked. No rules. He opened the glove compartment, found his pills, popped two Oxycodone, and swallowed hard. With the music turned up, going ninety miles an hour, he ruminated about what went down in Atlantic City. They were having such a great time until Chris caught him buying Anadrol and Oxy. Of all people! Chris, the boy wonder who did nothing wrong and everything right. Fucking Chris, whom he'd promised not to get hooked on anything.

He was sure Chris had called the cops on him. He'd been hiding because he'd left all his money at the craps table and couldn't pay for the drugs; when he saw cops all over the place, he assumed Chris had called them. He saw them haul crazy Michele away, then Nicole and Chris, Susanne and Dan stood in a circle talking, most likely about him. After they all left, the drug dealer showed up with loaded guns and two additional guys carrying baseball bats. He was still hurting badly.

He pulled into his parents' driveway and sat there for a few minutes, not knowing what to do next. Where was he going to live? He didn't have much money. He decided to go to the gym to see if any of the guys knew about an apartment. The Oxy was kicking in and his ribs weren't hurting as much. At the gym, the guys were hanging out by the juice bar. They took one look at him, and their jaws dropped. "Yo, Gee, what the hell happened to you?"

"Had a little disagreement with a baseball bat," he said, lifting his shirt to show them his bruised ribs.

"Damn, dude, you need anything for pain? You know I got it."

"No, bro, I'm good. But I am looking for a place to crash for a few days until I find a place. I gotta get out of my parents' house. It's cramping my style too much. I want to be out of there by Saturday. You guys know of anything?"

Mario, who owned the gym, said, "I know a guy who runs one of those apartment complexes over in Nutley. He works out here. I'll see what he can do for you."

"Mario, that would be perfect. Thanks," Giuseppe said. "Let me know as soon as possible, all right?"

"I'll call him now." Mario took out his phone and walked away, then came back and told Giuseppe that the guy had a two-bedroom apartment available.

As he got out of his Corvette at typical red-brick apartment complex, a Latino guy looked his car up and down. Giuseppe put the alarm on and went into the office. An older woman was sitting at the desk watching *General Hospital*. She looked away from the TV. "Damn, boy, you're a big one. What the hell happened to you? Did you lose your match last night or something?"

"Yeah, something like that. Hey, listen, I'm looking for Ray. Is he here?"

"He'll be right back. He just went to look at someone's AC. You lookin' for an apartment?"

"Yeah."

"Well, you might as well fill this out. Ray's gonna make you do it anyway." She handed him a clipboard with an application. He winced as he sat down to fill it out.

"Honey, you sure you're okay? Did you have a doctor check you out?"

"No, I'm good, but thanks." He decided to be nice. If he moved in, he'd need her on his side. Just as he was finishing the application, a skinny, clean-shaven Black guy walked in. Giuseppe thought he was a renter, but the guy asked, "You the guy Mario sent?"

"Yes, I am. Are you Ray?"

"No, muscle man, I'm a mind reader," he said, moving his hand around his head for effect. Giuseppe wasn't amused, but he knew he had to bite his tongue. He handed the lady the clipboard, and she passed it to Ray. "Hang on while I take a look at these," he said. "Do you do anything else to earn money besides the gym?"

"No, that's it, but I make decent money there."

"Yeah, I can see that. I didn't know Mario paid that good."

"I do personal training, which pays better than classes."

"I figured that, since you're so beefed up. All right, you wanna see the apartment?"

"Yeah!"

Ray grabbed a set of keys, and they rode his golf cart down the sidewalk to Building D. The apartment was on the first level, freshly painted white. It was an open-plan set up, with a small kitchen flowing into the living room and dining area. The bedrooms were spacious with plenty of closet space. The air conditioner was on and running great. He was beginning to think moving out of his parents' house wasn't such a bad idea.

"It looks good! How soon could I move in?"

"I have to do a credit check back at the office. If it clears, you can move in tonight," Ray said. "Do you have the security deposit?"

"Dude, I don't even know how much it is."

"Oh, I thought Alice filled you in. For a two-bedroom, it is going to be fifteen hundred a month. You pay for electricity, and we pay the gas. Anything else you may want, you pay for. I'll need a two-month security deposit. If nothing is broken when you move out, you get it back."

"Okay, sounds good. I'll have the security deposit and move in tomorrow." The rent was nearly everything he earned in a month. He'd have to figure out how to make a few extra bucks.

"Okay, let's go back to the office and I'll give you the rules and shit."

When they got back to the office, Alice was getting ready to leave for the day. "I did the credit check on Mr. Big here," she said. "It's on your desk. Looks good. I'll see you tomorrow."

Ray sat at the desk to check out the paperwork. Then he lifted his head and said, "Welcome to the Heights. Stop by tomorrow with your security deposit, and I'll give you the keys."

"Thank you, Ray," Giuseppe said, shaking his hand.

On the drive back to the gym, he popped two more Oxycodone. Mario was in his office. "Thanks so much, dude," Giuseppe said. "You helped me out of a bad spot."

"No problem, Gee. You'll be a little closer to the gym. So tell me, how did you get the shit kicked out of you? I thought you were on vacation with your family down the shore."

Giuseppe closed the office door. "I was at the shore. I was at a casino in Atlantic City with my cousins and decided to have a cigar on the boardwalk. I wasn't paying attention to the people around me, and the next thing I knew, a group of guys with fucking baseball bats surrounded me. I guess they thought I had money on me, but I left most of my cash back at the table with my cousin, so I only had about fifty bucks in my pocket, and they wanted more."

"Holy shit!" Mario said. "You're freakin' lucky they didn't have any weapons."

"I know, right? They knocked my legs out from under me then hit me with the bats. I must have a few broken ribs because they're killing me."

"Damn, boy, go home and chill."

"I can't. I got into a fight with my father, and he kicked me out, which is why I was looking for a place. I have to be out by tomorrow before they get back from the shore."

"Gather up the guys and get them to help you."

"That's the plan, boss! I'm going out to the gym to tell them I need their help."

Three trainers were working with their clients, and they all agreed to help. On the way back to his parents' house, he popped another Oxy and loved the feeling. Then it hit him. This was no longer his home. He thought about how his parents had tossed him out, knowing he had nowhere to go, and his mood went from sad to angry. An old family portrait hung on the living room wall. He spit on it. He went into the garage and gathered all the empty boxes he could find. Then he grabbed a can of spray paint from the work bench.

In his bedroom, he began packing his clothes. He took the TV off the wall and wrapped it up. He decided he needed a second TV, so he took his father's new 60-inch off the wall, and in the empty space, spray-painted, "Fuck you, old man!" Then he sprayed himself out of the portrait in the living room. He poured himself a drink from the liquor cabinet and packed up all his favorite bottles. He decided to take anything he might need—tools, soap, shampoo, anything he could think of. When he ran out of boxes, he threw stuff in garbage bags and lined them up by the back door. When the guys got there in the morning, they could grab the boxes and bags and take them to the apartment.

Chapter 4

Two weeks passed, and Chris still hadn't spoken to Giuseppe. He was disgusted when his uncle Mike told him Gee spray-painted the walls when he moved out. He thought if his cousin wanted to talk, he could find him.

He was building the third apartment complex he would own, this one near the Jersey City waterfront. His attorneys had been working on the project for almost a year and a half, negotiating all the permits. In a few days, they'd have a groundbreaking ceremony where the local officials would be photographed with shovels in their hands. The project manager, Alex, was with him in his office, going over the dates when the various phases of the project would be completed. Robin, his assistant, buzzed to tell him that his college buddy, Tony Rinaldi, was on the line.

"Rinaldi!" he bellowed into the phone, "What's up, man? How's NYC treating you?"

"Good, dude, really good."

"When the hell am I going to see you?"

"That's why I'm calling. It's been too damn long, and I'm hoping you and Nicole can come into the city Friday night to have dinner with Lisa and me."

Chris checked his calendar. "Looks like we're in luck. I don't see anything on my calendar. I just have to check with Nicole."

"Okay, great! But I have to warn you. This may be a working dinner."

"What are you talking about?" They'd both majored in business, but Tony had minored in restaurant and hotel management and now ran one of New York's most prestigious Italian restaurants. "What's this working dinner shit?"

"You'll see. Just come with an open mind."

"Oh jeez, you're scaring me."

"It's all good, my brother."

Chris cracked up. "Now that's better. I'll call you after I talk to Nic."

They'd been inseparable in college—studied hard and partied harder. He was looking forward to seeing him. He finished with Alex, then called Nicole.

"Are we free this Friday night to meet Tony and Lisa for dinner in the city?"

"Oh, that sounds great, we haven't seen them in a while. Schedule looks clear, hon."

"Great! He warned me it would be a working dinner, but that's all he would say."

"Maybe he's going to buy a restaurant and wants you to renovate it."

"I hope you're right. He needs to own it and stop working for that mob wannabe guy."

At the end of the day when the office emptied out, he called Susanne to check in. She was putting together a crew for the Jersey City project. He was worried about hiring new people to work on such a big project, but she kept reassuring him. He was always filled with anxiety at the start of a project. "Wanna come to the groundbreaking Friday morning?"

"I'd better stay here and make sure I have all my ducks in a row."

"Tell me we're all good. I really think we need a few experienced people on this."

"Chris, we're fine, and if you come in now and change the guys I scheduled, you're going to mess me up. I got it! This is not my first big project. Please stop freaking out and trust me."

"I got a lot of money riding on this."

"I know. I get it."

"Okay, we've got this. Is Dan around?"

"No, why? Do you need him?"

"I need to talk to him about his bachelor party. I can't believe how close your wedding is, and I can't believe my big sister is getting married."

"I know, right? I'll tell him to give you a call later."

Nicole was getting together with friends that night, so Chris thought he'd take Dan out to talk about his party, and they made a plan to meet for drinks.

Chris pulled his Jaguar F-Type AWD racing red convertible into the parking lot at Brady's. As he walked in, the two hosts looked up from the reservation list. "Hi, Chris, good to see you."

"You too. When Dan gets here, please tell him I'm at the bar."

Brady's was a typical Irish pub with surprisingly good food. It was close to Chris' office and not far from his house. Everyone knew him there, and he liked that.

When Dan joined him, he said he didn't want anything crazy at his bachelor party. Chris offered to fly a group of guys to Las Vegas for a long weekend, but Dan said no. He wanted to do dinner at a great steak restaurant with a cigar bar. Chris said all he needed was the number of guys.

"Have you talked to Giuseppe yet?" Dan asked as he signaled the bartender for a refill.

"No, he can find me if he wants to."

"So what do we do with him and this party?"

"I'll ask my assistant to call him along with the rest of the guys."

***

Two weeks had gone by, and Giuseppe's injuries were healing. His broken rib would take a little longer, but the bruises were fading. His apartment was coming together. He'd set up a bar behind the living room couch and hooked the big TV to a surround-sound kit he bought cheap from a guy who said it "fell off a truck." He was pretty proud of himself.

His mother called every day, but not a word from his father or Chris. He thought by now Chris would have called to iron things out. He still assumed he'd called the cops on him. If his cousin found out how much Oxy and Adderall he was taking, he'd flip. The thing that happened on the boardwalk should have been handled between them, not the cops. Chris' assistant had called inviting him to Dan's bachelor dinner. Fuckin' Chris didn't even have the balls to call him himself. Why didn't he offer to spring for a few nights in Vegas since he's so rich?

He was at the gym's juice bar waiting for his next client and had stashed his pills in the back of his locker. He popped two Oxy and two Adderall and washed them down with a protein shake. He never felt hungry, and had to force himself to drink a shake or two during the day. His client was now thirty minutes late, a high school kid trying to build up his muscles for football season. He called the kid, but it went straight to voicemail, so he decided to rip him a new asshole.

"Yo, Frankie, I'm here at the gym waiting for you and you are thirty minutes late. Where are you, kid? Do you think I have all fuckin' day to sit around waiting for you? I have clients who actually make it here on time. Call me back, you little prick." He slammed his phone on the counter, and it slid across and fell off just as a guy in a suit walked in. The suit bent over, picked up the phone, and placed it on the counter.

"Now, Giuseppe, what did this phone ever do to you?"

"Vinnie, is that you?"

"You bet your sweet ass it is." Giuseppe ran around the bar and wrapped Vinnie in a bear hug.

"Whoa, whoa! Easy on the wardrobe, man."

"Sorry, Vin, it's been too fucking long! How you been?"

"I'm good, Gee, incredibly good! How's the family? And my rich cousin Christopher?"

"Everybody's good. How's everyone by you? Mom and Dad good?"

"Thank God, everyone is good," Vinnie said, making the sign of the cross, then kissed his fingertips. "A little information made it to my ears that you are now living in this part of town."

"Yeah, I moved about two weeks ago. I needed to get out on my own and away from Mom and Pop."

Vinnie laughed. "Yeah, I hear ya! Well, I'm just going to come out and say it, Gee, and you can think about it and let me know within a week." Vinnie's father, Uncle Sal, no longer talked with Giuseppe's father because of his mob ties. Uncle Sal was now the boss, and Vinnie was a captain. "Now that you're not under your father's thumb, I was wondering if you wanted to do a couple jobs for us. Small jobs. I could use someone in this area."

Giuseppe didn't want to insult Vinnie by asking, but he had no idea what "small jobs" were. All his life he'd heard his father and Uncle John talking about that side of the family. Vinnie could see the blank stare in his eyes. "Gee, think about it. No hard feelings if you decide not to help us out. But I want to hear either way by Friday."

"Okay, Vin, let me think about it, but can you tell me what I'd be doing for you?"

Vinnie gave him a dead stare. "Small jobs, Gee, nothing crazy."

"Okay, but, Vin, I need a number to call you at."

Vinnie gave Giuseppe his cell phone number and they shook hands. Then his bodyguard opened the door and Vinnie got into a black Lincoln Town Car.

Giuseppe thought, *What the fuck just happened? How the hell did he know I moved into the area? What could small jobs mean? Collect money? Beat some heads in?*

Mario came out of his office and asked, "Where's your client?"

"He stood me up. I called him and ripped him a new asshole."

"Don't chase the customers away, Gee. We need them in here. Go out and find some new ones."

Giuseppe didn't like hearing that, but didn't reply.

His next client was a married woman in her early forties whom he'd fucked in the parking lot a few times. "Ready for a hard one today?" he asked her.

"As long as it's you who's hard," she said, grabbing his balls.

"There'll be none of that," he said. "Now warm up those muscles on the treadmill."

He thought about Vinnie's offer all through her session. Vinnie had come to him personally, so he must really want him to be part of his team. He needed the money now that he had to pay rent every month. He wished he could talk it over with Chris. Their fights never lasted more than a month, but he hadn't heard from his cousin in six weeks. Maybe it was time he got himself a new family.

When he left the gym, Giuseppe felt lonely, so he decided to buy himself a drink. In the car, he reached into the glove box. He was getting low on both Oxy and Adderall, but he popped two of each and washed them down with a Red Bull energy drink. At the local Italian restaurant, he told the host he was just going to the bar. "Jack and Coke, please," he told the bartender, then realized he'd said "please." He never said "please." Chris said that. He drank it down in one gulp and told her to hit him again and make it all Jack. She filled his glass, then waited, holding the bottle, while he gulped that down too. She poured him one more, then put the bottle down.

"You're new here, aren't you?" she asked.

"Yeah, I'm a personal trainer at Mario's Gym down the road. I moved to the neighborhood to be closer to work."

"Oh, that's cool. Welcome to the neighborhood. I'm Jackie." She offered her hand.

Giuseppe shook it and looked at her for the first time. "Nice to meet you, Jackie. I'm Giuseppe." She was cute.

"Rough day?"

"Yeah, you could say that. It's been a bad month, actually." She left to help another customer, then came back. Giuseppe was watching the TV. He looked around the restaurant and thought it seemed like a nice place. This could be his new hangout. He was starting to forget about Chris. He asked Jackie for one more Jack and Coke. He thought about Vinnie's offer. Maybe at this point in his life, he needed to do something different. The more he thought about working for Vinnie, the better he felt.

Chapter 5

C hris was already in his office at eight in the morning when his assistant came in. "Good morning, Robin," he said. "I'm going to run to Starbucks to grab a coffee. Can I get you one?"

He had a lot of questions, but he didn't want to hit her with them the minute she walked in.

"You never leave once you're here. What's up?"

"I'm glad you asked," he said smiling. "You know me so well. That's why we make a great team."

"Oh boy, now the compliments! This must be big."

"No, not really. But I am going for coffee first, so do you want anything?"

"Sure, a caramel macchiato, and thank you."

"Welcome! Nothing to eat?"

"No, I'm fine, thanks."

Chris returned with the coffee and scrolled through his emails. Still nothing from Giuseppe. It was starting to feel weird. His parents didn't even know where he was living. His mother was going crazy with worry, which made his father crazy, which made Chris' father constantly call him to ask if he'd heard from Giuseppe. Chris was starting to worry about him too. Giuseppe should have reached out to explain what was going on that night on the boardwalk. The next day was Saturday, so he'd have time to track him down.

"Okay, what suits do I have here in the office for this bullshit picture thing?" he asked Robin.

"You have a lightweight black with a pale yellow shirt and tie, or a lightweight blue with a teal shirt and no tie."

"Shoes too?"

She rolled her eyes. "Yes, Chris, you have a pair that goes with either suit."

"Did you just roll your eyes at me?"

"No, not I."

Chris laughed and she smacked him lightly on the arm. "You jerk, you always get me."

"Okay, a couple other things I need. Tonight, Nicole and I are going into the city, and I'll need a driver. Can you tell them to be at my house by six? Let them know it's to go into the city and it may be a late night."

"Okay, anything else? Do you want a car to drive you to this picture thing in Jersey City?"

"No, I'll drive myself there. How are we doing with the responses for Dan's bachelor party? How many do we have so far?"

"You invited thirty people, and they're all coming except one I haven't heard from yet."

"Don't tell me it's Giuseppe."

"Okay, but it's Giuseppe."

"That son of a bitch couldn't even call back. Why wouldn't he come? It's for Dan!"

"I knew you weren't going to like that bit of information."

"Not your fault. Thanks, Robin."

He pulled the blue suit from the closet in his office, changed clothes, and buzzed Alex.

"You looking for me, boss?"

"Yeah, we will drive together to this thing. I want to make sure those politicians see we're a united front and that we don't play games with jerkoffs looking to get their palms greased. Has anyone on any of our job sites mentioned my cousin Giuseppe? That fucker hasn't even responded to Dan's bachelor party invite."

"No, boss, but I'll definitely check around."

"I want to know where the fuck he's living and where I can find him."

"Okay, I'll put the word out right now."

Alex texted guys on various job sites. No one had seen or heard from Giuseppe, so he called a few other people who might have seen him. "Oh, really?" he said, clicking his fingers at Chris to get his attention and gave him a thumbs-up. He put his phone on speaker.

"Yeah, I think it was Wednesday night, I saw him at Mario's. He was working with this good-looking older chick."

"Have you talked to him lately?"

"No, not really. But I heard he's living somewhere in town."

"Where? In Nutley?"

"Yeah, he got an apartment somewhere down there."

"Hey, can you do me a favor? I need to know where he's living exactly. So, can you find out and let me know as soon as possible?"

"Yeah, sure, Alex."

"Listen, I don't want him to know I'm looking for him though."

"Yeah, sure! I'll get back to you later today."

Chris said, "Thanks, Alex. I was getting worried he was dead or somewhere in a gutter."

"No problem, boss. Now let's get this groundbreaking over with."

News reporters and TV cameras were already gathered when Chris and Alex pulled up at the site. A DJ was playing the latest hits, and a security officer was checking cars. Chris rolled down his window.

"Name?"

"Christopher Yacenda and Alex Romano."

"Which one of you is Mr. Yacenda?"

"I am," Chris said.

"Sir, I was told to tell you to drive straight to the police officer, and I'll let him know you're here."

"Okay, thanks."

"Welcome, Mr. Yacenda," the police officer said. "When you're done here, my captain would like to speak to you regarding security at this site." Chris knew that meant he was going to have to pay for a cop to be on the site. He was already paying a twenty-four-hour security company. Alex grabbed his arm to tell him to let it go.

"Okay, Officer, I'll do that," Chris said.

"Thank you, sir. You can drive straight up front. The mayor is already up there."

Chris put his window up again. "Motherfuckers! Everyone wants money from me."

When they got out of the car, they were surrounded by the press. The mayor shook Chris' hand. "Thanks for coming, Mr. Yacenda."

"Thank you, Mayor Cerrato. You know my site manager, Alex Romano." They smiled for the cameras. The TV reporters asked Chris a few questions and he answered, smiling, acting the part. After about an hour, Chris asked the mayor if they could begin the ceremony. "I'm sorry to rush you," he said, "but I have an important meeting at one."

"Sure, let me see what I can do. Please have a drink with me before you leave."

"Depends on what time we get done here," Chris said.

Half an hour later, Alex and Chris were hanging out at the bar of a nearby restaurant with the mayor, the chief of police, and Jersey City department heads, all of them excited about personally profiting from the project.

When they got back to the office, Robin asked how it went.

"Good, and glad it's done," Chris said. Alex went home to take care of his own business. He wanted to make love to his wife while his two boys were still in school. Chris changed clothes and called his father.

"Hi, Dad, I need a little advice."

"Sure, what's up?"

Chris told his father what he knew about Giuseppe and his plan to go to Nutley to talk to him. His father agreed that it was better to show up unexpectedly and talk to his cousin face to face. He was hopeful that the confrontation would start Giuseppe on the road to getting the help he needed.

***

Giuseppe left the gym and called Vinnie. He was nervous, but he figured it was time to make a change and he needed the money.

"Hey, Vin, it's Giuseppe."

"Hey, Giuseppe, what's the word?"

"I've decided to work for you, Vin. Can you tell me a little more about what you need me to do and what time you'll need me, so I can arrange my clients around your schedule?"

"How about you come here tonight, and we'll go over shit," Vinnie said.

"Sure, but I don't know where 'here' is."

"Newark. Across from the ports there's a restaurant called Luigi's. I'll be there eating. Tell Luigi you're there to see me, and someone will show you to the back. Be there at eight."

"Okay, Vin, I'll see you tonight."

Giuseppe's heart was pounding out of his chest when he hung up, and he tried to shake it off. He thought once he knew what he was getting into, his nerves would steady. He was going to show his father that he was a man now and didn't need his shit. He missed his mother, who had been calling him every day. And he couldn't believe he hadn't spoken to

Chris. Never in his entire life had he gone this long without speaking to him, but if that's the way he wanted it, then so be it. Fuck him!

He asked the guys at the gym to join him at the bar. Nick accepted the invitation. He was twenty-five, with degrees in nutrition and sports medicine, and he wasn't nearly as big as Giuseppe, nor as arrogant.

Giuseppe was happy to see Jackie behind the bar again.

"Hey, it's my 'Jack and Coke' guy," she said.

Giuseppe smiled a real smile for the first time in months. "This is Nick from the gym."

Nick ordered a Tito on the rocks, then asked Giuseppe how apartment life was going.

"Pretty good. I like it."

"Good! Have you talked to your cousin yet?"

Giuseppe was hoping he meant Chris. He didn't want anyone to know about Vinnie. "No, we haven't spoken since August. I really don't get it. But if that's how he wants it, I'm moving on and up with my life."

"Then here's to new beginnings." Nick raised his glass and Giuseppe touched it with his. They were more co-workers than friends and made small talk. Nick said he had to get going. He was having dinner with his girlfriend and a few other friends. He threw a twenty on the bar and patted Giuseppe on the back.

Giuseppe had a second drink, then realized it was time to meet Vinnie. The drinks had calmed his nerves.

He arrived in Newark half an hour early, found the restaurant, and went in. The bar was packed, so he decided to let Vinnie know he was there and spoke to the host.

"Wait here," he said. He went to the back room, and a few seconds later returned with two guys who told Giuseppe to follow them. A curtain divided the back room from the main restaurant. Vinnie was eating dinner at a round table with three other guys.

"Giuseppe! Come on in!" he said. "Glad you could make it." He stood up and shook his hand. "Have a seat." Giuseppe sat across from Vinnie and next to a guy in a suit eating linguini with clam sauce. "Pour yourself a glass of wine, Gee," Vinnie said. Giuseppe grabbed the closest bottle. "Victor, take a look at the body on this guy."

"Yah, Vin, he's fuckin' huge."

Giuseppe smiled and took a sip of the wine.

"We're almost done eating, then we'll get down to business, 'kay?"

"Sure, Vin, take your time. I'm early anyway."

The two guys who had escorted Giuseppe to the back were standing on either side of the room. Giuseppe was beginning to realize just how big his cousin Vinnie was in the mob life and was having second thoughts. But he also knew it was too late. He poured himself another glass and sat there silently while they finished their meal. A waiter came to clear the table and returned with three cups of espresso.

Vinnie said, "Okay, let's start this meeting. As you all know, this is my long-lost cousin, Giuseppe. I hadn't seen him or spoken to him in years until just the other day. My father and his father had a falling out an exceedingly long time ago, and let's just keep that there in the past. I think that he might be a good fit in our organization. He will *not* be given any special privileges, and he will have to work like we all worked to prove he can be trusted. Are we good so far?"

"Yah, Vin, I'm good with that," Victor said.

"Yah, I'm good too, Vin," the other guys said.

"Okay, good! Now, Giuseppe, this is not like the movies. You know that we may do a few things that may not be on the up and up, but we run a legitimate import/export business. We get all our drugs directly from Colombia. We'll need you to make a few runs to businesses throughout the state. You'll be picking up items and money and bringing them back to our office across the street at the port. You'll be working with Victor until you get the routine down. Your body size is why you're here. We need someone to put a little fear in certain clients. Nothing crazy, just put fear in their heads, and Victor will show you how it's done. Are you okay with all this so far?"

"Yes, Vin, I'm okay with all this so far." Giuseppe's palms were sweaty.

"Good! Like I told you when I came to see you Monday, nothing crazy, just a few runs to various places around the state. Now, do you two have any questions for Giuseppe?"

Victor said, "No, not at this time. Let's see how he does."

Another other guy said, "No, I'm good, but I just want to reiterate that this is not like on TV. We get guys coming to work for us who think it's like the movies or that HBO show, and we're not like that at all. We're just a bunch of businessmen."

Giuseppe said, "Yes, sir, I got that."

"We'll pay you cash for each run you do, a minimum of five hundred per night."

Giuseppe thought that was good money, but he tried not to show any emotion.

"Most of the runs are done at night, so it shouldn't interfere with the personal training thing you do."

"Okay, great! I'm in," Giuseppe said.

"Okay, good, Gee. Let's see how this goes," Vinnie said. "Let's drink to this venture. Four shots of Black Sambuca, chilled." The guy standing near the curtain went to get the server.

"Salute," Vinnie said, and his toast echoed around the table." Giuseppe shot the Sambuca down. Then Vinnie excused him, saying he'd be in touch. Giuseppe thanked each of the guys and shook their hands.

Back in his car, he felt really good about the way it went. He thought of it as a part-time job to help pay his bills. He kept hearing "nothing crazy." He'd be fine. He popped two Oxy and three Adderall and drove back to Nutley.

****

Chris was looking forward to seeing Tony. When he pulled into his driveway, Nicole's red Mazda Miata was already there. He went to the kitchen, expecting to find her there, but didn't see her anywhere. Then he heard her singing upstairs. "Nic, it's just me." She ran down to greet him.

"Hi, do you want a drink or your iced tea?" she said, wrapping her arms around him and kissing him. Chris lifted her off the ground.

"I could get used to this," he said, looking into her eyes. He'd thought that many times, but never said it before.

She kissed him passionately, then stopped. "Wait, wait, wait," she said, playfully pushing him away. "You could get used to me being here, or me making you a drink?"

He knew she was kidding with him. "Well, you'd have to be here to make me a drink."

"Ooooooh, I see." She unbuttoned her blouse, revealing her lace bra.

"Oh, come on, that's not fair," he said, reaching for her. She jumped behind the kitchen island and removed her blouse. He chased her around, but she didn't let him catch her. "Oh, I'm going to get you," he said,

"Oh, you think so?" she asked, taking a sip of the drink she'd made him.

"Hey, that's for me!" he said as they circled the island.

"I know, but I'm getting thirsty."

"Yeah, me too." He grabbed his drink and took a big gulp. "Oh, I have to say, you make a good drink."

"Yeah, I know. Mine is upstairs." She ran up the stairs and into his bedroom, with Chris right behind her. He lifted her in his arms and swung her around, pretending he was going to throw her on the bed, but he stopped mid-way and gently put her down, bent over, and kissed her breast through her bra, then kissed her lips and crawled onto the bed beside her. Nicole started to unhook his belt so she could feel him through his pants. He unzipped his fly, and she reached for his hardening penis, massaging him as he pulled off her pants and panties. Then he stood up to remove his pants and underwear, got on top of her, and entered her forcefully. She began to rock her hips. She was so wet that he almost slipped out of her, and she wrapped her legs around his ass. "Oh my God," she whispered. He picked up his pace, knowing she was on the edge. "Oh my God! Oh my God!" she screamed as she climaxed, and in a few seconds, so did he. He stayed inside her, staring into her eyes as they caught their breath. "I love you," they said together, then laughed. His phone rang from the pocket of his pants on the floor.

"Oh shit, I don't think I can move," he said with a laugh.

"Well, I know I can't move, so you'd better get it."

"Hello?"

"Hi, Mr. Yacenda. This is Jake, your driver. I just wanted you to know I'm in your driveway whenever you're ready."

"Oh, okay, Jake. We will be out in a few minutes."

They both giggled like schoolkids getting caught making out. Chris grabbed her martini and took a big gulp. "I think I'll make us another one and bring it with us in the shaker," she said, and ran out of the room bare-assed.

Chris shook his head. "Are you going like that?"

"Yeah, maybe I will," she yelled. "How do you think Tony would like my outfit?"

"I think he would love it, but that ass is for my eyes only, girl." He changed into a pair of black Abercrombie and Fitch slacks and a baby blue Loro Piana polo, then found his most comfortable pair of Salvatore Ferragamo loafers.

"Oh my God, I think that's the fastest I ever saw you get dressed," she said.

"We have a car waiting for us, so put your damn pants on, woman."

They made it into the city within fifty minutes, no traffic at all. Chris told the driver they'd be at least two hours, and that he'd call when they were ready to leave. Then he handed him a hundred-dollar bill and told him to find some dinner but no drinks.

Tony and Lisa were waiting for them at the bar. They'd begun dating in college when Tony was a senior and she was a freshman. For the past three years, they'd been living together in the city. Lisa was an OR nurse at Mount Sinai Hospital.

"There he is!" Tony called out. "There's my brother from another mother." The two men bear hugged.

"Damn, Tone, I miss you, man. It's been way too fucking long."

"Yes it has, man. Yes it has."

Nicole gave Lisa a big hug and kiss.

"Let's have a drink first," Tony said. They sat in big, comfortable bar chairs, drinking and talking, until Tony asked, "You guys ready to eat?" and waved at the host.

After dinner, Chris went to the bar to call the driver and tell him they'd be more than two hours. A woman made eye contact with him and winked. He smiled, went back to the table, and wrapped his arms around Nicole. "So, Tony, tell me this idea you have," he said.

"Well, I think it's the right time for me to make the move and open my own restaurant. I have some money saved and things are falling into place. A guy I know told me about a building going up for sale next month in Little Italy. I'm sure it's going to cost a fortune, but at the same time, it has a lot of potential as a huge income maker. Plus, room for my restaurant."

"That sounds great, Tone. I was hoping you'd 'grow a set' and go out on your own," he said with a big smile on his face.

"Shut the fuck up! Not all of us can do as well as you have. So anyway, I'm going to need a few financial backers, and you're the first one I thought of."

"Do you have any numbers yet?"

"No, I wanted to see if you'd be interested first. I don't want to do this alone. I need your expertise."

"I'm in! Whatever you need."

"Really? That was easy."

"Sure, Tony, I'm all for you going out on your own. I know how hard you work, and it's time for you to work for yourself."

"I one hundred percent agree with you, Chris," Lisa said. "It's his time."

"With someone like Lisa behind you, you can't lose," Chris said, winking at her. "Talk to your guy and get me some numbers. I know it's going to be in the millions, but don't let that scare you. It's just a number. If we can do this with just the two of us, that would be awesome. You and I acting like grown-ups instead of juvenile delinquents! Who woulda' thought?"

"It sounds like something you both would enjoy," Nicole said. "A venture together like the old days. Let's toast to that."

"Wahoo!" Tony yelled, getting the attention of everyone in the restaurant. "We should take a ride to Mulberry Street, and I'll show you the building."

Chris looked at Nicole. "Go!" she said. "Lisa and I will wait for you here."

"Let's do it another day," Chris said. "I'll come in one afternoon and we'll get someone to show it to us." He didn't feel like moving after eating that big meal and feeling a little drunk.

"Alright," Tony said, a little disappointed.

In the car on the way home, Nicole leaned on Chris, and he wrapped his arm around her. Her eyes were closed, and one of her breasts was popping out of her shirt. "You've *got* to be kidding me," Nicole said, not opening her eyes but feeling him growing hard beside her.

He laughed.

"Seriously, I'm so tired. It's not going to happen."

"I can't help it! You're just so beautiful."

She sat up and opened her eyes. "That's not going to work either."

They snuggled and fell asleep.

***

They got home around three in the morning, and Chris couldn't fall asleep because he was thinking about seeing Giuseppe. He had no idea what he'd say to him. Something told him his cousin was in trouble, and he'd do whatever it took to get through to him. His alarm went off at ten. He'd planned to get to the gym in Nutley at about eleven-thirty. He felt like he'd barely fallen asleep, but he went downstairs to make coffee. He brought a mug up for Nicole, who was still asleep, and placed it on the bedside table, then did his normal morning rituals—shit, shower, and shave, not necessarily in that order.

When he came out of the bathroom. Nicole was awake and watching TV. He threw on a pair of work jeans and a t-shirt, then sat on the bed to put on his sneakers. Nicole crawled over and wrapped her arms around him. "Good luck with Gee today," she said.

"Thanks, I hope I don't need luck and he'll just listen to me."

"He'll listen to you. He always does."

"I hope so, I really do. I don't even know what I'm going to say to him."

"Just offer to help him. Try not to provoke him or accuse him of being an addict."

"Thanks for the advice. I'm really going to try to keep my cool."

***

Mario saw him as soon as he walked in.

"Hey, Chris, how the hell are you?" He shook his hand and gave him a man shoulder bump. "What brings you to this side of town?"

Chris pointed to Giuseppe, who was working with a teenaged kid.

"He'll be done in about fifteen minutes. Do you want a drink from our juice bar while you wait?"

"Yeah, actually. I'm a bit hungover."

Mario laughed and mixed up a smoothie that would help. Giuseppe noticed and kept looking over at the juice bar. When he finished with his client, he came over. "What are you doing here? Isn't this place beneath you?"

"No, this place is not beneath me. I like Mario's Gym, and I'm here because I think it's about time we talk, don't you?"

"No, not really."

"Really? You don't want to talk to me?"

"That's not what I said. You asked me if I thought it was time we talked, and I said no. If it takes you this long to talk to me after calling the cops on me, then yeah, we don't really need to talk."

Mario took his cue and went back to his office.

"You want to play games here or do you want to talk?" Chris asked. "I never called the cops on you, and I never would."

"Now you're going to lie right to my fuckin' face?"

"Gee, I never called the cops on you."

"You're fuckin' lying to me, and if you weren't my cousin, I'd knock you out right here."

"You know what, Gee? I came down here to help you. To see if there was a way I could get through to you. I wanna help you with whatever you're going through. But you know what... Fuck you." Chris took his keys off the counter and headed to the door.

"If you didn't call the cops, why the fuck were they all around you and searching the boardwalk that night?"

"You still want to knock me out? Me? Did you say those fuckin' words to me? Fuck you, Gee! Find out yourself!" He pushed the door open with such force it slammed closed. Then he got into his truck and peeled out of the lot.

Mario came running out of his office. "What happened, Gee?"

"Fuck him! I don't need him anymore. I made new family connections! I don't need his shit, or my parents' shit! I'm done with them. Vinnie is now my go-to cousin."

"Vinnie? What are you, crazy?" Mario hadn't heard that name in a while. "Vinnie is bad news, bro. Stay away from him! Do yourself a favor and make up with Chris. He's really a good guy, and he came here to straighten things out. What happened?"

"He fuckin' lied to my face, Mario."

"Come on, really? He's not like that. Are you sure you didn't misunderstand something?"

"No, I didn't. Are you calling me stupid?"

"Listen, dude, step back. I'm just trying to help you."

Giuseppe left the gym and paced up and down for a while, then went to his car and popped a handful of pills. When his phone rang, he smiled. "You got good timing, Vin."

"Yeah, I've been told that before. Can you work tonight?"

"Yeah, what do you need me to do?"

"Come to the port at nine and meet up with Victor. He's going to show you the ropes. I just need you to go with him and listen to what he tells you. Got it?"

"Yeah, I got it, and I'll be there at nine."

Giuseppe wasn't feeling the love, but he was starting to feel high, so he really didn't care. He went back inside and found Nick, who was working with a client.

"Can I see you for a sec? Excuse me, kid, I just need one second of his time." He pulled Nick aside. "I need something a little stronger."

"Gee, let go of me. When I finish with this kid, I'll talk to you. Now get yourself together, dude."

Mario had been watching from his office. He'd seen Giuseppe pacing outside.

***

Chris called Nicole from the road. He was talking loudly, rambling.

"Woooo, slow down, Chris, I can't understand you."

"That motherfucker! He didn't want me there and doesn't want my help! He said if I wasn't his cousin, he'd knock me out. I went in calmly and waited for him to finish with his client, and he walked up to me with a major attitude. Then he accused me of calling the cops on him that night in Atlantic City. I told him I would never call the cops on him, and the motherfucker had the balls to tell me I was lying to his face. I told him to fuck himself and walked away before I knocked him out. I am done! Really, what else am I supposed to do?"

"Chris, take a breath! Are you driving like a crazy person?"

"I'm slowing down now. I am so pissed off. Why did I bother?"

"Because you love him, and he needs your help. Maybe he's just not ready to be helped."

"Well, I'm done! He'll have to find someone else to help him."

"Just come home! I'm here trying to put more things away for you."

"Yeah, I'm on my way. I am so pissed! What was I thinking?"

"You were trying to help someone who doesn't want help. You did the right thing. I love you for that."

"I'll see you in about twenty. Love you." He slammed his fist on the dashboard so hard he cracked it, but he didn't care. He pulled into his parents' driveway and went into the house.

"Hi, honey, this is a nice surprise," his mom said. She came toward him but stopped when she saw the angry look on his face. "What's the matter?"

"Where's Dad?"

"He's in the basement."

Chris went downstairs. "Dad, you down here?"

"Yeah, I'm over here by the workbench." John took off his glasses and put down the screwdriver he'd been using. "What's the matter?"

"Dad, I'm fucking done with Giuseppe! I tried, and I feel like a goddamn fool" He paced up and down, shouting the story so loudly, his mother could hear him in the kitchen. Even Susanne could hear him from her room on the second floor, and she came down to find out what was going on.

John said, "Chris, if you didn't care about him, you wouldn't be this pissed off."

Chris did not even hear that. "And he said he was going to knock me out. Really? Let him fucking try! Really, Dad, I'm done with him."

"Okay. Chris, take a breath. You don't have to talk to him."

"And you know what else? He thinks I called the cops on him that night Nicole got attacked. Everything is always about him. He'd better not show up for Dan's bachelor party. I'll fucking kill him."

"You're throwing the party, so he doesn't have to be invited," his father said calmly.

"But we already invited him. How do I uninvite him?"

"You said he didn't respond, so he probably isn't planning on going. Do you want a drink?"

"Yeah." Chris finally lowered his voice. "I gotta call Nic and let her know I'm here. I told her I was coming right home. She'll get worried." His father handed him a glass of Crown Royal as his mother and sister came down the stairs. "Mom, I'm sorry for yelling, but I'm really pissed and done with him. I can't help him."

"You're so mad because you're hurt," she said.

"I'm pissed because of the way he talked to me."

Susanne said, "Fuck him." Everyone looked at her in surprise because she'd summed it up.

"Susanne," their mother said, "that's not nice. We need to help him."

"I know, Ma. But I don't know what else to do," Chris said. "He's not our problem anymore."

"Christopher, he's family."

They heard Nicole come in the front door.

"Down here, Nic," Chris shouted.

"You okay?"

"Yeah, I'm calming down. We're talking about Gee again."

"As I said before," Susanne said, "fuck him! Chris, let's be honest. Maybe he needs to crash before he'll accept help from anyone. Look what he's put Uncle Mike and Aunt Annette through. They've given him everything and he does this to them. They don't deserve this! I truly feel terrible for them all, but I think Giuseppe needs to crash."

John said, "I think I agree with Suze on this one. Giuseppe may have to crash before he accepts help. Now, I hate to say that because that means there's worse stuff to come, and I'm not sure my brother can handle any more problems. I know Annette is at her breaking point. I was praying that when you saw him today, you could make him realize that we all love him. Remember, Giuseppe's not himself right now."

Chris nodded. "You can say that again."

"Your mother and I will concentrate on your aunt and uncle, and you guys just back off Giuseppe for now."

"No argument from me," Chris said, holding out his glass for a refill.

"Marie, can you please call my brother and see if they're going to be home tonight. After dinner we'll go over and let them know what happened today. I think if we leave them out of the loop, they'll feel like we're not doing anything. Do you agree with me, Christopher?"

"Yeah, Dad, totally agree."

"Can I *uninvite* Giuseppe to my wedding?" Suze asked. "I'm starting to worry about him showing up and causing problems."

"After today, Suze, I don't think he would dare show up," Chris said.

"Yeah, let's not throw gas on this fire, Susanne," her father said.

"I'm just thinking out loud, Daddy."

"I'll see if Mike and Annette want to play cards," Marie said, heading upstairs.

Nicole pointed to Chris' drink, and he handed it to her so she could take a sip. "Is there anything I can do?" she asked.

"Just keep this one calm," John said, patting Chris on the shoulder. "You did good, son. Thank you for trying."

"Dad, I feel like shit! I really thought he would listen to me, but he didn't even give me a chance to say anything."

"I know how you feel, but you did a good thing trying to help your cousin. Now forget about it. Take your beautiful girlfriend out to dinner."

Chris pulled Nicole onto his lap. "Good idea, Dad."

"Maybe I'll cook for you. What do you think about that?" Nicole asked.

"Wow!" John said. "If Marie gets a chance to eat out, she definitely doesn't say that."

"I'll meet you back at the house," Chris said. "I'll stop at the butcher and grab some steaks and we'll both cook."

"You two are so damn cute," John said. "Get the hell out of here and enjoy the rest of your day. I love you both."

Chapter 6

When Giuseppe arrived at the port, no one was around. He called out for Victor, but got no answer, so he walked around. He thought it was strange that there was a second parking lot behind the building with three big garage doors leading inside. There were no doors he could knock on, so he pounded on one of the garage doors. The sound echoed throughout the warehouse. After a few minutes, he heard someone inside ask, "Who the fuck is there?"

"Giuseppe! I'm supposed to meet up with Victor here at nine." The garage door opened slowly, squeaking as it rose. An average-looking sixty-year-old guy in jeans and a polo shirt was on the other side. "I'm Victor, come on in." He had a deep, raspy smoker's voice. He closed the garage door and headed to the back office. Giuseppe was unsure what to do, so he just stayed where he was.

"What?" Victor stopped and shouted. "Yo, kid, you comin' or not?"

"Yeah, I wasn't sure what you wanted me to do."

"I'm going to go over a few of the basics and what we're doing tonight. Follow me back to the office so we can sit. I just gotta make a quick call."

The dirty leather chair almost sank to the floor when Giuseppe sat down. "Yeah, watch that chair," Victor said. "Once you're in it, you can't get out. It's a piece of shit and I'm throwing it out next garbage day."

Giuseppe felt like an ass as he got up awkwardly and chose a different chair.

"My bad, I should have warned you about that," Victor said, and they both laughed a little.

"Yeah, it's me. The kid is here now. Do you want me to do our usual Saturday night run?" Victor said into the phone. There was a long pause while he listened to whoever was on the other end. He said, "Yeah," a few times, and then, "Okay, I got it. We're good. Talk to you later."

"Alright, kid. let's talk. We're going to drive around tonight and make a few stops. Some of these places can be nasty. We're supplying some, and others we will be getting payments for their shipment from last week. You got it?"

Giuseppe noticed that Victor never said what they were supplying, but knew better than to ask. "Yeah, I got it, but what exactly am I doing?"

"You're my protection."

"Oh, okay."

"You're a big guy, but just in case, you'd better take this." Victor opened up the desk drawer and pulled out a nine-millimeter handgun. "Do you know how to use this?"

"I've shot a gun, but only at the range."

"I'm not saying we're gonna need it, but take it in case." Victor grabbed another gun for himself. Giuseppe put the gun into his waist band at the small of his back.

They crossed the loading dock to Victor's black Cadillac Escalade. Giuseppe said, "Is it okay if I ask a few questions?"

"Of course, kid, ask away."

"What the hell are we doing?"

He laughed. "Well, kid, we're going to pick up some money from different people who we gave drugs to sell for us. Most of the time, there's no problem, but sometimes they don't have the money, or the right amount of money, which doesn't make our bosses happy. So sometimes we need to make the dude who owes us unhappy We also have to deliver drugs to our dealers without being seen."

Giuseppe said, "Okay, and what do I have to do?"

"For now, kid, you just follow me. I will do all the talking, *at all times*. If someone asks you something, just stare at them, and I'll answer. We're a team now, kid. You watch my back and I watch yours. I'll be teaching you the ropes. Got it?"

"Got it."

Victor held out his fist for a punch, then drove to their first stop in Newark at the corner of Martin Luther King Boulevard and Bright Avenue. He shut the headlights off but kept the car running.

"Alright, kid, we're going into this bar here. It's going to be really dark inside, so the trick is to look at the people sitting around the bar. It'll help get your eyes adjusted. We're walking around the bar to the office on the other side of the room where we're gonna collect money and drop off more drugs at the same time. Remember, no talking to anyone except me. I don't expect any problems here, so everything should be cool. Before we go in, I need to get the drugs out, so you'll be watching my back as I do that. If at any time something seems to be odd or going down wrong, our key word tonight is "cheeseburger." Say you're dying for a cheeseburger, and we get the fuck out of there. You're not only watching for fuckers looking to rob us, but also for the cops."

"Okay, I got it, Victor. Let's do this."

Victor used a remote to open the back of the SUV while Giuseppe stood by looking around. Three huge safes had been custom built into the back of the vehicle, each with a keypad on the front. Victor quickly punched in some numbers. The safe beeped a couple times and opened. He reached in and grabbed a bundle of drugs, put it in the front of his pants and pulled his shirt over it, then closed the safe and the hatch. He locked the car doors with the engine running, and they went into the bar.

Giuseppe did as Victor told him and looked at the people around the bar. His eyes quickly adjusted to the dark. He followed Victor into the office. Two big Black guys were on a couch watching TV, and three more were playing cards at a table. When Victor and Giuseppe entered the room, one of the guys watching TV grabbed a shotgun. Then he realized it was Victor, put the gun down, and went back to watching TV.

"There's my man Victor," one of the guys playing cards said and stood up to shake his hand. "How's it going?"

"Very well, Tyrone."

"I got ya money over here." Tyrone unlocked a desk drawer and handed Victor a thick envelope. Victor counted the money quickly. "So, Victor, who's this big guy with you?"

"He's my new partner."

"What happened to your other guy?"

"What the fuck, Tyrone. You writing a book? I'll take care of my business, you take care of yours. Okay?"

"Yeah, yeah, sure, Victor. I didn't mean nothin'."

"Okay, we're good here." He reached into his pants and handed Tyrone the bag of drugs. "See you in a week."

Giuseppe opened the door for Victor, and they walked through the bar area to the Escalade. Victor hit the remote and the hatch opened. He opened the other safe and put the money in it, then closed the hatch, and they got into the SUV. He looked around, checking for marked and unmarked police cars. He didn't see anything wrong, so he put the lights on and drove away. "That wasn't too bad, kid, for your first stop. Not bad at all."

"Thanks, Victor," Giuseppe said. "Where to next?"

"We have four more stops in Newark like the one we just did. Then we have to go over to Elizabeth and do three stops. The ones in Elizabeth are done on the street, so I won't count the money 'til we get back to the office. The street stops, we need to have our eyes all over the place. Look for cops. Look for people coming at us. Watch for cars coming at us. And watch for trunks opening up. Street stops are a little more dangerous. You gotta have eyes everywhere."

"Okay, Victor, I'll do my best."

"You're doing great, kid. Relax."

When they entered the office of the fourth bar, no one was there. The lights were off, and a soft glow was coming from the computer. As soon as he saw that the lights were off, Victor said, "Boy, I could go for a cheeseburger, how about you?"

Giuseppe backed out of the office with Victor in front of him, put his hand on Victor's shoulder, and pulled out the gun. Once they were outside, Victor slammed the door shut. Giuseppe held the gun by his side and let go of Victor's shoulder. They turned and started to walk toward the car when the door opened, and out walks the guy Victor is looking for.

"Jamal, where the fuck were you?"

"Sorry, Victor, I had to take care of something."

Victor didn't look happy. He followed Jamal back to the office, then stopped at the door, staring at the back of Jamal's head. Jamal went into the office and flipped on the lights. Victor placed his gun against the back of Jamal's head. Giuseppe followed them into the office and closed the door.

"Yo, Victor, no need, man, no need," Jamal yelled with his hands up.

"You know the rules. You wait in this office until I get here, and we do our business," Victor said, not moving the gun.

Jamal kept his hands up and said, "Yo, man, I'm sorry, I'm sorry. It won't happen again."

"It fuckin' better not," Victor said, lowering his gun. "Kid, check the room for other people." Giuseppe checked the room and told Victor it was all clear. Victor counted the money Jamal gave him, handed him a bag of drugs, and turned to leave.

"Yo, Victor. The next time you put a gun to the back of my head, you better blow my brains out, because I'll fuckin' kill ya," Jamal said.

Victor stopped in his tracks and turned around. "Is that a threat? You showing off for my new partner?"

"I ain't showing off for *nobody*. Don't you ever point a gun to the back of my head again."

Giuseppe still had his gun by his side. Victor walked back to Jamal, and Giuseppe closed the office door again. Before he had the door completely closed, Victor had Jamal in a chokehold and held it until Jamal passed out, then dropped him to the floor and kicked him in the face and ribs. Blood dripped from his nose and the corner of his mouth. Victor pulled out a chair and calmly sat, waiting for Jamal to come to. As Jamal's eyes started to open, Victor spit in his face. Jamal tried to get up, but Giuseppe pushed him down with his foot. Calmly, Victor said, "Jamal, I don't want to have any problems with you. We never did, and this is your only warning. If you don't want to continue our business agreement, just let me know. But don't you *ever* talk to me in a disrespectful tone again. Do I make myself clear?"

"Yeah, yeah, I got it," Jamal said softly.

"Kid, make sure he doesn't forget what I said."

Giuseppe kicked Jamal in the ribs like he was kicking a football. Jamal screamed as his ribs cracked.

"See you in a week, Jamal," Victor said.

Back at the Escalade, they repeated the routine, putting the money into safe number two, unlocking the car doors, and driving off. Victor put his fist out to Giuseppe.

"Excellent job, kid, excellent job."

"Thanks, Victor," he said, fist bumping. He was on an adrenaline rush, feeling like he could do anything. He thought back to when Vinnie came to see him at the gym and laughed out loud.

"What's so funny?" Victor asked.

"I gotta tell you, when Vinnie came to see me about working for him, he said I wouldn't be doing anything crazy, just light stuff. Well, if this is the light stuff, I'd hate to see what the fucking heavy stuff entails." They both laughed.

When they got to Elizabeth, Victor said, "Alright, we're almost done for the night, but this is where we'll be meeting with associates right here in the SUV. They'll come to us. I'm gonna pull over here to get the bundles outta the safe so we can make the exchange fast and clean. I'm gonna give you the bundles, and when our associate gives me the money, you hand me one bundle. Got it?"

"Got it! I have to watch for cops and for people coming to fuck with us."

"Exactly, kid, and again, I don't really expect any problems, but ya never know." They were in a dark section of Warinanco Park, and a bunch of people were walking around like it was midday. Three guys were hanging out, smoking cigarettes. One of them got up and walked over to the SUV. Victor rolled the window down and said, "Yo, Dee, how's it goin'?"

"Good, Victor. This is for you, and do you think next week I could get a double shipment?"

"Absolutely," he said as he handed the money to Giuseppe. Giuseppe handed him the bag. "You want double now?"

"Yeah, if you got it."

"I got it right here." He snapped his fingers at Giuseppe, who handed him a second bundle.

"We good here. See you next week." He shook Victor's hand with some cool handshake and went back to the bench.

As they pulled away, Giuseppe was feeling confident, but he was craving his medicine. He thought about all the drugs in the safe, but knew he'd have to wait until he got back to his car. They did the last two stops without problems.

As they drove back to the Newark docks, Victor asked Giuseppe if he was hungry. All he could think about was getting some Oxy, so eating was not in his plans. He told Victor he wasn't.

Back at the office, Giuseppe asked, "Hey, Victor, how the hell do I get in this place? There're no fucking doors."

Victor laughed. "The same way you did tonight! In time, kid, we'll give you a remote to open the doors. But for a while, we need to keep the number of people who have access limited."

"Okay, cool. I get it."

"Do you want to get out of here, or do you want to help me count the money?"

"Do you mind if I head out? I gotta meet up with a friend of mine back in Nutley."

"No, I don't care. You did really great for your first time. Follow me." Victor opened the safe and told Giuseppe to put the gun in it. Then he pulled out a roll of money wrapped in an elastic band. "Vinnie told me to give you five hundred for tonight, but because you handled yourself so well, I'm giving you a little extra." Victor counted out ten one-hundred-dollar bills and handed them to Giuseppe.

"Woo, no shit?" he said.

Victor laughed and told him to get the hell out of there and have some fun. He said either he or Vinnie would call him when they needed him again.

"Sounds great! Call anytime." Giuseppe got into his car and popped two Oxys before he even started the engine. Driving home, he felt great for the first time in months. He decided to go to the Italian restaurant back in Nutley to see that cute bartender. Maybe it was time for him to find a girlfriend. He hadn't thought about a woman in more than a month. He had to change that too.

When he got out of his car, two girls were smoking in the parking lot, watching every step he took. As he got closer, he said, "Hello, ladies," opened the door to the restaurant, and went straight up to the bar. A different bartender was there. He looked around the place, but there was no sign of Jackie. The bartender asked for his order. "Jack and Coke. Is Jackie working tonight?"

"No, she's off. She and Jenny had tickets to see a show in the city."

"Oh, cool. Who's Jenny?"

"The other owner," she said, hesitating. "Her girlfriend."

"Wait. Girlfriend as in *girlfriend*? Did you say, 'other owner'?"

She laughed. "Yeah, girlfriend as in girlfriend, and other owner as in other owner of this place. You're new here, aren't you?"

"Yeah, moved to the Heights a few weeks ago. I work at Mario's Gym as a personal trainer. My name is Giuseppe."

"Nice to meet you, Giuseppe. I'm Dana. Let me ask you something. Do you even know the name of this place?"

He laughed because he didn't.

"It's JJ's. Get it? Jackie and Jenny."

"Oh my God! I feel so stupid! I had no idea. I was in here a few days ago, and Jackie made me feel so comfortable."

"Yeah, that's Jackie. She's such a sweetheart. Jenny is too, but she's more of a boss. She keeps things under control around here."

"Well, thanks for straightening me out."

"Sure, anytime. Want another Jack and Coke?"

"Yeah, why not?"

"Yeah, why not?" she repeated with a wink.

Giuseppe thought about his day, from his fight with Chris to working with Victor. He decided it was time he made his own happiness, time to make a new family, starting with

Victor. It was getting late, and he was tired. He finished his drink and asked Dana for the bill. It came to forty-five dollars. He decided to give her a nice tip, since he'd made some extra money, and threw a hundred-dollar bill on the bar. "Dana, I hope I see you again soon. Thanks again for the info. Have a good night."

"You too, Giuseppe. See you soon."

Chapter 7

Chris and Nicole decided to have lunch with his parents. Chris was much calmer by now, and being around his parents was still his comfort zone. Chris' dad recently retired from working with an insurance company as a "do it all" type of position. He was their top general maintenance/fix-it guy. He could do it all. He had experience in all fields, such as construction, electrical, and plumbing. He was the reason Chris was doing what he was doing. As he grew up, his dad would teach him how to fix and diagnose anything from cars to houses.

After lunch, Chris ran to the butchers and Nicole went to the grocery store. They met back at his house. His back yard was beautiful, with a big patio and a built-in outdoor kitchen. He had a swimming pool with a small waterfall at one end and a small jacuzzi at the other. The two of them decided to go in the pool for a few hours before they cooked dinner. They both had their favorite raft to float around on. They talked for hours about everything—her job, his new apartment complex plans, Giuseppe,

and Suze and Dan's wedding. Chris fell asleep on his raft for about an hour when Nicole woke him up and told him to get out of the sun before he got too tan. She would tease him about having olive oil in his veins, which made him get the best tan.

Chris got out of the pool and went inside to grab his favorite beverage: iced tea. He grabbed Nicole a glass of wine. As he walked back out toward the pool, Nicole was getting out of the water, and boy was she beautiful. He handed her the glass of wine and she was very happy to accept. It turned out to be a relaxing afternoon, which was exactly what he needed after his meeting with Gee this morning. Every time he thought about his cousin, he just couldn't believe where they were now. They thought of each other as brothers, and now he couldn't even have a conversation with him. He was mad, but he was sadder than anything else. He was always able to fix whatever little fight they ever got into, but not this time. He knew that Gee needed help with his anger, but he never thought Gee would ever turn to drugs.

Chris fell asleep again in the shade as Nicole floated around the pool, talking on her cell phone with different friends, getting caught up on things. It was getting close to dinner time, so Nic woke Chris up with a light kiss.

"You better wake up, sleepy. It's almost dinner time."

He woke up and grabbed Nic from behind.

"You want to take a shower with me in the outdoor shower?"

"Oh, now that sounds like fun."

They walked over to the shower attached to the back of his house. Chris put the water on a nice cool but comfortable temperature, and they both took their bathing suits off, got under the water, and made love for the first time in his outdoor shower.

Chapter 8

Chris spent the day of Dan's bachelor party in meetings with his accountant, Stu Rosenberg, and the investors, presenting their quarterly report. The numbers were terrific, but he was careful not to look too ecstatic. The rental properties were generating enough income to pay for the initial costs of the Jersey City project. The investors were elated.

Chris walked them to the elevator, waited for the doors to close, then let out a scream. "WaaaaHooooo! My dreams are coming true!"

"Christopher, you are one courageous, hardworking young man," Stu said. "And you're not afraid to get your hands dirty. You deserve this."

"Thanks, Stu. You ain't' so bad at what you do either." Chris gave him a big bear hug. "I know you're not a hugger, but I am, and damn it, I'm your boss!"

Stu laughed.

"How about a drink?"

"Absolutely, my friend, absolutely!"

Chris kept a bottle of eighteen-year-old Glenmorangie in his desk drawer. They sat in his office, talking. Chris asked Stu when he could give Robin and Susanne raises.

"In January," Stu said.

"Okay, and what about the project managers, field bosses, and their teams?"

"So you want everyone to get a raise? Is that what you're asking me?" Stu laughed.

"Yeah, that's what I'm asking. I want to reward the good workers. Without them, I wouldn't be in this position."

"You don't give yourself enough credit, Chris."

"I just know how to keep my troops happy. I have a project for you. I want to venture into a business with a close friend. I don't have the time to put much into it, but I want the money available so he can get the construction started. I'm going to be a silent partner. This is his project, not mine. I'm basically his banker."

"What type of business are we talking about?"

"Restaurant. I need you to reach out and set up a meeting with him, then come back to me and give me the details. Tony and I go way back, and he deserves a helping hand with this."

"Okay, Chris, I'll get on it first thing Monday morning."

"Great, and thank you in advance for your help. I'll take care of you, Stu."

"You always do, my friend. You always do."

"I got one more thing I need you to help me with, and you're the only one who knows this… I'm thinking of asking Nicole to marry me."

Stu raised his glass. "Mazel tov!"

"Thanks. I'll need money for a ring, and I'm thinking about a prenup. What's your opinion on that?"

"My cousin for the ring, and a prenup is a definite."

"I don't know how to bring that part up to her."

"Chris, a man in your position must protect himself. She'll understand. She's an attorney, right?"

"Yeah."

"I bet she'll bring it up before you even have to."

"Yeah? You think?"

"I really think so. When will you need money for the ring?"

"I'm thinking in a month. Is that okay?"

"Of course. It's your money, my friend."

Robin came into the office. "I hear congratulations are in order."

Chris thought Robin was talking about his plans to ask Nicole to marry him. He hadn't told her yet, so how did she know what he was thinking? He just looked at Robin with a puzzled look on his face.

"I mean about how well things are going around here."

"Oh, oh, yeah! Sorry, my mind went somewhere else."

"Really? I know you better than that Chris. What's going on?"

"Ahh, nothing…" Chris had a big smile on his face.

"Oh, okay! I'll mind my own business."

"I didn't mean it that way."

The look on Robin's face made Chris crumble. "Okay, but you can't say anything."

Robin rolled her eyes. Everything she did for Chris was confidential.

"I'm going to ask Nic to marry me."

"I'm so happy for you! Nicole is a great girl, and you make a great couple. Details, Chris. I want details."

"I can't give you any details yet because I'm just thinking about it. I haven't figured it all out yet."

"Great! I can help with whatever you decide."

"Thanks for the congratulations."

"Just reminding you, your haircut appointment is in thirty minutes."

"Okay, I'll head out now. Do I have clothes in the back for tonight?"

"You're all set."

"You're the best, Robin. Thanks." Chris and Stu finished the last of their drinks and walked out of the office together.

Chris pulled up at the Prestige Salon in his Jaguar. Trish, the owner, was a close friend of Nicole. "Just clean it up for me today," he told her. "I need a hot towel shave also."

"How's my girl doing?" Trish asked.

"She's great. When are we getting together?"

"I don't know. I have to give Nic a call, and we'll set it up."

After he was done at the salon and on his way back to the office, he called Nicole. She didn't answer, so he left a message for her. "Hey, I'm wondering if I'm going to see you before this party tonight. I just left Trish's place, and I'm heading back to the office."

He'd been back at his desk for a few minutes when he looked up and was happily surprised to see Nicole standing at the door. "What are you doing here?"

"I'm here to remind my guy *not* to have too much fun tonight."

"Do you really think I would do anything with those girls?"

"Aha! So girls will be there?"

"Was that a test?"

"Yes, actually it was, and you failed."

He grabbed her waist and pulled her onto his lap. "I failed, huh? Why would I go there when I have the best at home?"

"That's nice."

"I'm not trying to be nice. It's the truth." They were kissing when they heard a soft tap at the door.

"I'm heading home," Robin said. "Your clothes are laid out in the back room, and I have one more thing to tell you... Behave yourself tonight!" Chris rolled his eyes because not only was Nic telling him to behave, so was Robin. "Also, Tony asked if you'd call him when you're on your way into the city. A total of thirty-six guys have been confirmed. They'll be at Dan's house at six-thirty, and the bus is leaving at seven."

"You're the best, Robin. But why is everyone telling me to behave myself?"

"Because we know you."

Nicole and Robin high-fived each other.

Nicole said, "No surprise trips to Las Vegas in the middle of the night."

"Exactly," Robin said. "Have a good time! See you Monday."

"Seriously, hon, please promise me you will not get any crazy ideas in your head and charter a plane and fly away somewhere for the weekend," Nicole said.

"I wouldn't do that."

"Yes you would. When you get drinking and having fun, you get big ideas."

"Yeah, I guess you may be right there. I'll be good, I promise."

"That's what I wanted to hear. Thanks, I love you. By the way, your haircut looks awesome."

"Thanks, but all I did was sit there. Trish did all the work."

"Yeah, she really knows her stuff. I'll call her tonight."

Nicole worked on her phone while he dressed for the party. He sat beside her to put on his shoes. "You are so freaking hot in your business clothes. Come to think about it, you are so freaking hot out of your business clothes." He started to unbutton her blouse, but she stopped him.

"You gotta go to Dan's, and I got dinner plans with Trish."

"You do?"

"Yes, I just made them," she said. "Now, let's go. I'll see you at some point tomorrow morning."

The party was in full swing when Chris got there. When Dan saw him, he shouted, "Hey, the best man finally got here!"

"You know me, I have to be fashionably late."

"Someone get this man a drink."

"Hey, Dad!" His father handed him a glass of champagne. "Is Uncle Mike here?"

"Yeah, he's sitting over there."

Chris walked around saying hi to everyone. The party bus arrived, and they headed to Tony's restaurant in the city, where they'd reserved the private room. Sexy waitresses wearing tight uniforms were holding trays of whiskey and single malt scotch. Servers came in with trays overflowing with shrimp, crab, lobster, and clams on ice. A buffet table offered baked clams, mussels marinara, eggplant rollatini, fried calamari and stuffed mushrooms, freshly made mozzarella, roasted peppers, prosciutto, salami, and sausages. Tony stopped by, and Chris assured him that everything was better than fine.

As the servers were carrying the empty platters away, Chris picked up his glass and hit the rim with a spoon.

"Can I have your attention for just a minute? Grab your drinks so we can toast the poor bastard who's marring my sister." He smiled and winked at Dan. "I want to wish you all the happiness and love two people can find in this lifetime. You have become my brother, my dad's 'other' son, and the only person in this world who can keep my sister quiet. My family welcomes you with open arms. We love you, bro. Congratulations! Now let's eat some more!"

The room erupted in applause, and the guys found their seats at the tables and ordered steaks or lobsters.

Chris had reserved an area at a gentleman's club within walking distance. A few of the older guys, like Chris' dad and uncle, had had enough for one night and went home on the party bus.

At the club, they were ushered into an area with sectional couches separated from the main space with curtains. Dancers were performing at one end of the space, and bars were strategically placed along the walls. The guys were already a little drunk and ready to party. Someone ordered a round of shots.

Chris was at the bar with Dan watching the dancers up close. "Thanks for this great party," Dan said. "Tony did a great job, and your speech really hit home. I love you, bro." They hugged and slapped each other's backs.

Their bar stools spun around, and two women began to lap dance on them, while the other guys in their party yelled and cheered, and Chris and Dan high-fived each other. Dan grabbed the dancer's ass and pulled her into his crotch.

"Would you like a private lap dance?" she asked. "I hear you're single for a limited number of days."

"Yes, I think I would like that." She led him away.

When Dan rejoined the group, Chris noticed that he didn't seem to be enjoying himself. "You okay?"

"Yeah, I'm just drunk. I wanna get out of here. Can you call the bus?"

"Sure, I'll get right on it." Chris rounded up the guys and told them to help get Dan on the bus. One of them, a professional firefighter, carried him over his shoulder. Chris sat beside him to make sure he was okay.

At four in the morning, when the bus pulled up at Dan's house, most of the guys were asleep. The driver announced their arrival and turned on the lights. Dan was snoring loudly. The firefighter carried him into the house and plopped him on his couch. Chris gave the driver a three-hundred-dollar tip, then fell asleep next to Dan on the couch for the night. Some of the other guys also crashed at Dan's because they were too drunk to drive.

Chapter 9

Giuseppe was lying in bed thinking how good he felt about himself. Working for his cousin was going to be great. Then he thought about the cute bartender he'd met the night before. He laughed out loud when he thought about Jackie being a lesbian. He looked at the clock and remembered that he had a client in an hour. He jumped into the shower, dressed, and made himself a protein shake. Before he left, he grabbed his pills and put them in his pocket.

Saturdays were always busy, and the gym was rocking. Giuseppe headed to the back office, turned on his computer, and looked at his schedule. He had an appointment with twin boys, wrestlers at the local high school, then a girl on a weight loss program, and the married woman he'd fooled around with a few times. All the appointments were back to back. When he headed to the gym floor, he saw Mario making himself a juice.

"Hey, Gee, how's it going?"

"Good. Just waiting for my twins. I really need some coffee and I'm trying to figure out if I have enough time to run over to D and D's."

"What time do they start?"

"In five minutes."

"Go. I can set them up."

"Okay, I'll be right back." Giuseppe sprinted across the street. When he got back with his coffee, the twins still hadn't arrived.

Mario asked, "How did it go last night?"

"Good." Giuseppe didn't want to say too much, and luckily, at that moment, the twins came in with their mom.

"Giuseppe, I am so sorry we're late. It's my fault," the mom said.

"No problem. You gave me time to run across the street and grab a coffee."

"That's exactly where I'm going while they're here with you."

"Get your asses on that treadmill" Giuseppe barked. Then he put them through jumping jacks, crab walks, and squats. When they were panting and sweating, he told them to grab a drink, then put them through a circuit with free weights. When he walked them out to the parking lot, their mom was in her SUV on her cell phone. "I really pushed these two today," he told her. "Make sure they drink a lot of water, and they may need an Advil or two."

"Okay, will do! Thanks again for your help, Giuseppe." As he headed back to the gym, she said something about his ass to whoever she was on the phone with, and he looked back to let her know he'd heard her.

Back in the office, he tossed three Adderall and washed them down with what was left of his coffee. He still had five pills in his pocket. When his next client came in, the phone in his pocket was ringing, so he sent her off to warm up on the treadmill. Mario had a strict policy about leaving phones in the office while training, so he shut off the ringer and returned to the office. As he was about to put it on the desk, he saw it was a call from Victor. Just as he was joining his client on the treadmill, she somehow tripped, and as she fell, she knocked over a fifty-pound weight, which landed on her arm. Mario was the first to reach her. She was screaming in pain, and he told her not to move. The instant he removed the weight, her arm blew up like a pillow.

"Don't move, honey, I'm going to call an ambulance," Mario said, taking his phone from his back pocket.

Giuseppe knelt beside her. "Janet, what happened?"

"Where the fuck were you?" Mario barked. "Get outside and guide the medics to her when the ambulance arrives." Within minutes, the EMTs were working on Janet, who was in excruciating pain.

Mario and Giuseppe stood in the parking lot as the ambulance pulled away. "What the fuck?" Mario asked. "I saw the fucking thing happen!"

"Then you saw I forgot I had my phone in my pocket. It rang, and I went to put it in the office. I was only away from her for a second."

"Enough time for her to fucking fall."

"Yeah, but I was right there, Mario. She tripped! Even if I'd been standing there, I wouldn't have been able to do anything."

"You *should* have been standing there!" Mario walked away.

Giuseppe didn't think it was his fault. It had been an accident. He decided to work out some of the anger he was feeling, so he went inside and pumped iron for the rest of

Janet's hour. He went back to the office dripping with sweat and took two more pills, then headed to the shower.

Mario saw him coming out of the shower and waved him over. Giuseppe thought he was going to yell at him again, but Mario said, "What time is your next client?"

"In fifteen minutes."

"Alright, can I see you in the office for a sec?"

Mario closed the office door. "I'm sorry for jumping on you before. I just got nervous when I saw her arm."

"Wow, I wasn't expecting that. I thought you were going to suspend me for having my phone on me while working with a client."

"No, I saw the whole thing. Your phone rang, you grabbed it and went to put it in the office. She tripped and fell. I'm sorry for taking it out on you."

Giuseppe felt much better after hearing that. "Okay, we're good."

"Can you do me a favor and check on Janet at the hospital when you get a break?"

"Yeah, I was going to do that anyway."

"Great, let me know how she is."

After his next client, Giuseppe headed to the hospital.

Janet was lying on a bed, waiting for the results of her x-rays. The hospital had a lot of patients everywhere in beds. He asked the receptionist where he could find Janet and he peaked around the curtain.

"Hey," she said, happy to see him. "I'm sorry that happened."

"Sorry? What are you sorry about?"

"I'm sorry I'm such a klutz."

"Stop it. That's not true. Accidents happen. I'm just making sure you're okay."

"I'm glad they gave me pain medicine. I feel like I've been waiting here forever."

"Let me see if I can find out what's happening." He went to the nurses' station and waited at the empty desk, tapping on the counter. A gorgeous woman carrying a clipboard walked by, and he locked eyes with her. A nurse appeared at the desk. Giuseppe said, "Excuse me, I was hoping you could tell me how much longer it will be until my friend Janet's x-ray results are available."

"Let me check for you."

The gorgeous woman stepped behind the desk. Giuseppe stared at her. Her brown hair was tied up in a bun and her blue eyes sparkled. She smiled, then asked the other nurse what was going on. "Dr. Ross just read the results. I think he's going to put a cast on her arm."

"Oh, okay, great," Giuseppe said and went back to Janet. "I got good news, and I got bad news. Good news, the doctor is coming in just a minute. Bad news, he's putting your arm in a cast."

"Well, that's not shocking news. I figured it was broken."

Dr. Ross came in. "Okay, Janet. Sorry this took so long. You've fractured your arm, so I'm going to align the bone, and then protect it with a cast. First, I'm going to get you more pain meds, and I'll need a nurse to help me."

When he returned, the beautiful nurse was with him.

"Don't worry, Janet, this injection will make your pain disappear. Just look at your friend and it won't hurt. Okay?"

Janet asked Giuseppe, "Can you come closer?"

Giuseppe stepped closer and took her hand. The nurse stood at Janet's shoulder, holding her arm. The doctor pulled it quickly and, with a loud *pop*, straightened it.

"You okay, Janet?" Dr. Ross asked.

"Yes, I'm good and I'm ready."

Giuseppe laughed a little. "It's done, Janet!" The doctor was right. She hadn't felt a thing.

When the cast was completed, the doctor told Giuseppe, "She can't drive for at least twenty-four hours. Can you make sure she gets home?"

"Absolutely. Her car is back at the gym, so I'll get it, and then I'll take her home."

Janet said in a loopy voice, "You're the best, Giuseppe. Thank you so much."

The nurse asked, "Are you one of the trainers at the gym on Broadway?"

"Yes, at Mario's."

"I was thinking of checking out that gym. I'm Lisa, by the way."

Janet said, "Oh, you have to work with Giuseppe. He's the best."

"Yeah, come check us out," Giuseppe said. "I'd love to show you around." He handed her his business card.

When he got back with Janet's car, Lisa was busy with another patient, and Janet was in a wheelchair. Giuseppe drove her home and got her settled on the couch with the remote, water, her cell phone, and a bunch of pillows. He told her to call him if she needed anything and then jogged the two miles back to the gym.

He was feeling a bit sad. Suzanne and Dan's wedding was the next day, but he wouldn't be going. He hadn't spoken to his parents since they'd told him to get out of their house. He'd lost Chris—his whole family, really—over what? He didn't even know anymore.

When he got home, it was getting dark and the apartment was quiet. He poured himself a Jack Daniel's, drank half and refilled the glass, then turned on the TV and checked his phone for messages. Nothing. He clicked around the TV channels. Nothing. He took two more Oxycodone. He knew alcohol enhanced the effect of the pills, so he drank the rest of the scotch in his glass. Tears rolled down his face.

Chapter 10

Susanne and Dan's wedding went off without a hitch. Susanne was beautiful, and Dan was as proud as any man could be. At the reception, Chris danced with his sister and each of her bridesmaids. Annette and Mike were watching from their table when Giuseppe arrived and stood there like he was going to make a speech. Mike saw the fear in his wife's eyes, and his jaw dropped. Susanne saw him and stopped dancing.

Giuseppe was standing at the entrance, dressed in his everyday clothes. Annette started to run to him, but Mike grabbed her arm. Dan grabbed Chris' arm and said, "I'll handle this."

He went to the entrance. "What are you doing here, Gee?"

"I just wanted to stop by and see my loving family."

"Listen, Gee, if you're here to make a scene, you can turn your ass right around and get out. I'm not kidding around. This is my fucking wedding. If you want to have a drink and be cool, I have no problem with that."

"To be honest with you, Dan, I don't really know why I'm here, because I fucking HATE everyone in this room! I just wanted them all to see I'm doing FINE! Actually, better than fine! I found a new fucking family that doesn't turn their back on me or toss me out like a piece of SHIT! Just thought you all should know that my new family is the 'other' side of the family, Vinnie! So..." Giuseppe yelled out for everyone to hear.

Mike walked up to him. "I worked my whole life to stay away from that, and you come here to push it in our faces? Those people are animals."

Dan asked the maître d' to get rid of Giuseppe. Within seconds, five bouncers appeared. As he was being escorted from the room, Giuseppe smiled and pointed at Chris, who started to go after him, but Nicole stepped in front of him and cupped his face in her hands. "Let it go, Chris. This is your sister's wedding." He nodded, took her hand, and led her to the bar. His father, Uncle Mike, and Susanne and Dan joined them.

"The fucking balls on that guy," Susanne said. "To do that at my wedding! I'm sorry, Uncle Mike, but who does he think he is?"

"Suze, I'm so sorry! I feel terrible." Mike had tears in his eyes.

"It's not your fault, Mike," John told his brother. "The boy is making some really bad choices, and he'll have to live with them. You and I decided a long time ago to stay away from that life. Giuseppe's a grown man. You have to let him go."

Susanne said, "Let's not let this ruin the rest of the night."

Everyone in the room was tapping the rims of their glasses with a spoon, demanding that the bride and groom kiss. And they did.

As the band played "The Godfather Waltz," Susanne grabbed Mike's hand. Everyone cleared the floor, leaving it to Susanne and her godfather. He was crying and she was wiping his eyes. The whole room was filled with love. The band picked up the pace with "Luna Mezzo Mare," and the guests made a circle around Susanne and Dan, clapping as the men cut in one by one to dance with her. The reception was getting back on track.

Chris was still at the bar with Nicole and his father. "Dad, what the fuck do you think that pointing at me was all about?"

"I don't know, Christopher. Let it go for tonight. We'll talk about it tomorrow. Order Sambuca for all of us, and I'll get your mom."

Nicole said, "I'm so proud of you! You were the bigger person here tonight. It would have been much worse if you and Giuseppe had gotten into it at your sister's reception."

"I know. You stopped me. I would have reacted without thinking,"

He was kissing her when his parents arrived. "Get a room, you two," his father said with a wink.

"We already have one," Nicole replied, and they laughed. Uncle Mike, Aunt Annette, Susanne, and Dan joined them at the bar.

Susanne yelled, "Were you really going to do a shot of Sambuca without all of us? No way, baby!"

"Line 'em up," Chris said. "To you two. Family is family...until you decide to join the other side." They emptied their glasses, then ran out to the dance floor as the band played "That's Amore." The band's singer sounded just like Dean Martin.

Chris whispered in Nicole's ear that he needed to sit down. She nodded and continued to dance with the other guests on the floor. He plopped into a chair, watching her; drunk as he was, he wanted to rip off her dress. Two songs later, when Nicole danced over to him, he had his legs up on another chair, his tie off, and his shirt buttons open to the middle of his chest.

"You okay?"

"Yeah, I'm good. Just a little drunk."

"Just a little?" She leaned over and kissed him.

"You wanna be the next ones to get married?" There it was, his big secret. As soon as he said the words, he wished he hadn't opened his big mouth. That wasn't the way he wanted to propose. If he could, he would have kicked his own ass, but he knew he would just fall over if he tried to get up.

"Boy, you are drunk!" She laughed and gave him another kiss. "You stay here. They're about to cut the cake. I'll get you a piece and some coffee."

John sat down beside him. "Dad, please make sure he doesn't fall off that chair," Nicole said.

"Okay, I got him." He slapped his son on the back and Chris almost hit the floor. "Damn, boy," his father said, and they both laughed.

The night was coming to a close. Susanne and Dan were about to head to the honeymoon suite. Most of the family had reserved rooms at the hotel so they wouldn't have to drive. Susanne surprised Chris with a kiss. "Thank you to the best brother in the world."

"Oh, you must have gotten my gift."

"You shithead, no! I haven't opened my gifts yet! I was thanking you for not going after Giuseppe and letting Dan handle that bullshit. But since you mentioned it, how much did you give me?"

"Four hundred, to cover Nicole and my dinners," he joked. "Go enjoy your wedding night. Nicole and I are heading to the room. I think I may need a little sleep."

"You think?" his father asked.

Chapter 11

Chris woke up around ten and reached for a bottle of water. When he sat up, the room was spinning, and his head felt like a sledgehammer had fallen from the ceiling and hit him between the eyes. Nicole was coming out of the bathroom, putting on her earrings, dressed and ready to go. She asked him how he was feeling. "Not good! I think I'm still drunk."

She laughed and handed him a bottle of Tylenol. "We're meeting everyone for breakfast at ten-thirty. I knew you wouldn't make it, so I figured I'd represent us."

Chris fell back on the pillows.

"Go back to sleep, maybe you'll feel better later." She pulled the covers up to his shoulders and kissed him.

The family were assembled in a private dining room. John was carrying a plate of scrambled eggs. "Where's my son? Hungover?" he asked, smiling.

"He told me he's still drunk, so I think he has a way to go before he gets up."

"His loss. Marie and I saved you a seat. Follow me." He led her to a seat opposite Dan and Susanne, who were in a hurry because they were catching a plane to Italy. The honeymoon was Chris' gift, along with ten thousand dollars in cash.

Susanne gently kicked Nicole under the table to get her attention. "Is Chris going to behave himself about that Giuseppe thing?"

"I hope so," Nicole said. "I have to be honest, I just don't get it. This feud Giuseppe is creating is getting crazy. It doesn't make sense. What are they fighting about in the first place?"

"Chris isn't doing anything," Susanne said. "It's Giuseppe. He has it in his mind that Chris called the cops on him. He's doing drugs, and he knows Chris is really against that. He's messed up in the head, and I feel bad for Chris because Giuseppe was like a brother to him."

The hotel manager appeared. "*Scusate m* , Ms. Susanne. There is a problem. I must speak now to Mr. Yacenda," he said in a heavy Italian accent.

"What's wrong?"

"We called his room, but there is no answer."

"Which Mr. Yacenda are you talking about?" Susanne asked. "My dad or my brother?"

"I am looking for Chris."

"He should be upstairs in the room sleeping," Nicole said. "I just left him there. Maybe he shut the phone off. What's the problem?"

"Is his car," the manager said.

"Oh boy, did someone hit his Jag?"

"Aaaaa, no, I must speak to Mr. Christopher Yacenda."

John overheard the conversation and joined them. "I'm Chris' father. What's going on with his car?"

"*Scusate, signore.*" The manager put a hand on John's shoulder and walked him away from the other guests. "Mr. Yacenda's car was in the protected area, but somehow, some-one... The sunroof was broken, and someone..."

Susanne, who had been watching them, came over and asked, "Dad, what is it? Is everything okay?"

"Honey, don't you have a plane to catch? Everything is fine here. It's just a little damage to Chris' car. Not a big deal. You go and catch that plane and have a great time, my sweet daughter." He kissed her forehead. "I'll take care of Chris' car."

"Dad, you sure everything is alright?"

"Sure, it's all good. Now go find your husband and get the hell out of here."

"Okay, Dad. Love you. I'm going to go say goodbye to everyone." Susanne gave Nicole a big hug and kiss and went off to find Dan. John beckoned Nicole to follow him to the parking lot with the manager.

"What's going on?" Nicole demanded.

"Someone broke Chris' sunroof."

When they saw his car, they both clapped their hands over their mouths. There were footprints on the hood. The sunroof was shattered, and glass was all over. An empty five-gallon bucket had been turned over and shoved through the broken sunroof. It smelled awful. The leather upholstery was covered in feces, and a layer of shit covered the paperwork Chris had left in the back seat. On the driver's side door, the word "family" had been spray-painted in red, and red question marks were all around the exterior.

Nicole broke out of shock, and her attorney side took over. She began taking photos with her phone and asked the manager if he'd called the police yet.

"I wanted to first tell Mr. Yacenda."

"I'm not sure Mr. Yacenda can handle this right now," she said.

"Giuseppe," John said. "He did this."

"I have to agree with you. I'm gonna go wake Chris."

When she got to their room, Chris was snoring lightly. She sat on the edge of the bed and slowly rubbed his back to wake him. "How do you feel, honey? Any better?"

"I'm not sure because I'm not awake. What time is it?" he asked, stretching.

"It's eleven-thirty."

"Did you eat breakfast?"

"No, not exactly. I didn't have a chance."

"Why?"

"The manager came to our table and said he needed to speak to you about your car."

"Did someone hit my car?"

"Someone did some damage to it."

"Did someone break into my car?"

"Not exactly."

"What is it? What's up with my car, Nic?"

"This is hard, but here goes." She took a deep breath and told him.

"Did you say 'SHIT'?"

"Chris, it's bad! *Really* bad."

He jumped out of bed, grabbed his head, and waited for the room to stop spinning, then threw on his jeans and sneakers. "Let's go."

In the elevator, he said, "Seriously, fuckin' Giuseppe did this. You know that, right?"

"I think so too. The manager hasn't called the police yet, but..."

"Not sure I want to involve the police."

The manager and John were waiting for Chris. He walked around and around the car. "I'm going to kill him," he said.

"No you're not. It's just a car and it can be replaced," his father said.

"Fuck that, I'm going to kill him," Chris repeated. "That motherfucker destroyed my $150,000 car! Who throws shit in someone's car? Who does that? He needs to be taught a lesson, and I'm going to be the teacher. He thinks he's all gangster. Look at my car, Dad! Look!"

"I know, Chris. Let's call the cops and get this whole thing documented."

"Not sure I want the cops involved. I want to handle this on my own."

"That's not a good idea. We really should call the police, plus you're going to need a report for the insurance company."

The manager said he was obligated to call the police.

"Fine, call them."

When the police arrived, John did most of the talking because Chris was too angry to do more than answer their questions. When the officer asked if they had any idea who might have done this, Chris said, "Yes, I know exactly who did this. His name is Giuseppe Yacenda, and he lives in Nutley somewhere. He works at Mario's Gym, also in Nutley. You can find the son of bitch at work, or they can tell you where he lives."

"Okay," the officer said. "Are there surveillance cameras here?"

The manager said he'd burn a copy of the video for the police. Nicole gave him her card and asked when they could pick up a copy of the report.

Chris was walking toward the hotel entrance. She called for him to wait, but he ignored her, so she ran to catch up. "Chris, please slow down. Where are you going?"

"Just give me a few minutes to myself. Please, leave me alone right now."

She stopped in her tracks, turned, and went back to the dining room where the family was finishing breakfast. She filled a plate with fruit and sat beside Marie. John was already there, telling her what had happened.

Marie could see that Nicole was upset. She leaned over and put her arm around her. "What's up, Nicole?" she whispered. "I see it all over your face. I know how Chris gets when he's angry. Come on, what happened?"

"Nothing, really. It's fine. He's upset about his car, and I understand that."

"But..."

"He told me to give him some space. He hurt my feelings a little, but I'll be fine."

John nudged Marie's arm and gave her a questioning look.

"*Your* son hurt her feelings," she said.

"He's pissed off, Nic. Don't let anything he says right now bother you. He's not thinking right."

"John," Marie said, "that's no excuse to take it out on Nicole. She's trying to be there for him. You know how he can be when he's upset."

John went to Chris' room and knocked on the door. "Chris, it's Dad." He opened the door with his cell phone up to his ear.

"Yah, that's what I'm thinking. But I'll have to get back to you. I'll call you later today and we'll set it up."

"I know you're pissed off," his father said, "but remember who you're mad at."

"What are you talking about?"

"Nicole is sitting downstairs with her feelings hurt. She should be by your side through this. What is wrong with you, boy? She's the best thing you've had in a long time. Stop being so independent and let her help you."

Chris sat on the bed. "I just needed to make a few phone calls."

"So why couldn't she be here while you made those calls?"

"I didn't want her to hear what I was saying, Dad! I need some payback for Giuseppe."

"So next time, you make those calls when she's not around, but don't tell her you need space. That just creates a space you don't want. Do you get me?"

"Yeah, I think I got it."

"Now, you'd better do something to make her forget what you said." John slammed the door as he left.

Chris flopped back onto the bed and stared at the ceiling for a few minutes, then pulled himself together and went to find the manager.

"Sir, I need a favor," he said. "Can you use some of the flowers from my sister's wedding to make me a really nice arrangement?"

"Sure, give us a few minutes," the manager said. "Stay right here." When one of the desk clerks appeared with a beautiful flower arrangement, Chris tried to tip her, but she refused to take it.

"I hear you've been through a lot," she said. "Please allow us to do this for you."

When Nicole saw him heading toward her table with the flowers, she suppressed a smile. He got down on one knee. "I'm so sorry. I didn't mean to push you away. I just needed a few minutes, and I didn't say it right. I was so pissed off, I wasn't thinking straight. Will you forgive me?"

"Yes, of course."

Marie smiled at him, and John gave him a wink. Chris put his arm around the back of Nicole's chair and pulled her as close as he could, whispering, "I'm really sorry." Then his phone rang. "Yeah, okay ... When? ... There's a garage no one can get to... Okay, tell them to get a move on. I don't want to be here all day waiting for them... Okay, thanks, Alex."

"What's going on?" Nicole asked.

"I called Alex to get someone he knows to tow my car to a garage on one of our construction sites. I want it in a locked garage where no one can see it."

"Why don't you just send it to the dealership so the insurance company can get to it?"

"Because I have plans for that car," he said, not looking at her.

"Oh boy! Do I want to know what those plans are?"

"Probably not."

"Okay, I won't ask." She kissed his cheek.

Chapter 12

Giuseppe kept thinking about the nurse he'd met at the hospital. For the first time in his life, he hadn't had a line to get her attention. He'd been making good money working for Vinnie and was feeling strong. This would be the day he got up his nerve and asked her out. He only knew her first name, and had no idea if she was dating someone or even married. But he was ready to make his move.

He was in the office and found Victor drinking coffee, when he glanced at the surveillance camera and saw Vinnie pull up to the garage, get out of his car, and bang on the door.

"Oh shit, he's not looking happy," Victor said and jumped to his feet. When he pulled in, Vinnie tossed his remote to Giuseppe.

"Change the fucking batteries," he barked, "and wipe that fucking look off your face or I will. Victor, get in the office. We gotta talk."

Giuseppe headed for his car to buy batteries.

Vinnie slammed the office door. "You want to tell me why our profits are down in your division? Maybe you haven't noticed, or maybe you have. I just want answers."

"I knew we were a little low last month, but I also knew we were higher the month before," Victor said.

"Really, balanced out, huh? What fucking math are you using? According to my figures, your division is down a quarter percent in profits since Giuseppe joined up."

"Vin, I hate to correct you, but that can't be true. Since Giuseppe joined, we've been doing good with our clients. They see him step out of the car and they pay for their product even if they didn't sell it all. Before, I had to give them time to sell it before they paid."

"Okay, if it's not him, then what's the fuckin' problem? Something's happening and I want to know what it is."

Victor unlocked the desk and took out his ledger. The figures showed the opposite of what Vinnie was saying.

"Vin, look." He showed him the spreadsheet. "I gave OJ sixty-five thousand in June, then eight-nine thousand in July, seventy-five thousand in August, and a hundred and twenty thousand in September. I have the receipts from him right here stapled to each month." Vinnie looked over the receipts and Victor's spreadsheets without saying a word, which made Victor nervous.

Vinnie tapped his fingers on the spreadsheet, then closed the book and looked away.

After a while, he said, "Well, this is not good. Does that mean that OJ is skimming off the top? And if so, who else is he taking from? Oh, this is not good."

OJ had been Vinnie's cashier for years. He'd always been organized and kept great records. Choosing his words carefully, Victor asked, "Do you really think he would do that? He's been with us for a long time."

"I don't know, but I'm going to find out," Vinnie said and went back to his car. Giuseppe was waiting for him and handed him the remote. As Vinnie pulled out, Giuseppe said, "Nice to see you too, cuz."

"Shut your mouth, Gee. Never say shit like that out loud."

"Okay, but what the hell was that all about?" Giuseppe asked.

"Nothing for you to worry about."

Giuseppe let it go and went back to thinking about the nurse. He thought maybe he would bring a big bouquet of flowers to the hospital and ask her out to dinner. Maybe that would be overdoing it. Then he thought of balloons. Maybe that would be overdoing it too. Maybe just one smiley face balloon.

When he got to the hospital, he stopped at the coffee shop on the first floor. He didn't know how she took her coffee, so he bought a vanilla black coffee with cream and sugar on the side. He walked up to the nurse's station on the floor where Lisa had been. A nurse behind the desk looked up at the young man holding a smiley balloon and a take-out coffee.

"Can I help you?"

Giuseppe put his charm in high gear. "Yes, please, I'm looking for Lisa. Is she by any chance working today? She helped a friend of mine and I wanted to thank her."

"Oh, that's nice of you. She just ran to the pharmacy. She should be right back. You can wait here if you like."

Giuseppe flashed her a big smile.

Lisa came back and rushed right by. He looked at the nurse behind the desk, who shrugged. "The patient really needed that medicine." She left the nurse's station and went to find Lisa.

Lisa reappeared. "What are you doing?" she asked, laughing.

"I thought you might like a coffee," he said. He held out the cardboard coffee holder. "Mine's the one on the right." As she went to grab it, he said joking, "No, no, my right."

"Thank you," she said as she took the coffee from the holder.

"I wasn't sure how you took it, so there's cream in that small cup, and sugar and Splenda in my pocket."

"Why are you bringing me coffee, and who gets the balloon?"

"Oh, this. That's not for you."

"I'm sorry," she said.

"Just busting you. It's for you, but first agree to have dinner with me, and that will put a smile on my face."

"Oh my God, that is the corniest invite I've ever gotten."

"Really? Does that mean I get a date?"

"Yes, you win a date with me."

Giuseppe pumped his fist up and down. "Yes!" Lisa gave him a high-five and they both laughed. They exchanged phone numbers and agreed to dinner the following Friday.

On the way to the gym, he reached for his pills without thinking. It was more a habit than a need. That evening after work, he went to JJ's for a steak and a drink. The bar was packed, so he caught the bartender's attention. She told him a big group was celebrating a birthday and they'd hired a band for the night. She found him a seat at the bar and set a placemat in front of him.

He drank his Jack and Coke and surveyed the crowd. A girl was checking him out. He winked at her, and she winked back. As he finished his dinner, the girl came over. "Wow," she said, "you really devoured that steak."

"Yes I did! I was hungry." She sucked on her straw until she finished the drink she was holding. Giuseppe asked if she'd like a refill. "What's your name?"

"Casey."

"Hi, Casey. I'm Giuseppe. Whose birthday are you all celebrating?" Casey pointed to one of the guys in the group. "Anna told me you hired a band."

"Yah, they should be setting up soon. They're really good, wait 'til you hear them."

"So, Casey, what do you do?"

"I work at a bank, but I don't plan to stay there much longer."

Giuseppe was thinking that he hadn't had a good blowjob in a while. They made small talk, then he reached for her, kissed her neck, and asked if she was tired of standing. She smiled and rubbed his muscular thighs, then slipped her hand over his dick. He pulled her on to his lap. She leaned back and whispered, "You're poking me."

"I know." She smiled and kissed his open mouth. The band was playing and the lights in the bar were turned down.

"Casey, you're driving me crazy. You're beautiful and I want you. What do you say we take a walk somewhere outside?"

"I was just thinking the same thing."

Giuseppe helped her to her feet and gave Anna his credit card.

As soon as they got out the door, Giuseppe pushed Casey up against the wall and kissed her neck, her mouth. He felt her tits under her fitted shirt. They were still in public, but he didn't care.

"Do you want to get into my SUV?" she asked.

"Absolutely." As she unlocked her car, he kissed her neck. She turned and unbuttoned his jeans, reached in, and found him ready for action. She pulled his pants down and jerked him off a little as he stood there. He leaned back against the car as she moved faster and faster. He closed his eyes and moaned. "Damn, girl! That feels great." She continued until he released, then crawled into the back of the SUV. Giuseppe kicked off his jeans and threw them into the SUV. She stripped to her underwear. He unhooked her bra and pulled her damp panties off, then slid his finger into her. He put another finger in and rocked her. Then he reached for his pants pocket on the floor and pulled out a condom and put it on. Neither of them cared that they were in a car in a parking lot.

When they finished, he was about to get off, but she grabbed his ass and pushed her hips against him, forcing him deeper inside her. He was not expecting that. "You want some more?"

"Hell yeah, big boy."

Giuseppe decided he was going to fuck this chick until he couldn't climax again. She pushed one of the seats back to give them a little more room and spread wide open. He crawled over to her and whispered in her ear, "You want me?"

"Yes, I want you."

"You want me hard?"

"Yes, I want you hard!"

"Wanna' taste me?"

"Yes, I want you in my mouth."

She reached out to him, took the condom off, and licked the tip of his dick, making circles with her tongue. She gently massaged his balls as she took him into her mouth as deep as she could. He ran his hands through her hair. She knew what she was doing, and he was loving it. He thought his head was going to explode. She started to suck him harder and he burst in her mouth. She kissed his muscular stomach and continued to kiss her way up his chest as she got to his ear. She whispered, "You wanna fuck me hard now?" Giuseppe wasn't sure he could, but he was sure he was going to try. He reached for his second condom and put it on faster than fast. He grabbed her and, like a rag doll, flipped her over onto her stomach, and got her up on all four, entering her from behind. She mumbled, "Harder...harder." Giuseppe grabbed her shoulders and pounded himself into her. She moaned and came, which set Giuseppe off. They got dressed and stepped out of the SUV. She snuggled up to him and said, "I gotta tell ya, *that* was fun." And she poked his chest.

"Well, thank you... I think," he said with a laugh. "You were good too." He felt awkward telling a woman she gave a good blowjob. They started to walk back to the restaurant, then Giuseppe stopped, kissed her, and told her he was done for the night. She didn't seem to mind. Her friends were still dancing and partying, so she went to join them.

In his car, Giuseppe laughed. He wanted to tell someone about his amazing luck, but when he lost his friendship with Chris, he lost all his other friends. He turned on the radio to stop that thought from bringing him down. He grabbed his pill bottle, popped two Oxys, and headed home, tapping on the steering wheel to the music blasting through the speakers.

Chapter 13

Chris was bent over a set of blueprints when Nicole called.

"Hi, hon, I'm just reminding you that we're having dinner with my parents at Bella Italia tonight."

"I'm gonna quit in a few and head home. What time will you be finished?"

"I'm pulling into your driveway right now. I got done a little early."

"Make yourself a drink and I'll cut out of here."

As he was locking up, his buddy at the Jaguar dealership called. "Hey, Billy. Did you find me one?"

"I did. I found the car you're looking for. However, it's next year's edition. Does that matter?"

"No, that's fine. But I want to see it before I sign."

"Sure. It'll take me at least four weeks to get it here from Solihull."

"It's in freakin' England?"

"Yeah, still on the factory line."

Chris laughed. "Let me ask you something. Can I make any changes to this car to make it a custom-built vehicle?"

"Depends, but I'm sure we can make some changes."

"What's the biggest engine I can put in that car?"

"Supercharged 5.0 liter, V8, 470 horsepower."

"I want that. Can you make that work?"

"I'll make a few calls and get back to you tomorrow. Is that okay?"

"Absolutely, let me know tomorrow, and I want a fair price."

"Honey, I'm home," Chris yelled in a joking voice.

"Good," Nicole yelled back, "because I've been cooking all day in this little kitchen, just for you."

Chris walked into the kitchen. "Funny, I don't smell anything cooking!"

"Well, I did whip this up." She handed him a martini.

"Damn, that smells so good! You are one hell of a cook, my love." They both laughed.

While Nicole changed clothes, he made two more drinks in a shaker and carried them up to the bedroom. Nicole was in her underwear, standing in front of the mirror, taking off her earrings. He kissed her back in the spot that made her melt. She tried to ignore him, but he wrapped her in his arms and told her he loved her very much. She turned to him. "I love you too, Chris, more and more each day."

They drank the tumbler of martinis as they got dressed.

They were only five minutes late to meet Nicole's parents. Chris had a reputation for being late. After the "shit episode," he'd begun asking valets to keep his car at the front of the lot. Chris owned several fancy cars, but his Jaguar was definitely his favorite.

He'd decided to ask Nicole's dad, Jim, for permission to marry his daughter. He just had to figure out a way to get him away from the table. He knew his whole family loved Nicole. Halfway through his meal, Chris sat back in his chair and said, "I'm so full! I love the food here." Jim and Chris ordered Cognac, and Nicole and her mother ordered Sambuca. It was Chris' moment. He invited Jim to join him for a cigar.

The restaurant's smoking lounge was furnished with brown leather easy chairs and small tables topped with ashtrays. Chris pulled two cigars from his jacket pocket and offered one to Jim. They chatted about business for a few minutes, then Chris said, "I need to ask you something important."

Jim took a sip of his Cognac. "Sure, Chris, what's up?"

"It's about Nicole."

"Is she okay?" he asked, leaning forward.

"She's fine. I'm sorry. I didn't mean to scare you. Well, I don't have a big speech to recite, so I'm just going to say it the way I feel it. Jim, I love your daughter with all my heart. I think she's the most beautiful, smart, compassionate person any man could marry. I want to make her my wife. I want her to be part of my life forever. I'd like your blessing to ask your daughter to marry me."

Jim had a tear in his eye. "I'd be honored to have you as my son-in-law!" He stood up and opened his arms, so Chris stood too, and they shared a long hug. Then Jim stepped back. "Oh my God, Chris, I can't even tell you how happy I am!"

"Thank you, Jim, really, thank you! But Nicole has no idea I'm even thinking about marriage. You can't say a word. Not even to Carol. You know those two."

"Yes I do. I won't say a word, but I must tell you, it's not going to be easy. I'm truly blessed to have you join my family."

They went back to the table as the server arrived with the dessert menu. Nicole asked, "Can we get two desserts and four spoons?"

At the end of the meal, Chris handed the server his credit card. Jim started to put up a fight, but Chris insisted. While they waited for the valet to bring their cars, Nicole said she was cold. He opened his jacket and she snuggled against him.

In the car, she put her head on his shoulder and fell asleep. When they got back to the house, she stumbled upstairs and was sound asleep by the time Chris got into bed.

Chapter 14

Giuseppe and Victor had finished their rounds and were hanging in the office while Victor counted the money. "So, Vic, is this all you do for Vinnie? I mean, collecting and replenishing. I don't mean any disrespect. I'm just wondering if this is all I'm going to be doing."

Victor looked up at him. "What do you think this is, a TV show? We do whatever we're asked to do. And if that means collecting and replenishing, then that's all we do."

"But is this the only thing you've ever done for him?"

"First of all, I started working for your uncle Salvatore, and I still do. A lot of people forget that Salvatore is still in charge. He may be aging, but trust me, he's still in charge."

"Really? I would have bet that Vinnie had taken over."

"Like I said, Gee, Sal is still running the show. This business is all I know. I started doing runs when I was still in high school. I'm quite happy just collecting and replenishing, as you put it."

"I don't mean any disrespect, Victor. I was just wondering where I'm heading here."

"Patience, my boy. Patience. I'm sure you'll be asked to do more, but in this business, you have to prove yourself before they find a spot for you. They'll ask, and you'll have to do whatever it is."

"Okay, cool. I was just thinking about my future. I'm enjoying the extra money. It's helping me out a lot."

"What about me, dude?"

"You know I love you, man!" Victor had become his best friend. Giuseppe got up from his chair and gave him a hug. Victor laughed and smacked him away.

"Don't you have a date tonight, Gee?"

"Oh shit, yeah, I do! I gotta go."

"Okay, go have fun and don't screw it up."

Giuseppe sped home, jumped in the shower, and then started to pick out his clothes. He was never nervous on a date, but something about Lisa made him feel a little off his game. He chose his Roberto Cavalli jeans, a Hugo Boss button-down shirt, and black Hugo loafers. He always wore a gold necklace and a ring on each pinkie finger.

In the car, he put Lisa's address into his GPS, threw on some dance music, and turned up the volume. Then he shook two pills out of the bottle, hesitated for a second, and threw the bottle back into the glove compartment. When he pulled up at Lisa's townhouse, he decided he needed those pills after all.

Lisa opened the door looking totally different; better, if that was possible. Her brown hair fell to the middle of her back, and the makeup she wore made her sparkling big blue eyes pop. Her white blouse was partly unbuttoned, leaving her chest bare, and her black slacks flattered her high, round butt.

He was impressed with her house. Comfortable brown leather couches faced a big flat-screen TV. On the other side of the room, a small bar was installed beside the fireplace.

"Would you like a drink before we go to dinner?"

"Rum and Coke, if you have it," Giuseppe said. "And I have to tell you, I love your place."

"Thank you. I bought it about a year ago." Another girl passed by, said hello, and continued to what Giuseppe assumed was a bedroom.

"That's my sister," Lisa said. "She's being nosy. She knew I was going on a first date tonight."

"Oh, so this is our first date, meaning we might have a second?"

She laughed and handed him his rum and Coke.

In the car, she asked, "Where're we going?"

"That depends on you. I made two reservations, one at a nice seafood place on the water with a view of the Manhattan skyline, and the other at a steakhouse on the Green. It's your choice."

"Hmmm, what do you feel like? Because I like both ideas."

"Oh, no. This is your choice."

"Okay, let's do seafood on the water. That sounds really nice."

He down-shifted the Corvette and floored it. Lisa grabbed the door handle with one hand and Giuseppe's arm with the other.

When they pulled up, Giuseppe told the valet, "No joy ride, boss. And can you keep it out front here?"

"Yes, sir." He pointed to the first spot next to a Porsche.

"Thanks," Giuseppe said and handed him a twenty-dollar bill.

It was a crystal-clear night, and their table was beside a window, so they had a perfect view of the lights across the Hudson River.

Lisa sat back in her chair and sipped the last of her wine. "Now that I told you all about my crazy family, tell me about yours."

Family was the last thing Giuseppe wanted to talk about. He was saved by the server, who arrived for their dessert order. They both passed and asked for coffee.

"So, how long have you been a nurse?"

"It's been about four years. I love it except for the occasional obnoxious patient. How about you? I feel like I've been doing all the talking. Do you have any siblings?"

Giuseppe took a deep breath. "Well, my family situation is a bit complicated. I'm the one and only."

"What do you mean? Did your parents pass?"

"No, no, nothing like that. I'm sorry, it's a touchy subject. My parents and I had a big argument a few months ago, and we're not talking." He looked at her. "Like, not at all."

"Oh no, Giuseppe, I'm so sorry to hear that."

"Yah, it sucks, but let's not talk about that. I just want to say how beautiful you look tonight, and I'm having a great time getting to know you."

"Me too."

"Would you like to take a walk along the river?"

"That sounds perfect. I need to walk off some of this food."

The river walk extended for miles. Lisa wrapped her arm around his back, and he kissed her, smiled at her for a moment, then took her hand and they continued walking. As he helped her into his car, he stole another kiss.

"Would you like to take a ride into the city, or should we head home?" he asked.

"I'm a bit tired. Do you mind if we head home?"

"No, not at all. I'm feeling a bit tired myself." He drove back much more slowly, holding her hand. At her house, he kissed her passionately, then asked, "So, do I get another date?"

She laughed shyly. "I think that sounds awesome."

He walked her to the door and kissed her again.

"Call me tomorrow," she said, closing the door.

Giuseppe stood with his hand on the door, thinking, *What a great night! What a great girl!*

Giuseppe stood with his hand on the door, thinking, *What a great night! What a great girl!*

Chapter 15

Chris woke up extra early. He was bothered that he hadn't told his father he was planning to ask Nicole to marry him, and he had a lot to do. Nicole was still asleep, so he was careful not to wake her as he got out of bed, but she grabbed his arm. "Where are you going so early?"

"It's not that early, actually. I have a lot to do today, and I couldn't sleep. I'm going to get in the shower and get started. You sleep, I'll keep the noise down."

"Don't have to tell me twice. I'm tired today." She rolled over, pulling the covers up to her shoulders. Chris kissed her forehead, grabbed his cell phone, and headed into the bathroom. He called his parents and his mom answered.

"Morning, honey! You sound very awake for eight on a Saturday."

"Yeah, I know! I have a lot to do today, so I thought I'd get an early start. I have to go into the city to meet with Tony and the builder."

"Oh, how is my Tony? Tell him I said hi."

"Will do. Is Dad around? I want to ask him to come with me."

"He's downstairs playing on one of his machines. Hold on a minute."

His father was always in the basement doing something, usually sneaking a drink of Crown Royal, but it was way too early for that.

"Hey, Dad, I was wondering if you could come into the city with me to meet with the builder and Tony."

"Aaaaaah, yeah, I could come with you. What time?"

"I got to be in the city by ten. I'm jumping in the shower now and I'll get you."

"Okay, I'll be ready."

On the way to pick up his dad, he stopped at Starbucks for coffee. As he was walking back to his car, coffee in hand, he noticed a girl staring at him and his car. He realized she was checking him out, standing closer to his car than he liked. He opened his car door and said, "You may want to move away from my car so I don't hit you."

"Oh, sweetheart, you can hit me anytime."

"Not with a ten-foot pole," he said and got back into his car.

"Fuck you, dick!" she yelled back at him as he pulled out of the parking spot. What a way to start a day! But nothing was going to bring him down. He was on a natural high, thinking about picking out an engagement ring for Nicole.

As they drove into the city, Chris said, "Dad, I gotta ask you something. How would you feel if I asked Nicole to marry me?"

"I would be honored. I already love her like family."

"Really?"

"Yes, really! Did you think I was gonna try talking you out of it? I know you're afraid of that word—*marriage*—but I'm thrilled you're finally ready, and Nicole is the right one for you."

Chris had always been afraid of marriage because he didn't think he could ever have what his parents have. But he was sure of his love for Nicole.

"I wish I could give you a hug, son, but you always buy these fancy small cars, and I can't even move."

"I'll take that hug when we get out. Or do you want me to pull over?"

"No, the hug can wait." They chuckled.

When they got to Tony's apartment, he had coffee brewing, donuts on the counter, and blueprints spread out on his dining room table. He was incredibly happy to see Chris' father. "You brought the big guns with you today."

"I'm just here for the ride and to see you," John said.

"So, tell me a little about this builder before he gets here," Chris said.

"Well, we've been friends for about five or six years—not like us, but friends. He's had his construction business as long as I've known him. He does a lot of apartment renovations, knows all the inspectors, which ones we need to grease and which ones we don't. He's a good guy, Chris. You're gonna like him."

Pat arrived wearing a Fighting Irish jacket. He explained that he owned O'Brien's Construction with his older brother and offered to show Chris any of the projects they completed. Chris was impressed with everything he said they'd do, and he liked the way he answered his questions. "So how much do you need to get this started?" he asked.

"Well, I have it broken down in phases." He handed Chris a timetable. "First phase is $500,000, and that's firm. Then if you look at the other three phases, there's room to play with the figures a little."

Chris looked it over, then handed it to Tony. "I have a meeting with my accountant, Stuart, on Tuesday. He'll wire $500,000 to your account on Wednesday. Is that okay with you?"

"That would be great. We've already applied for the permits, which should be approved sometime next week."

"Okay, great. Give Tony the account information so I can give it to Stu, and let's make this happen." Chris stood up to shake Pat's hand.

"I'll do that."

Tony was smiling from ear to ear. He'd been an employee for too long.

After Pat left, Chris finished his coffee and told Tony he had one more appointment in the city.

"What else are you doing in town? Isn't your name already all over New Jersey?"

Chris laughed. "It has nothing to do with construction or business. I'm going to see a jeweler."

"Don't tell me...don't tell me...you're going to ask Nicole to marry you! *You,* who said you'd *never* get married."

"Yeah, yeah, yeah. It's time."

"No, it's overdue," John said.

"If you're both done with the jokes, let's go."

Tony gave him a hug. "Thanks, man. I wouldn't want to do this with anybody else."

"I'm happy to help you, Tone, but I get to pick out the colors," he said with a wink.

The relative Stuart had mentioned had a store in the diamond district. Amos was expecting them, ushered them to the back of the store, and offered champagne. "So please, tell me what you're thinking about."

"Well, I'm not sure exactly," Chris said with a nervous laugh. "That's why I'm here. I need your help."

"Stuart told me you would say that. How many carats are you thinking?"

"A total of five, but I want the big stone to be four carats with little diamonds around it."

"Damn, boy!" John said. "Don't show it to your mom."

"See, you do know what you want. Now let's design it." Amos drew a sketch of what Chris had described. After only half an hour, they'd agreed on the ring, and Chris put $50,000 on his credit card.

When they got back to his parents' house, Chris told his mom, and she cried with joy, kissing his face over and over.

Chris said, "You both have to promise you won't say a word to anyone until I ask Nicole. No one! I know it's going to be hard, but you can't even tell Susanne. I'll tell her when I get the ring."

John and Marie promised.

***

At the office, Victor was reading his daily newspaper when Vinnie called him. He hung up the phone, folded the newspaper he was reading, and headed over to see him. He walked into Vinnie's office and found two big bouncer types were sitting at the round table, and another guy was tied to a chair with duct tape over his mouth, looking terrified.

"Victor, come in, and shut the door," Vinnie said.

Victor sat in the chair in front of Vinnie's desk.

Vinnie said, "That money I talked to you about being missing the other day has been found. OJ decided to help himself to a little of my money. Now I need you to help him remember who he stole from."

"What are you thinking, Vin?"

"Take Frick and Frack with you to hold him down while you take off a few fingers."

Victor looked at the guy tied to the chair, realized it was OJ, then back at Vinnie and nodded. "Alright, I'll take care of it."

He looked at the big dudes sitting around Vinnie's table and said, "Bring him over to my office." They got up and grabbed OJ with the chair attached to him. "Yo, dummies, I don't need the fucking chair!" They cut the ropes that tied OJ to the chair.

A car pulled into the garage, and the two big guys got out carrying OJ into Victor's office.

"Sit him down in that metal folding chair," Victor said. OJ had his hands tied and duct tape over his mouth, but he was still able to slip away and tried to make a run for it. Victor ran and got him before the two big guys could get out of their own way. He threw them a dirty look. "Useless! You two are fucking useless. Now hold him here and don't let him move."

Victor carried over a garbage can with a black plastic liner. OJ started to scream through the duct tape and tried to get out of the chair, but this time, the two big guys held him down. Victor asked him if was left-handed. He shook his head.

Victor asked him again, "Are you a lefty or a righty?"

He tilted his head to the right. Victor said, "Give me his left hand and hold him tight." He fought with the guy to get him to unclench his fist, then took a hammer and board from his toolbox. "Last time I'm going to do this nicely. Either you give me your hand opened, or I will break the bones before I take some fingers off. It's your choice." OJ just kept a fist and tried to get away. Victor put the board over his fist and started to pound on it. OJ screamed, but Victor kept hitting his hand like he was tenderizing a chicken cutlet. Then he grabbed the pinky finger, took the wire cutter from his back pocket, and cut it off in one quick snap. The finger fell into the garbage can, and a stream of blood flooded in. OJ was fighting not to pass out, still screaming under the duct tape. Victor grabbed his middle finger, and with another quick snap, it fell into the garbage can. Since he'd broken most of the bones in OJ's hand, he figured that was enough. He grabbed two towels and tossed them at the big guys. "Wrap him up and get him out of here."

"What are we going to do with him?" one of them asked.

"You two are really smart, aren't you? Fucking take him back to wherever you found him. Get him out of here, NOW!"

They threw him in the back of the car and drove off. Victor took the bag from the garbage can, tied it up, and tossed it into the dumpster. He cleaned the wire cutters in the bathroom and put them away, then sat behind his desk and finished reading his paper. After he was done, he called Giuseppe, who didn't answer, so he left a message. One job done, now on to the next. He sat back in his chair and spun it around while he waited for Giuseppe to call back.

Within a half-hour, he got another call from Vinnie. "I gotta job for you and your sidekick. It's in addition to what you've been doing. I'm not sure Giuseppe is going to like this, so you need to keep a close eye on him."

"Alright, Vin. He was just asking me the other day if we ever get to do other things. I think he'll be okay."

"Yah, but I didn't tell you what I need you to do yet. This is going to be real close to his home front."

"He's not close to anyone right now. What's the job?"

"You know that new apartment complex being built in Jersey City?"

"The one Chris Yacenda is building."

"Yeah, Giuseppe's cousin, the millionaire of the family." Chris was also Vinnie's cousin, but he didn't acknowledge that. "He's refusing to pay us. He thinks the security he hired is enough to protect the site. We've been warning him since they started building, but they're being stubborn. I need you and Giuseppe to convince them their security sucks. I've given them plenty of time to come to their senses, but I think they need a push. I was thinking a fire might help convince them."

"We can do that. When do you want this to happen?"

"Case the place for a few days, then let me know when you're doing it."

"Alright, Vinnie, I'll take care of it," Victor said.

Giuseppe was telling Mario about his date with Lisa. "Good for you, Gee. I'm happy for you. You need a good woman by your side. Maybe she can keep you out of trouble for a while."

"Yeah, I doubt that," he said with a big smile on his face. He went back to his client. He was a high school kid getting in shape for the upcoming baseball season, and Giuseppe told him they were done for today. Then he went to the office and started to gather his things when he saw he had a message from Victor. He yelled to Mario and the two other trainers that he was leaving for the night and headed out. It was freezing, so he sat in his car and called Victor while it warmed up.

"Yo, Victor, it's me."

"Are you available tonight? Vinnie gave us an extra job that I want to talk to you about. It requires a little bit of preparation."

"Yeah, I'm good for tonight. Let me just run home and take a shower and I'll head over."

"See you soon."

"So, what are we doing, boss?" Giuseppe asked as he walked into the office.

"Have a seat, we gotta talk first. I was told a construction site isn't paying what they should be, and Vinnie wants us to light a fire under their ass."

"Okay, so what does that mean? Do we need to break some heads?"

Victor laughed. "You're always ready to beat in a few heads, aren't you? No, we need to sit and watch so we can see what the normal routine is around the site. Then light it up."

Giuseppe sat still while the information connected with his brain. "We're going to torch the place?"

"Yeah, you okay with that?"

"I'm fine with that." He was glad to be doing something new.

"I have one more thing to tell you... The construction site is your cousin's in Jersey City."

Giuseppe looked at the floor for a minute, then started to laugh.

"What the fuck is wrong with you?"

"You asked me if I'm okay lighting up Chris' construction site. Hell yes, I'm okay with that! Fuck that son of a bitch!"

"This goes without saying, and I know you already know this, but you *have* to keep your mouth shut. Not a single word to anyone, or you could find yourself in deep shit with not only Vinnie but the cops too, and if I were you, I'd worry about Vinnie more."

"Yeah, of course I'm not gonna say a word to anyone. I may be stupid, but I'm not *that* stupid."

"Okay, so let's go sit down by the site and watch what goes on so we can make a plan."

Victor found a parking spot in the shadow of a tree. While they waited and watched the construction site, Giuseppe told him about Lisa. Victor was looking at the site and taking notes, but he listened enough to tell Giuseppe he was happy for him. Then, for the first time, he told him a little about his wife and family. Giuseppe had never asked, figuring that if Victor wanted him to know about his personal life, he'd tell him. Victor said he'd been married for twenty-six years and his only child, a daughter, was married with no kids. Giuseppe told him a little bit about what happened with his family. Three hours later, Victor decided he'd seen enough, and they went back to the office. When Giuseppe headed for his car, Victor asked, "Where you going? You wanna get paid?"

"Hell yeah, I do."

In the office, Victor opened the safe and handed Giuseppe a pack of money with a thousand-dollar strap.

"Thanks, man."

"There'll be more when we get this done."

"You can count on me, Victor. I'm all in."

"Good. See you tomorrow night, same time."

Chapter 16

Monday morning, Chris met Alex at the Jersey City site to do a walk through. The wind was fierce, and it had just started to snow, so he decided to leave half an hour early. Route 280 was dicey in bad weather, and snow almost always meant accidents, but he got there without a problem. When he arrived at the office trailer, no one was around, so he sat behind the desk to wait. After a few minutes, the door opened, and a young woman blew in struggling not to spill a tray of coffee. Chris jumped up, grabbed her arm, and took the tray.

"Oh, thank you," she said, closing the door behind her. "I hate this fucking weather. Can I help you with something?"

"You don't know who I am, do you?"

"No, dude, I'm assuming some sort of inspector. Alex should be right back. He had to check on a pipe that burst in one of the buildings. And seriously, do not let Alex see you sitting behind his desk. He'll rip you a new asshole."

"I'm Chris Yacenda, so I don't think Alex will mind that I'm sitting behind his desk."

She stopped slurping her hot coffee and looked up.

"Oh my God! I'm so sorry, Mr. Yacenda. What a freaking idiot I am! Alex told me you were coming down this morning, but I didn't expect you until ten. I should have realized."

"No worries. What's your name?"

"I'm Andi. Well, Andrea, but everyone calls me Andi."

"Nice to meet you, Andi."

"I am such a moron," she said, hitting herself upside the head.

The door opened again, and frigid air rushed in carrying Alex. "You better have one of those for me," he said, pointing to the coffee tray. "It's freezing out there."

Andi handed him a coffee.

"Is there an extra one for me?" Chris asked.

Alex turned and saw Chris at his desk. "Jesus, boss, you scared the shit out of me!"

"Sorry, now pass me a coffee."

"You're early."

"I wanted to beat the weather. What's this about a broken pipe?"

"It's the cold. It froze. No biggie. We got it under control. Do you want to do that walk-through before it gets any worse out there?"

"Yeah, just let me drink this coffee. In the meantime, show me which inspections have been completed and approved." Alex reached behind the desk, grabbed a file, and handed it to Chris, who began to look through it. "Andi, can you do me a favor and fax these approved inspections to my office? Send them to Robin. You have her number, right?"

"Yeah, I'll take care of that for you right now."

"Okay, Alex, let's go see our luxury apartments." He handed Andi a twenty-dollar bill. "Thanks for the coffee, and be safe by that door," he said, smiling.

One section of the apartment complex was in the final phase, while others had only been roughed in. Chris liked what he saw. He told every worker he ran into that they were doing a fantastic job and thanked them.

By the time they finished the walk-through, the snow was coming down hard. Chris was about to leave when Alex asked, "When do you want to take care of your car thing?"

"As soon as I get the insurance check."

"Cool. Just let me know, because my guy is ready and waiting for your word."

"Tell him very soon," Chris said with a wink.

"You got it, boss."

Chris slipped on icy roads as he drove slowly back to his office. He thought about Nicole driving home and got a sick feeling. As he pulled into the parking lot, he called her. "Have you seen the weather out there?"

"Yeah, and you'll be very proud to know that I left the office, and I'm at your house working out in the gym."

"Holy shit! That's a first."

"I know, right? Why don't you come home and join me?"

"That's very tempting, but I've been at the Jersey City site all day, and I need to do a few things here. Then I'll come home. I promise,"

"Okay, your loss. I was thinking about working out in the nude."

"Really? Well, you'd better put a towel down. I don't want you to get my new equipment dirty with your ass prints." They both laughed.

Chris always threw a big bash at Christmas. He called Robin in and asked her how it was going. "I'm not sure," she said. "Do you want me to check in with the party planner?"

"Yeah. When you have her on the phone, I want to talk to her about an idea. I might need her help."

Tara had been planning Chris' parties for years and was a close friend to Nicole. Chris got on the phone and explained he was going to ask Nicole to marry him, and he wanted to make it a night to remember. She was thrilled to help and promised not to say a word. First, she'd have to find out if what he wanted was even possible.

***

A couple days later, the insurance company payment came through. Chris had made a deal to accept a smaller payment so he could keep the car. He called Alex. "I'm ready for that tow truck."

"I'll call him right now, but I'm sure he can do it anytime. Can you find out when he's at the gym?"

Alex called back within minutes. "He said he's ready to do it today."

"Okay. I'm thinking Gee is probably working all day. Tell the tow guy to hook up the car, and I'll call you right back." Chris knew Mario would recognize his voice, so he asked Robin to call the gym and check on Giuseppe's schedule.

"He is at the gym until five," she reported. "Should I even ask what you're up to?"

He called Alex back. "Let's get this done, and I want a video."

"You got it, boss. I'll call you when it's done and send you the video."

Alex went to the garage where they stored all the company equipment. Within a few minutes, the tow truck pulled in and rolled the Jag onto the flatbed. Alex jumped into the passenger seat.

When they pulled up in the parking lot at Mario's Gym, Alex went across the street, focused his phone, and hit record. The tow truck backed up to where Giuseppe's car was parked. The driver unhooked the chains holding Chris' car, got back into the cabin, and hit a few buttons. The flatbed tilted and the car slid off, crushing Giuseppe's Corvette. The alarm on the Corvette went off, and all four tires popped like balloons. Alex recorded the whole thing, then ran to the tow truck and jumped in as they raced away. By the time Mario and Giuseppe got out to see what was going on, they were gone, and the Corvette had been reduced to a pancake.

"No, no, no!" Giuseppe screamed. "Fuck! I'm going to fucking kill that motherfucker! Oh my God, I'm going to kill him!"

He ran around screaming, and kicked the door of the Jaguar. It opened, pouring shit over his feet.

On the way back to Jersey City, Alex sent the video. Chris texted him to pay the driver a thousand bucks and take a thousand for himself that he left on Alex's desk in an envelope. "The boss says good job, and we both just made a quick grand," he told the driver, and they high-fived.

At the gym, all the clients were standing by the windows. "Show's over!" Mario said. "Get back to work." He slammed the office door behind him.

One of the other trainers went out and asked Giuseppe if he wanted him to call the police. "No, I don't need the fuckin' cops here," he said.

"Then you'd better get these cars out of here, because Mario is really pissed."

"What? Really?"

"You know he always tells us not to bring our personal problems to the gym."

"Fuck him! Like I wanted my fucking car crushed."

"Man, I'm just trying to help you. Get the cars out of here."

Giuseppe called for two tow trucks, then sat on the curb. How was he going to explain this to Lisa? He'd have to come up with a story. After the cars were towed away, he went back inside. Mario yelled from his office, "Giuseppe, get in here!"

"Close the door. What is my number one rule?"

"Not to have our cell phone on us while we're training."

"That's my number two rule. My number one rule is, never bring your personal stuff to my gym. And you just broke that rule big time. Having your car crushed in my parking lot brought a *lot* of your personal shit to my gym. I don't know what you've got going on with your family drama, but I'm not waiting to find out. You are a good trainer, Gee, but you're done here. Get your stuff and get out. I'll take care of your clients."

"Wait, Mario. I had no idea that was going to happen. Fuckin' Chris set that up."

"It's always somebody else's fault with you, Gee, and I'm tired of it. I'm sorry, but you're done here."

"You're fuckin' firing me? I can't believe you're firing me."

"Sorry, I just can't do this anymore."

"Fine, I got no car and no job. What a great fuckin' day!" Giuseppe opened the office door, and swung it closed so hard, it broke the glass in the frame.

Mario yelled, "Get out of here NOW!"

Giuseppe just kept on walking, grabbed his personal things out of his locker, and went around the corner to JJ's. Anna was behind the bar and poured him a large Jack Daniel's, which he drank down like water. "Give me another one." He downed that too.

"One more?" Anna asked, holding the bottle up.

"Yeah."

"Wanna talk about it?"

"Not yet. I just need to sit."

"Okay, can I pour you some Coke to go with that JD in your stomach?"

He looked up with half a smile. "Yeah, sure, thanks." After a while, he called Victor. "You got some time for a friend who had a terrible day?"

"Absolutely, kid. Where are you?"

"I'm at a place called JJ's in Nutley, just down from the gym."

"Hang tight. I'm on my way."

Giuseppe ordered another glass of Jack. He had no family, no friends, no job, and no car. If he left this earth, no one would care.

Victor patted him on the back. "Hey, kid, how's it going?"

"Not good, man, not good at all."

"Alright, so fill me in. What happened?" He listened to Giuseppe's story. "Yup, you had a shitty day."

"Oh, speaking of shit, the Jag was filled with it, and it poured all over the shoes I was wearing."

Victor let out a hearty laugh. "Are you kidding me?"

"Do I look like I'm in a kidding mood?"

"Why was there shit in the car?"

"Well, that's a whole 'nother story," Giuseppe said, emptying his glass. Anna came over and Victor ordered a Johnny Walker Red. "Seriously, Victor, I have nothing right now. I have no family, no friends, no job, and no car. I don't know..."

"If you got no friends, what the fuck do you call me?"

"I don't know what to call you, Victor. My other boss?"

"Well, you little fuck! If I'm not your friend, then why am I here?"

"Come on, dude, you know what I mean. I called you to stop me from stepping off a ledge somewhere."

"Okay, kid, I'm just teasing. Take a deep breath and let's figure this out. Tell me the whole story about the car."

Giuseppe told Victor about showing up at Susanne's wedding and telling off his entire family, but he left out the part about destroying Chris' Jag. He said he missed his mom but had a lot of anger for his family. Then, for the first time ever, he admitted he might have a drug problem.

Victor was a little shocked about the drug problem. He put a hand on Giuseppe's shoulder. "Okay, so we have to fix a few things here, but that doesn't mean you need to throw in the towel. I have an extra car sitting in my driveway. You can use it 'til you get yourself another one. You got your shit together when it comes to being a personal trainer, so I'm sure you can find another job tomorrow. Take a ride with me to get the car. Do what I do... I allow myself to feel bad for one day when things go wrong, then I pick myself up and do whatever I need to do to carry me through to the next thing. I'm here for you, man, so don't ever think about stepping off any ledges, you hear me?"

"Yeah, I hear you," Giuseppe said with a fist bump.

Victor decided to have a little talk with Mario at the gym. When he pulled into the parking lot, he saw a big oil spot where Giuseppe's car had been crushed. It was close to closing time, and the door was locked. He took a small tool case from his back pocket, and used a screwdriver to unlock it, then walked slowly to the office. He could hear Mario on the phone rescheduling Giuseppe's clients and waited in the doorway until he hung up.

Mario looked up and grabbed his chest. "Damn, man! How did you get in here?"

"I let myself in. Mario, do you remember me?"

"Yeah, you're one of Vinnie's guys."

"Good. I have a question for you. What the fuck did you do to my boy Giuseppe today?"

"I fired him..."

"I don't think what happened today was within his control, Mario. And I was thinking you were wrong to fire him. So, what can *you* do to rectify ***your*** error?"

Mario was scared out of his mind.

Victor slammed his fist on the desk and repeated the question. "How can we fix this trivial problem you created?"

Mario jumped out of his chair and stood with his back against the wall. "Victor, I'll hire him back if that's what you want."

"I was thinking more on the lines of you retiring." He sat in Mario's desk chair. "I was thinking, maybe it's time Giuseppe took over the business."

"Ummm, I don't want to retire. I'm too young to retire."

Victor took out his gun and laid it on the desk. Then he stood up and got within smelling distance of Mario. He leaned in as though he were about to whisper in Mario's ear and said in a loud voice, "You made a big mistake today."

"Please, Victor; I'll hire him back right now if you want. I can't give him my business."

Mario paced around the room, pretending to be thinking. "For *now*! But you're going to help him buy a new car. And in about a month, you're going to give him a nice raise. Don't you think that's fair?"

"Ummm, yes, yes! That's a great idea, Victor. I'll call him right now if you want me to."

"No, the poor guy had a really rough day, and I think he's sleeping off the drinks we both just had. I don't want you to bother him tonight. But I ***do*** want you to call him tomorrow and tell him the good news, that you had second thoughts on what happened today and want to fix things."

"Yeah, okay, I won't call him tonight, but I'll take care of it tomorrow, first thing. And how do you want me to help him get a car?"

"Money!"

"Money? You want me to give him money to buy another car? I didn't have anything to do with the car thing. I was told it was payback for something Giuseppe did to his cousin's car."

"What do you mean? What did he do?"

"He went to his cousin's wedding and created a scene with his family. He wasn't invited, and he went there just to cause a problem. He cursed out the entire family and everyone else. When he was leaving, he saw Chris' Jag in the parking lot, and he destroyed it. He broke the sunroof, poured a bucket of shit into the car, then spray-painted the sides of the car."

"Wait. Giuseppe threw a bucket of shit into Chris' Jag?"

"Yeah! The car was totaled."

Victor shook his head. Then he started to laugh. Giuseppe never told him he'd started the fight. "That's something I would have done at his age. Okay, this is what you're gonna do. I want you to get fifty thousand bucks together within the next week and see that Giuseppe gets it without knowing it came from you. That way, you can make up for ***your*** little lapse in judgment. What do you think, Mario? Fair? You keep your business, give Gee his job back with a raise and ten thousand cash. We'll call this whole difficult day *done*."

"Yeah, yeah, sure, Victor. I'll take care of it tomorrow."

"Good. I'm glad we could come to an agreement without anyone getting hurt. I like it better that way. I heard you were a decent guy, so I'm genuinely glad I didn't have to hurt you." He put his gun away.

"Me too," Mario said, faking a laugh.

Chapter 17

The phone woke Giuseppe. He was dizzy and his head was pounding. "Hello?"

"It's Mario."

"Yeah."

"I was thinking about you and our situation all night. I was a bit too quick to react the way I did."

"You think?"

"Yeah, well, I wanted to see if we could work things out. I'm offering you your job back."

"Are you fucking with me, Mario?"

"No, dude, I need you here, and I was wrong. You didn't know what was going to happen in the parking lot yesterday."

"Damn, Mario, I didn't think you would ever admit you were wrong."

"Well, I am. Do you want to come back or not?"

"Yeah, I'll be in later today. I have my schedule here, so I'll be there."

"Okay, cool. I'll see you later."

"Yeah, cool, see you later… And, Mario, thanks for calling." Giuseppe shook his head, grabbed a bottle of water, and guzzled it down. He reached for the pill bottle, but stopped, jumped into the shower, and started to feel a little better. He was getting dressed when his phone rang again.

"Hey, Gee, how ya doin' this morning?" Victor asked.

"I'm a bit hungover, but doing okay. I gotta thank you, man, for coming to talk me off the ledge last night! I don't know what I was thinking."

"No problem, kid. That's what friends do."

"Hey, get this. I just got a call from Mario, and he offered me my job back."

"Really? No shit? Good."

"Yeah, I never thought Mario would admit he was wrong, much less say he needed me at the gym."

"Good for him for being the better man. I'm glad to hear you're back working. So, that's one problem solved. I want to talk to you about something else you said last night. I'm concerned about your drug use."

"No worries, Vic, I don't have a problem. I take a few painkillers every now and then, but I don't have a problem."

"Really, just like that? Tell me, how did you fix yourself? Quite a few people would like to know your secret. How did you do that *overnight*?"

"I don't really have a problem. Seriously. I was just having a pity party for myself last night, and I told you something I was just thinking."

"Kid, listen to me, and listen good. If I'm gonna take you under my wing and show you this business, I must have full trust in you. But I do not, I repeat, **I do *not*** work with people who use the shit we are selling. Do I make myself totally ***clear*** to you?"

"Yeah, Vic, I got you. No more Oxy. I got it." Giuseppe was pacing around his apartment.

"I'm not fucking around with you, Gee. If you need help, I will help you, but do not fucking lie to me, now or ***ever***."

"Okay, man, okay. I got it."

"Good. Now, back to business. I'll see you tonight around nine. We have to continue staking out Jersey City, but we're getting close to actually doing the job."

"Cool, Vic. I'll see you then." He emptied two bottles of pills down the toilet.

When Giuseppe walked into the gym as though nothing happened, the other trainers looked up from their clients and gave him a nod. Mario was at the juice bar, doing paperwork. "Glad to see you, Gee" he said, and shook his hand.

"Thanks, Mario. And for what it's worth, I'm sorry for yesterday."

At the end of the day, Giuseppe was craving Oxy bad. He'd left a bottle in his glove compartment, but now it was smashed under a ton of metal. He could always get more, but he really wanted to straighten out his life and stay on Victor's good side. When he took his phone from his locker, he saw that Lisa had called twice without leaving a message. He should have called her by now, but he didn't know what to tell her about his car. He decided to call her as he walked home.

"Hey, good looking."

"Hey, Giuseppe, I was starting to wonder what happened to you."

"Yeah, I'm sorry I disappeared for a couple days. I had a little accident with my car at the Port while I was working for my buddy Victor. My beautiful Vette is no longer, and I am walking back from the gym as we speak." He left out the part that he already had Victor's spare car.

"Are you okay? What happened?"

"It's a long story. I'm fine, but my car is totaled."

"Well, if you need a ride somewhere, I can take you."

"Oh, thanks, but I'm all set for now."

"I'm here if anything changes."

"Thank you. Do you think we could have dinner tomorrow night? I'd love to make it up to you for not staying connected."

"Sure, I'd like that."

"Great, I'll see you around seven tomorrow. By then I'll figure out my car situation."

"Sounds like a plan. Glad you're okay and I'll see you tomorrow."

Giuseppe hadn't felt this happy about a girl in a long time. He made himself a protein shake and headed out to meet Victor.

When he pulled up to the garage, he saw Vinnie's car. Never a good sign. He waved to the driver as he walked by. He could hear Vinnie yelling.

"When the fuck are you going to get this done, Victor? I told you to do this two fucking weeks ago!"

"Vin, I want to do this right. I do not want anyone in the building when we light it up. The last thing we need is more attention pointed in our direction."

"Fuck the attention! We should make sure they know it's us, so they pay up when we tell them to pay. I want you to take care of this tonight. Do you hear me, Victor? TONIGHT! No more excuses. While you're casing the place, who's doing the collection and supplying our distributors?"

"Me and Giuseppe are keeping up with it all. Everybody got their usual deliveries and paid up. We're on this, boss! I didn't know there was a timeline on this new thing. I'll take care of it."

"Tonight!"

"Okay, tonight."

Giuseppe tapped on the open door, and watched Vinnie pull out his gun. Giuseppe raised his arms and said, "It's just me. May I come in?"

"Yeah," Vinnie said, and put the gun back into his shoulder holster. "I'm done here anyway."

When he heard Vinnie's car pull out, Giuseppe said, "He's such a nice guy! So happy to call him my cousin."

Victor laughed. "You'd better shut up. Vinnie is one arrogant prick who has no clue how to run this business. His father gave people respect, but not him." Most of the lieutenants all felt the same way. Vinnie was too arrogant to be in his position in the business. "I paid my way to my position a long time ago. Sal gave me this garage so I could get away from the daily crap. Vinnie can't undo that, and it burns him up. We gotta do this job tonight, so I can get that little prick off my back."

Giuseppe was taken aback. He'd never heard Victor speak of Vinnie disrespectfully.

"I just want to make sure *no one* is in that building, or I'm not torching it. Get the cases from the back room and put them in the Escalade. Be careful. Don't let them fall over."

"Got it," Giuseppe said and headed to the back room. He saw three boxes containing upright wine bottles with paper towels under the corks. He opened the back of the Escalade, put a blanket on the floor, and very gently placed the cases on it. Then he found a few bricks and placed those around the boxes to keep them from moving. As he was closing the hatch, Victor came out of the office and got into the driver's seat.

As they drove to Jersey City, Victor explained, "Okay, so this is how I want to do this. I want to sit tight and watch the building. Do you know which one I mean?"

"Yeah."

"I want to make sure no one is in that building. I know the security guard does his walk through at ten. I've never seen more activity after that. The place is empty until the workers come back in the morning. So, after the guard is done, we'll wait another hour to make sure no one's around. The overnight guard stays in the trailer most of his shift and watches the cameras. He'll do a few circles of the property in a little pickup truck. If the pickup isn't parked next to the trailer, he's out doing his checks of the property. Now, what we're going to do is move the cameras that are set up on that building in a slightly different direction. They have to cover part of the building or the guard in the trailer will know something's off. We just have to point them away from the areas where we're gonna go. We'll do this together, step by step. After the cameras are turned away, we'll bring the bottles to three different areas of the building. The main entrance, the second-floor lobby, and the top-floor boiler room. The fuses are different lengths. The bottles with the longest fuses go to the top floor. Medium fuses go on the second floor, and then the shortest ones at the main entrance. As soon as the cases are set, we'll move fast, light the fuses on the top floor, then run down the stairs to light the fuses on the second floor, and run down to the fuses at the entrance. We got seven minutes from the time we light the first fuse to get outta there, or we blow up with the building. I want us in the Escalade driving when the top floor explodes. The second floor will go up thirty seconds later, then the entrance."

"Okay, I got it," Giuseppe said.

"Stick close to me and keep your eyes open. If you see anybody, get my attention and point them out. I'm going to be focused on what I'm doing."

"Okay, Victor. We got this."

***

Chris and Dan had a habit of meeting at Brady's after work, but lately they hadn't gone there as often. Tonight, they'd decided to have a drink together. Chris arrived first and ordered a Crown Royal and ginger. He texted Nicole to let her know where he was, and she texted back with a smiley face saying she was still at the office. He settled in to chat with the bartender and watch TV. After forty-five minutes, he called Dan. No answer. He waited a little longer, then called his sister.

"Suze, do you know where Dan is? We were supposed to meet at Brady's for a quick one, but he never showed up."

"No idea where he is. He must still be at the job site. He has been coming home a little later than usual. He told me he had to fix something." As Chris' top structural engineer, he'd been working on the plans for a new complex in West Jersey near the Pennsylvania border. Chris was surprised to hear there were problems.

"Alright, Suze, let me call him and see what's going on." He called Dan again, but it still went to voicemail. That didn't bother him, because he knew signal was spotty in that part of the state, which was quite rural. He left a message asking him to call and saying he wondered what was going on.

He pulled into his driveway just as Nicole was getting out of her car dressed for a court appearance. He watched her as she bent over to reach for her briefcase in the back seat. Her skirt rode up and he got a look at the best legs he'd ever seen. When she turned around, she saw Chris staring at her and smiled. Chris grabbed her ass as they walked into the house.

"Would you make me a drink, please? I didn't have the luxury of hitting the bar before I came home, like some people," she said.

"What would you like?"

"Anything with alcohol," she said, flipping off her high heels and plopping down on the leather couch.

"Rough day?"

"Yeah, I got a case where a gang member went up and punched an older man in the back of the head as he was walking down the street minding his own business. He knocked him out cold and he sustained a head injury. The problem is, the police didn't have enough evidence to prove it was him, and the judge dismissed the case. I feel terrible for the old guy and his family. They looked at me like it was my fault that the case got dismissed. I tried to explain it to them, but they didn't want to hear it. They just wanted someone to be held accountable. I told the police to keep looking for evidence. Not sure they liked me telling them what to do, but come on."

"That had to suck."

"Yeah, but it comes with the territory, ya know?"

"Yes I do, my love. Yes I do." He told her what happened with Dan, and they decided to order dinner from the Chinese restaurant down the street and eat in. Just as they finished eating, Dan called.

"Hey, man, I'm so sorry about Brady's. I didn't notice the time and my phone wasn't working right."

"No worries. It just wasn't like you to stand me up."

"Sorry, just got caught up with what I was doing."

Chris noticed that Dan was not saying anything about fixing anything but decided to keep that information to himself for now. "No biggie. We'll do it again sometime soon. It's been too long."

"Okay, cool."

Chris looked at Nicole and shook his head.

"What?"

"I don't know. Something has been off with him lately. I'm not sure what it is. He's probably wrapped up with the plans for the West Jersey project."

Chris fell asleep on the couch, and Nicole woke him to go to bed, then locked up the house and armed the alarm system. He was already asleep when she went upstairs.

Victor and Giuseppe saw the security guard pull away and head to the trailer. "Okay, that should be last person in that building for tonight," Victor said. "He'll watch the cameras from the trailer. One more guard will be in that pickup truck." He pointed to the lot about a hundred yards from their car. "That guy falls asleep every night in the truck. Before we do anything, put this on." He handed Giuseppe a black sweatshirt; Victor already had his black sweatshirt on. "I'll do everything. You'll just assist me. Be as quiet as you can and keep your eyes open."

Victor opened the safe in the back of the Escalade and gave Giuseppe a gun, then took one for himself. "Grab that box and follow me," he said. They'd parked in a dark spot, but the building they planned to destroy was lit up. It was the only completed unit in the project, and the sleek hallways were decorated with shiny marble floors and elegant fixtures. Giuseppe heard his heart pounding in his ears. They placed their backs against the building to stay in the shadows. Victor whispered, "Stay here while I unlock the door." He went to the huge glass doors, reached up to the security camera, and pointed it away. Then he took a tool from his back pocket and picked the lock. Ten seconds later, he signaled Giuseppe, who carried in the box of bottles.

Victor took two bottles and headed for the stairway. They climbed six flights to the boiler room on the top floor. "There's gotta be a camera here," Victor said. "Find it." Giuseppe found it fast and turned the lens away. "Good eyes, kid! Now the cameras on each floor, you need to point them in a different direction while I place the torches. Then I'll light them, and we head to the Escalade."

"Okay, got it."

Victor put the two bottles on the roof beside the door to the stairs and they headed down to the second level. Giuseppe easily found the camera and turned it in the opposite direction. Victor placed the bottles in the middle of the hallway near the elevator. They went to the next floor, and they did the same thing. Victor tossed him the keys to the Escalade, and Giuseppe ran through the main entrance, left the last two bottles by the double doors, and headed to the car. He started it, then got into the passenger seat. Meanwhile, Victor ran back up the stairs to the roof and lit the fuses on the two bottles he'd left by the door, then ran down to the second floor and lit the fuses that were in front of the elevators, and finally lit the two at the front entrance.

As Giuseppe was getting into the passenger seat, he saw the small security pickup truck heading toward the building. He opened the back door of the SUV and grabbed the baseball bat they used when making their deliveries. Then he moved into the shadow of the building. Victor was about to step through the doors when he saw the security guard approaching. He took a step back as the guard pulled on the doors to make sure they were locked. When they opened, the guard lost his balance and fell onto his back.

Giuseppe stepped out of the shadow and stepped on the guard's shoulder, pinning him to the ground with his foot while holding the bat up against his throat. Victor stepped out and said, "We gotta go."

"What about him?"

"Let him up." As the guard got to his feet, Victor took out his gun and put it to his head. "This is your lucky day," he yelled in the guard's ear. "I'm about to save your life. Give me your wallet so I can find you if you **ever** say a word about seeing us here." The guard reached into his back pocket and handed Victor his wallet. Victor grabbed it and screamed, "Get the fuck out of here! This place is going to blow." The guard ran to his pickup truck, and Victor and Giuseppe ran to the SUV. Just as they got in, the top floor went up in flames. Wood, metal, and glass flew everywhere. Then the second explosion tripped the third, and the building was engulfed in fire.

Victor drove fast to avoid the flying debris. Giuseppe looked back and was amazed how fast that building was burning. Victor pulled into a parking spot and shut off the lights but kept the engine running. He pulled the driver's license from the guard's wallet, then threw the wallet out the window. He was about to pull out onto the road when he saw a police car speeding toward the construction site. He waited for it to pass, then calmly drove off.

Giuseppe didn't know if he was allowed to talk, but he was dying to scream. He felt like he'd just hit the home run that won the World Series.

Victor pulled into the garage and closed the door behind them, then looked at Giuseppe and let out the scream. They began laughing like schoolkids and high-fived each other. "I can't believe we just did that!" Giuseppe yelled.

"Yes we did, kid. Yes we did," Victor said, and turned serious.

"What?" Giuseppe asked.

"That fucking security guard."

"Oh yeah. I forgot about him for a minute. What do we have to do about that?"

"Hopefully nothing. If he says anything about seeing us, we'll have to make a visit to his house. That's why I took his driver's license."

"Wow! That was smart thinking, Victor."

"Thanks, kid, but I've been doing this a few years."

"Yeah, yeah, I know, just saying."

"Come on, let's call Vinnie and let him know it's done."

***

At one-thirty in the morning, Chris woke up and sat up in bed for a minute before he realized his phone was ringing. He swung his legs over the side and answered. Nicole sat up and listened.

"Oh my God! How bad is it? What? Okay, I'm on my way."

"What happened?" Nicole asked.

"There's been a fire at the Jersey City complex. Alex said it looks like arson. They hit the completed building! Son of a bitch!"

"Do you want me to come with you?"

"Yeah, maybe you better." He threw a sweatshirt over his head. Nicole jumped out of bed and threw on her clothes. As they were getting off the Turnpike, they saw the flames and smoke from five miles away. "Oh my God, Nic! We can see it from here!" She grabbed his hand.

Police were stopping everyone at the gate except emergency vehicles. Alex was standing with one of the police officers and yelled, "Let him through, he's the owner."

Chris parked, jumped out, and looked at Alex. "What the fuck?"

"I have no idea. I got a call from the Jersey City police telling me the building was on fire. It was even worse when I got here. The flames were everywhere, and the smoke was so thick, I couldn't breathe, even from this distance."

"I don't know for sure," the police sergeant said, "but it looks like someone lit it up."

Nicole grabbed Chris' arm and held on as they watched the building burn. Chris asked the sergeant, "Did anyone get hurt? What about the security guys?"

"No, sir, everyone is safe."

"Thank God for that. Any idea how this started?"

"No, sir. The fire chief is just trying to knock the fire down for now. After it's out, we may be able to answer your questions." Another officer motioned for the sergeant to come with him. The two officers huddled for a moment outside the ambulance, then got in. The security guard was on the stretcher getting checked out. The officers heard the guard talking about who started the fire.

"An older guy took my wallet while another big guy held me down." he said. "The older guy said he'd come after my family if I said anything about them being there." An officer was taking the report, writing down everything he said.

"Can you tell me what they looked like?"

"Not really, except the older guy had salt and pepper hair, and the big one had brown hair." He started to cough a lot and the EMTs said they needed to get him to the hospital and ended the interview.

***

As the sun rose, the fire department had the blaze under control. The sergeant told Alex, "We may have a lead on who set the fire. One of the security guards saw two men as he was about to check the building for the last time this evening, but they threatened him and his family, so he's closed-mouth right now."

"Boss," Alex yelled to Chris. "You gotta hear this." He made the officer repeat what he said. Chris just listened and shook his head in disbelief.

The fire trucks and ambulances were moving out. Chris couldn't do anything else, so he and Nicole headed home smelling of smoke. He called his father from the car.

"Listen to me, Chris," his father said. "This is why you spend all that money for insurance."

"But, Dad, my investors won't want to hear we're insured when the building was just about to open and start making money."

"I know, but it happened, and the only thing you can do is rebuild. Right?"

"Yeah, I know. I'm pissed this happened. Plus, one of the cops told me that two guys were seen leaving the building and they threatened the security guard's family. Now who does that sound like?"

"What? Really?"

"Tell me that doesn't sound like Vinnie and his boys."

"Oh God, it does. Let's just see what the police investigation turns up."

"Dad, I don't know what I'm going to do if it turns out that Vinnie's boys did this. I really don't. I'll kill him myself."

"Stop that kinda talk! I know you're upset, but we don't joke about that stuff."

"Dad, I'm not fucking joking. I gotta go because I'm almost home, and I need to shower and get to the office."

Nicole reminded him what a smart businessperson he'd become and how much he'd accomplished, but he was too upset to hear it.

By eight that Saturday morning, Chris was heading to his office. He called Robin from the car and filled her in. She told him she'd meet him to go over the insurance papers and she'd ask their attorney to join them.

A couple hours later, Chris had calmed down enough to order lunch, and he called to invite Dan and Suze to join them so he could fill them in. When he told them, Suze suspected Giuseppe. She was still angry at him for crashing the wedding. Chris didn't want to think about Giuseppe being involved, but it made sense. He told Dan they'd have to put the West Jersey project on hold for a while and make rebuilding in Jersey City their priority. He wanted to show whoever torched the building that it wouldn't stop him. Now he was angry.

Chapter 18

A month after the fire, Victor and Giuseppe were in the office counting the cash they'd just collected from the route when they heard a car entering the garage.

"Who the fuck is that?" Giuseppe asked.

They looked at the monitor and saw Vinnie's bodyguard opening the passenger door for him. Victor buzzed him in. When Vinnie came to the office, it usually meant trouble. If things were running and money was rolling in, he left Victor alone.

Giuseppe asked, "Should I stay or get the fuck out of here?"

"Keep counting the money."

Vinnie didn't even look at Giuseppe. "Victor, we got a problem."

"What's up?"

"I heard from one of my cop informants that the security guard is talking. You wanna tell me why I shouldn't put a bullet in both your heads right now?"

"Wait a minute... You mean to tell me that prick is squealing? I warned him to keep his mouth shut. I took his driver's license so I could find him if he did something stupid."

Vinnie shouted, "But why the fuck did you give this guy a chance? You shoulda taken care of this when it was happening. What the FUCK is wrong with you, Victor? Are you getting soft in your old age? This motherfucker is talking! From what I was told, he gave the cops a very good description of you both. He told them you said something about saving his life. Why didn't you just give him your fuckin' name and address and explain what you were doing there? What the fuck am I supposed to do with you, Victor? Back in the day, we wouldn't be having this conversation because nobody could give a description of you."

Victor was getting too old for this shit. If Vinnie's dad were still in charge, he wouldn't be doing this anymore. "I'll take care of it," he said.

Vinnie got closer, pulled out his gun, and put it next to Victor's ear. "You'll take care of it? You. Will. Take. Care. Of it!" Victor swung his arm back, spun toward Vinnie, and took his gun. Then he pushed him so hard that Vinnie lost his footing and fell. Victor pointed the gun into Vinnie's mouth and released the safety.

Giuseppe jumped out of his seat and started yelling. "Whoa, whoa, whoa! Victor! Step back, man. Hold up a second!"

Victor knelt down. "If you ever point a gun at me again, you better pull the trigger, you little fucker. Outta respect for your father, I'm gonna let you go. Just remember who you're dealing with, you little cocksucker. You're a fucking child, and you do not deserve the position you're in. You haven't earned it. You're not your father and you never will be. You have NO FUCKING RESPECT!" He pushed Vinnie to his side and stepped back. Vinnie stood up, brushed off his overcoat, and left without trying to recover his gun.

"Dude, are you okay?" Giuseppe asked. "What the fuck?"

"I know! I just couldn't take that prick anymore. I'm probably a dead man now."

"No, don't say that! We'll fix this. I don't know how, but we'll fix this."

"Glad you're so optimistic."

"I am, Vic. We'll fix this together."

Victor laughed in his face. He was pissed that he'd let his temper get the best of him. "Maybe I shoulda killed him. Maybe then I'd get the respect I deserve. Yeah, I think I shoulda killed him because now he has to kill me."

"No one has to know what happened here," Giuseppe said.

"He's not going to let that go! I gotta see Salvatore, and I have to do it now. Are you done counting that money? I'll bring it directly to Sal."

"I'm almost done. Give me five minutes."

Victor sat behind his desk, took out his scotch, and drank it out of the bottle.

"Yo, Victor, can I ask you something? What are we going to do about that security guard?"

"Probably kill him, if I don't get killed first."

"You really think Vinnie would do that?"

"Not Vinnie, but he'll order the hit for me. Without a doubt, that arrogant motherfucker will take no responsibility for what went down today. He fucking pointed a gun in my ear! I gotta get out of here. Are you done yet?"

"Yeah, here, take it."

When Victor arrived at the house, Sal was in the back yard smoking a cigar. He turned to Victor and shook his head.

"You know already," Victor said.

"Of course I know. What do you think? Just because I'm not in the office, you think I don't know everything?"

"I've wanted to talk to you about Vinnie for some time, but I didn't think it was my place. The kid has **NO RESPECT**. He's gonna ruin everything we worked for, Sal. I keep my distance from him. I do what he orders me to do. Maybe he doesn't understand where we've come from and what we've done, but he acts like a self-righteous prick."

"YO!" Sal yelled. "That's my son you're talkin' about."

"I'm sorry, I'm sorry, Sal! Forgive me. I lost my temper. Really, I'm sorry. But do you know that he stuck a gun in my fuckin' ear less than an hour ago? Now, I ask you, is that respect?"

Sal took another puff from his cigar. "Okay, tell me exactly what happened. *Everything* as if I'm standing right there watching."

When he finished, Victor placed Vinnie's gun next to Sal's ashtray. "I don't know how to fix this one without your help. Your son and I do not see eye to eye to begin with. But I respect him as my boss, your son. My actions today were a reflex from having a gun pointed at my head. I didn't intend to disrespect him. Honestly, Sal. And I know he's not gonna let me apologize." Victor sat beside Sal and exhaled.

Sal's wife poked her head out the door and asked Victor how his wife was. They used to be close friends but had a falling out when Sal made Vinnie the boss. "She's good, Fay, thanks for asking." Fay nodded and closed the door.

"Sal, I'm asking for your help with this."

Sal nodded. "You're not the first person to tell me about Vinnie not handling himself right. I was hoping with experience he'd get better. I've talked to him before about his temper."

Victor held up a finger. "If I can ask you something... Vinnie obviously told you about today before I got here, right? Did he tell you anything about sticking a gun in my ear?"

"No, he didn't tell me that part."

"Well, now he's disrespecting you. At least tell the fuckin' truth! That's what I am trying to say to you, Sal, he's not you, and he's not running our business properly. He fuckin' has someone drive him around in a limousine with a bodyguard to open doors for him. What kinda shit is that?"

"I know, I know. He likes to show off."

"But we're not in business to show off! What happened to the days of keep a low profile?"

"I think it's this generation. They have to show off."

"But showing off is going to land somebody in jail."

"I know, Victor, you're right. I'll talk to Vinnie, and I'll take care of what went down today."

"Really? I would be so grateful. We go back a long way, and I really don't wanna be looking over my shoulder to see who's comin' after me. We did that for too long back in the day. I think I've earned at least a little respect."

Sal put a hand on Victor's shoulder. "You have, my friend, you have. I'll tell Vinnie to leave you alone and let you handle the business with that security guard. You're gonna take care of that, right?"

"Yeah, I'll handle that without a problem."

"Good." Sal took Vinnie's gun and put it in his pocket. "You wanna share a cigar with me for old time's sake?"

"Of course I do, of course."

Chris was at the Jersey City site with Alex and Dan watching the bulldozers knock the building down. He'd halted all the other ongoing construction and moved every worker here to clear the place and build it back as quickly as possible. The police had classified the fire as arson, but he had no idea the security guard was talking to them. His focus was getting the renters into the building so he could start a cash flow. Suze was working with Andi to line everything up for the reconstruction.

When his phone rang, he didn't hear it because of all the noise from the machines. He headed back to the office to find out where they stood on the permits. He was meeting with Suze when his phone rang again.

"It's Detective Franco from the Jersey City police."

"Yes, sir, how can I help you?"

"I was hoping to speak to you sometime today regarding the fire."

"Are you available now?"

"Perfect."

"See you in a half hour."

"Suze, you wanna come for a ride?"

She looked at him over her glasses. "Really? I'm in the middle of a lot of shit here, Chris. Where we goin'?"

"Jersey City Police Department."

"Oh, hell yeah, I can finish later." She was convinced that Giuseppe had something to do with the fire.

"I wanted to update you on our investigation," Franco said. "I'm not sure if you're aware that one of your security guards came face to face with the two individuals who started the fire."

"Really? No, I had no idea. Who was it?"

"Slow down," Franco said with a laugh. "We don't know exactly who it is yet, but we're thinking it may have been someone connected to organized crime. Were you approached by anyone asking for money?"

"Detective, I'm always being asked for money."

"Okay, well, maybe someone thought you should pay for extra protection or something like that?"

"I did get asked for that, and I told them to get out of my face. I knew who they were, and I had my own security in place."

"Do you remember who approached you? What did they look like?"

"I'm sorry, but I truly have no idea. I speak to so many people when I'm opening a job site of this size. I can ask my manager if he remembers. Can you tell me what the security guard said they looked like?"

"One was an older man with salt and pepper hair, average build, approximately five foot ten. The other was younger, like in his twenties, big, muscular build, and taller, like six-two, brown hair. The younger one had a baseball bat with him and held the security guard down on the ground. They both were wearing black."

Chris shot Suze a look to shut her up. "Wait, what about the cameras I had installed? They were everywhere. I'm sure we got something."

"We got the footage the night of the fire. These guys knew exactly where each camera was, and they moved each lens as they approached the area. So we didn't get any faces, just arms as they moved the lenses."

"But they knew what they were doing?" Chris asked.

"It looks like they knew *exactly* what they were doing. Well, if you come up with anything that can help us, please call me." He handed them each his card.

"Okay, I will definitely let you know, and thank you for your help," Chris said, shaking the detective's hand.

Back in the truck, Suze went off. "I told you that motherfucker had something to do with this. He definitely did this! What a piece of shit. What happened to him? Oh my *God*! He burned your five-million-dollar building down."

"Suze, get a grip. We don't know for sure if it was Giuseppe."

"Are you fucking kidding me? *Really?* Tell me that description didn't sound like Giuseppe. Tell me! Do *not* try to convince me that it wasn't him."

Chris knew in his heart it had been Giuseppe, and it made him terribly sad to think what had become of his cousin, his best friend. He also knew that he hadn't started the fight between them and that he'd tried to talk it out.

"And now that we know this," Suze said, "I think we should beat the shit out of him."

"No, Suze, we're not going to do anything to him. Now you sound like Gee. We're going to let the police handle this while we get the building back up and the renters in. That's the only thing we're gonna concentrate on. The investors want their money, and I want those buildings back up. Fuck Giuseppe! Hopefully the cops will catch them, and they'll get locked up for a long time. It's not worth our time or energy."

"I hear you, but I don't know how you can be so calm."

"Calm? You think I'm calm? I want to put a bullet in Giuseppe's head, but I can't."

"Okay, I'm sorry for saying that. I love you more than anyone in this entire world. Don't tell Dan. You're the best brother anyone could have. I'm here for you if you ever need to let it out."

Chris fought to hold back his tears. He started up his truck and headed back to the job site. Suze kept touching his shoulder as he drove in silence. He pulled into a Starbucks and asked her to get him a coffee so he could get himself under control.

Back at the office, Victor got out the guard's driver license, took his nine-millimeter gun from the safe, and twisted a silencer onto the barrel. As he was pulling the Escalade out of the garage, Giuseppe pulled in.

"How'd you make out with Sal?"

"Good, he said he'd talk to Vinnie and tell him to leave it alone."

"Do you think he will?"

"I fuckin' hope so! What are you doing here?"

"I was concerned about you. Thought I'd hang around 'til you got back."

"I'm good. I gotta go."

Giuseppe could tell that something was up, but he knew better than to ask any more questions. As Victor was closing his window, he let out a loud whistle to get Giuseppe's attention.

"I'm comin' with you."

"You know where I'm goin'?"

"I have a pretty good idea."

"Okay, it's your life."

Within fifteen minutes, they were outside the guard's house. Victor told Giuseppe to stay in the car. The sound of clattering pots and pans came from the kitchen window. Victor pulled out a ski mask, put it on, and leaning against the house with his gun in his hand, he stared at the back door. He wanted to put a bullet in Vinnie's head, not this security guard's. He'd thought he wouldn't have to kill anybody else at this stage in his life. Half an hour later, he heard someone unlock the inside door. A kid around thirteen years old came out carrying a garbage bag with both hands. When he saw Victor, he dropped the bag and screamed. Victor grabbed him and put a hand over his mouth. He heard someone running and pointed his gun at the back door. He hit the security guard's head with one shot. He flopped down the back stairs of the house and landed on the ground with blood pouring out of the side of his head. Victor knew he had to shoot the kid too.

Giuseppe heard the scream and ran to the house, thinking Victor might need help. He saw one of his young clients struggling to get free from Victor's grip, and the guard on the ground with blood pouring from his head. Victor let the kid go, raised his gun, and pointed it.

"No, wait!" Giuseppe yelled.

Victor lowered the gun. "I have no choice, Gee! It's either him or we both end up dead." He raised his gun again.

"Wait, I know this kid. I'm his trainer."

The kid was on his father's body crying.

"Jesus Christ! Are you fucking kidding me?"

"No."

"Gee, if he knows you then we *have* to kill him."

The kid took off running to the front of the house. Without hesitating, Victor fired into the back of the thirteen-year-old, who fell to the ground with a thump. Giuseppe stood there in shock. Victor grabbed Giuseppe's jacket and led him back to the Escalade. They both jumped in, and Victor took off for the Parkway.

Not a word was spoken as they drove back to Newark and into the garage. Victor shut the car off and turned to face Giuseppe. "Listen, kid, the last thing in this world I want to do is kill anyone. I've done enough of that already, and I am too old for that kind of shit. Killing a kid is the worst thing I ever had to do. I feel like shit, and I'm sorry you had to see that. But it's part of our business. If I didn't kill that security guard and his kid, Vinnie would have no problem killing the both of us, and that I promise you. He's just looking for a reason to kill me, and since you're my partner, you would also be killed, just for being part of my responsibilities. I'm really sorry, Gee, but you asked for more things to do. Well, this is what we do."

Giuseppe was quiet for a while. Then he said, "Yeah, I know. But I never meant shooting a guy and his son. That's a fuckin' lot for someone to take in. That kid was one of the better ones I train."

They sat in the SUV, staring straight ahead in silence. Finally, Victor said, "Come into my office and we'll have a drink." Victor pulled out the bottle of scotch and poured them each a glass. They tapped glasses and drank it, then refilled them again, and again.

Chapter 19

Every year, Chris looked forward to the company Christmas party. It was his way of thanking everybody and he went all out. This year, he had to work hard to put on a happy face so he could reassure his investors that everything was back on schedule and looking great. And he had to make sure his employees knew how much he appreciated the extra work they'd been putting in. He'd give some sort of bonus to every one of them, which was a lot of money coming directly from his own pocket.

He and Robin left the office early to be there before the guests arrived. As he drove home, he thought about how supportive and helpful Nicole had been. She was everything he was looking for in a partner. He was surprised how much he loved and depended on her. He'd never trusted anyone the way he trusted her. He knew he was making the right decision to marry her. After the trauma of the fire, he was finally beginning to feel like himself again.

When he pulled into his driveway, it was only three o'clock and Nicole's car wasn't there. He decided it wasn't too early for a cocktail and mixed one of his favorites, Amaretto di Saronno and Ketel One vodka over lots of ice. He let it sit on the counter for a few minutes as he went through his mail. He noticed a letter addressed to Nicole at his address. She didn't usually use his address for mail. Whoever sent that letter must have known this would eventually be her address too. He tossed the letter on the counter and went upstairs. After his shower, he was resting in bed in his underwear when he heard Nicole come through the garage door. He yelled, "I'm up here." She came up the stairs and into the bedroom carrying her dress in a garment bag.

"Look at you, all relaxed! I'm running around like a nut, and you're showered, shaved, and drinking a cocktail! What's wrong with this picture?"

Chris took a sip of his drink. "Do you need help?"

"No, I'm good, but thanks." She scurried around the room, getting organized. He just laid back and watched her get ready.

"Your hair looks fantastic, you going to the party like that?" Chris busted her.

She had forgotten that her hair was still in rollers. "Oh my God, I forgot to take these out before I left my house."

"But it looks fantastic! You should leave it."

She slapped his chest lightly. "You are such an asshole." They began to kiss and talk about the party. She lay beside him, and he rubbed her back. Then she jumped into the shower and Chris began to get dressed.

When she got out of the shower, she glanced in the bathroom mirror and saw him in his shirt and socks. She thought to herself, *How did I ever find such a great guy?* "Hey, handsome," she called.

"Yesssss," he answered.

"Can you make us one of those drinks to share? I don't want to get too tipsy before the party, but that sip was delicious."

When he returned to the bedroom, Nicole was still finishing her hair and makeup, leaning over the bathroom counter in her bra and panties. He went into the bathroom, grabbed her from behind, and kissed her back. She turned around and kissed him. His hands roamed her body.

"Chris, we can't, we *have* to be on time! You said you wanted to be there before anyone showed up."

He knew she was right, but he was already hard as a rock. Nicole saw how hard he was and decided to help. She got behind him, reached around, took his cock out of his underwear, and began to pull on it. He moaned softly and started to breathe faster. She kissed his back. He stood up straight and reached climax.

Nicole handed him the fresh cocktail. He kissed her and went back to the bedroom to finish getting dressed without missing a beat.

She wore a long black fitted dress with crystals on the bodice and left sleeve, a deep V-neckline, and a slit up to her right thigh.

"You look absolutely amazing, my love," he said, transfixed.

"And so do you, the most handsome man in the world."

They arrived at the party in Chris' new Jag. The table settings were designed to mimic snow, adorned with tiny sparkling lights and, in the center, a tall lit candle on a pedestal. The chairs were wrapped with red and green ribbons, and a huge tree with white angels and ribbons glowed in the corner. A nine-piece band was setting up.

Chris went to Robin and kissed her on the cheek.

"Oh my God! You scared me."

"Sorry about that," Chris said as Nicole leaned in and they traded cheek kisses.

"You two look amazing," Robin said.

"So do you, and so does this place," Chris said.

"Is Tara around?" Nicole asked.

"She's around here somewhere."

As Nicole walked away in search of Tara, Chris followed her with his eyes.

"You two are such a cute couple," Robin said.

"Yeah, she's alright," he joked. "I appreciate you more than you can ever know, Robin. Truly, thank you for everything you do for me every day." He gave her a huge hug and handed her an envelope with her bonus in it.

"It's my pleasure," she said. "You're the best boss anyone could ask for. Bill and I wouldn't be in the financial position we're in without your generosity."

Chris introduced himself to the band. He greeted the bartenders as they were setting up and asked for a large glass of water—he did not want to get drunk at his own party. He spotted Nicole and Tara talking and joined them. "Tara, you've outdone yourself," he said. "I didn't think that was possible after last year's party."

"Thanks," she quipped, "but wait till you see the bill."

Dan was helping Susanne with her coat as her parents arrived. Marie said, "This place looks like a fantasy winter garden."

Soon, the room was packed. More than five hundred guests had been invited, from construction workers and their wives to the mayors of the towns Chris was building in, to his attorneys, accountants, lenders—everyone who played a part in his business. Chris whispered to Nicole, "It's time for my speech." The band stopped playing as he approached the microphone. He wished everyone a happy holiday and thanked them for coming. He thanked his employees for all they'd done and mentioned the fire and rebuilding. He told them about their bonuses, which were double the previous years, and drew a laugh when he said the money had come from his own savings account. He thanked the mayors and the police departments of each town, then wished everyone happy holidays. He received a standing ovation. Truly humbled, he went to his table and sat between Suze and Nicole.

As the night was coming to a close, Chris headed to the bar to get Nicole, Suze, Dan, and himself a Sambuca. His accountant, Stu Greenberg, approached him.

"Want to join us for a shot of Sambuca?"

"Love to! I heard from my cousin Amos. Your ring is ready. He'd like to deliver it himself."

"Oh man! That's great news! Tell him to come over whenever it's convenient."

When the band announced the last song, Nicole and Chris got up to dance. Nicole looked up at him. "I am so proud of you. You're the best in every way, and I love you with all my heart. You make me so happy and I'm proud to say I'm with you, Mr. Christopher Yacenda."

"No, Nicole, I'm the one who's proud to have you in my life. You're beautiful, smart, supportive—everything I could ever ask for in a partner." He was tempted to get down on his knee right there on the dance floor, but he didn't have the ring. He had to get Tara alone before she left to ask if she'd had any luck with Luke Combs' manager. His proposal vision was to have the country singer performing "Beautiful Crazy" and "Forever After All" when he proposed.

Chris walked Nicole back to their table, then found Tara near the stage and pulled her aside. "I had a very hard time," she said, "but I finally got in contact with his manager. It just so happens that Luke has a concert scheduled in New York City in February. He'll do it. But we have to confirm the plans by January with his manager so he can arrange the time in Luke's schedule. And you have to pay him cash."

"You're the best. Just let me know how much he wants, and I'll have it that night. Oh man, I'm getting excited to do this," Chris said.

"Nicole and I have been close since college. I'd do anything to help you guys." They gave each other a big hug, then walked away like they'd never had a conversation.

Chapter 20

That night, Giuseppe couldn't sleep. He kept turning the TV on, thinking the news would have a story about the shooting. In the morning, there it was. "The shooting of a man and his son in their own back yard is being investigated by the police." His stomach dropped. He was scared out of his mind and didn't know what to do. Victor was his only friend, so he had no one to talk to. He went to grab his Oxy, then remembered he'd flushed it down the toilet. He stayed in bed watching the news repeatedly. When the phone rang, he jumped out of his skin.

"Kid, I'm just checking on you. You doin' okay?"

"Fuck no, I'm not okay!" Giuseppe yelled. "Are you seeing the news? It's all over the place that the cops are investigating. The father is dead, and the son is in the hospital, possibly paralyzed. The kid knows me! I'm so fuckin' screwed."

"Gee, calm your ass down. We'll be okay."

"Really? How the fuck are we going to be okay, Victor? The kid saw me!"

"I know, but we'll figure it out. I'm meeting Vinnie in a few minutes. I'll call you when I'm done."

Giuseppe knew he'd really screwed up this time. Why had he gotten involved with Vinnie? He said, "I'm going to jail," over and over as he paced the apartment.

When Victor walked in, everyone in Vinnie's office left. "You go to my father like a fucking cry baby?" he asked. "Tell Vinnie to leave me alone. Wa-wa-wa! You're one of the biggest pains in my ass."

Victor got really close to him and said through clenched teeth, "That's because *I should be in your position, and you should be beneath me*. Then the business would be run properly."

Vinnie pushed him away. Victor raised a fist to punch him but stopped. Vinnie held up his hands like a little kid.

"Can we get down to business?" Victor asked. "I'm not in the best mood."

"Yeah, yeah, yeah. Just relax yourself."

"Last night, Giuseppe and I went to take care of that security guard business, and it didn't go as smoothly as I wish it had. I waited outside the back of the house for the guy to come out. When the door opened, it was his son. The kid saw me with a gun pointed at him and started to scream, so I grabbed him and held his mouth shut. Then the father came out to see what was going on. I shot him right in front of the kid. I struggled to hold the kid still, and Giuseppe came to see if everything was good. The kid got loose and started to run away, so I had to shoot him too. I fuckin' hit him right in the back."

Vinnie held up a hand. "Wait. You shot the security guard, then you shot his kid?"

"Yeah, because the kid recognized Giuseppe. He knows him. I had to do something with him. But here's the problem: the father is dead, but the kid survived. He must'a talked to the cops as soon as he woke up from surgery."

"Is that what I heard on the news this morning?"

"Yeah, I'm afraid so. It's all over the news. So that's why I'm here. I'm coming to you as my boss, Vinnie, to see what you want to do with all this heat."

Vinnie laughed a fake laugh. "***Now*** I'm the boss? You and your boy fuck up royally, and you want me to fix your problem? You're some fuckin' jokesters, aren't you?" Vinnie's eyes were big and bulging and his breathing was fast. He pulled a gun from his waistband and pointed it at Victor's face.

Victor backed away, but with every step back, Vinnie moved forward. Victor reached for Vinnie's gun and grabbed his arm, pointing the gun toward the ceiling, and it went off. Two bodyguards standing outside the door came running in and tried to break up the fight. The gun went off again, this time into the wall. Victor's grip on Vinnie's arm was so powerful the guys couldn't pry it free. The gun went off again, hitting one of the guys in the thigh. Vinnie looked at the guy, who had dropped to the floor, and Victor elbowed him in the eye, forcing him to bend over in pain. Vinnie raised his hands to his face, letting go of his grip on the gun. Victor pushed the gun into the back of Vinnie's head and pulled the trigger. Brains splattered all over the floor and Vinnie dropped to the floor with blood pouring out of his head. The other guy put his hands up and backed up. "STOP!" Victor yelled, and the guy stopped in his tracks. The guy Vinnie shot was trying to crawl away.

"Let's all take a breath. RELAX and no one else will get hurt," Victor said. The guys looked at Vinnie's brains on the floor. Victor pointed to the injured guy. "Take care of him. There are bandages in the closet. Fix him up, NOW."

Victor threw Vinnie's gun onto the desk and helped the injured guy into a chair.

"I *DID NOT* want this to happen! I came here for Vinnie's help, and this is what he does? This is not how we run our business, and things will change. I do not want you two to be involved in cleaning up this mess. I will handle that. What I want you to do is call all the lieutenants and tell them we have an emergency meeting tonight at eight. It's a mandatory meeting, and whoever doesn't show will have to deal with me. Now get me some cleaning supplies and a body bag. Then get the hell out of here and be back at eight." Victor barked the orders to guys whose names he didn't even know. The unhurt one ran off to get cleaning supplies. The injured guy just sat in the chair, nursing his thigh. Once Victor had what he wanted, they both took off and Victor called Giuseppe.

"Gee, get your ass down to Vinnie's office now. We have a little cleaning up to do."

"I'll be right there," Giuseppe said, thinking Vinnie had come up with a solution to their problem.

When he got to the office, he smelled bleach. A body bag was on the floor and Victor was mopping up.

"Who's in the bag?"

"It's Vinnie."

"What the fuck, Victor?"

"Things got out of hand."

"Oh, ya think?"

"I need you to help me get him into the trunk of my car. I'll pull up to the door."

"Okay, then what?"

"Please, Gee, stop asking questions and do what I say right now. I'll explain as soon as I get this body out of here."

Giuseppe had been thinking he was going to jail. Now he thought he was going to die.

Victor came back and lifted Vinnie's body over Giuseppe's shoulder. They laid Vinnie in the back of the Escalade and pressed the button for the door to close.

"Now what?"

"Follow me." They jumped into their cars and drove back to their office at the port.

At the office, Victor poured himself a large glass of scotch, drank it down and poured another one, then told Giuseppe what had happened.

"I know this is not what you wanted," Giuseppe said, "but any idea what we're going to do now?"

"I'm taking over. I have a meeting tonight at eight with all the lieutenants. You will be my right-hand man."

Giuseppe wasn't sure he wanted to continue in this line of business, but he knew this was no time to bring that up, so he nodded.

"I'm hoping this doesn't start a mini war amongst the group," Victor said. "I know Sal will be putting out a hit on my head, and there's nothing I can do about that. I'll need good people to protect me, and I'm counting on you being my top man. You can pick others you trust."

"I don't know any of these guys," Giuseppe said. "How can I trust them with your life?"

"I have a few in mind, and we'll get them on board. Now, do you think you can help me get Vinnie's body out of my car, and dump it into the water by the big crane on the dock?"

"By myself?"

"Do you need me to hold your hand? Gee, you gotta toughen up a bit."

"Okay, okay, I can do it." Giuseppe took Victor's keys off the desk, drove to the crane, and backed the Escalade up to the dock. There, he popped the back hatch, grabbed Vinnie's body, and tossed it as far into the water as he could, muttering, "Thanks for the memories, cuz."

As he drove to the meeting with the lieutenants, Victor filled him in on which guys to trust and which ones to not turn his back on. His head was spinning. He knew the only way out was in a body bag. He was trapped.

Giuseppe had never seen any of the lieutenants. They were each accompanied by their right-hand men, all of them sitting at the bar, drinking. When Victor walked in, they stopped talking and stared.

Victor said, "All heads, get into Vinnie's office, and everyone else stay out here." Giuseppe wasn't sure if he was allowed in the meeting, but Victor motioned with his head, inviting him.

The men sat around a large table. Giuseppe stood with his back against the wall.

"Let me start by saying, this is not what I wanted to happen today," Victor began.

"Who the fuck are you trying to kid here, Victor?" someone yelled. "You wanted this to happen a long time ago. You thought you were next in line when Sal retired."

Victor stood up, took his gun from his waistband, and pointed at the guy mouthing off. "Are you done? Anybody else want to tell me what I did and didn't want? I'll listen." He glanced around the table, the gun still pointed at the man who had spoken out. No one said a word, so he put the gun back into his waistband. "As I was saying, this is not what I wanted to happen, not now, not ever. Did Vinnie and I have our problems? *Yes,* we did. But today I came to him with a problem, as he was my boss. Instead of offering to help with the situation I brought to his attention, he decided to try and shoot me. He said I was his biggest pain in the ass. Instead of helping me, he threatened me. I ask you, is that any way to run this business?"

The men began to mumble. "No, Victor, it's not."

"I had to defend myself, and we fought a bit over Vinnie's gun. It went off and hit Vinnie in the head. If any of you doubt me on this scenario, Vinnie's bodyguards were in the room and can tell you it's the truth. I didn't want this to happen, but now that it has, we have to move forward. I want to know if you guys can accept me as the boss, or are we going to have a war? I don't want you to answer me now. I want you to think about what I am asking. I will promise you all, this business will be run with a strict hand, but you'll make more money than you made under Vinnie's control."

Eight men were sitting around the table. Six of them said, "I'm in." The other two were silent.

"You need more time to think about it?" Victor asked.

One of them said, "I'm just having a hard time that you killed the boss, and that it seems to be okay with everyone else."

"I get that. So, what do you think should happen to me?"

"I'm not saying we need to do anything to you. I'm just saying we need to give Vinnie the respect he deserves."

"If the motherfucker hadn't attacked me, he'd still be here. But that's not what happened. He fucking went after me, and I had to defend myself. He never gave me any respect, so I'm done respecting that little prick. If you want to do something to give your respect, go do it. All I want to know is, are you with me or against me?"

The two men looked at each other. "We're with you."

Victor opened the door and called the bartender for a bottle of scotch and glasses. He poured a shot into each glass and passed them around. "Here's to a new generation. We are all brothers. We will respect and protect each other from here on out." He held up his glass, said, "*Salute,*" and walked around tapping glasses with each man at the table, patting their backs.

After they all left, Giuseppe asked Victor if this would be their new office. Victor said they'd stay where they were at the docks, but this would be a secondary headquarters.

Giuseppe was lost. He had no idea what his position was or what was expected of him. He thought of saying he wanted out, but he knew Victor was counting on him.

"Can I ask you something else?"

Victor was going through Vinnie's desk drawers. "What?"

"What are we going to do about the security guard and his son?"

"I got an idea, but you gotta give me a few days to get things organized around here. If all goes as I hope it does, we'll have a solution to our problem. If Vinnie would have just listened to me, my plan would already be in action. But since that's not the case, you need to lay low for a few days. No working at the gym. Tell them you're sick or something. The only place I want you to be is either home or right here with me. And always carry your gun. Once Sal realizes his son has disappeared, he'll come after me, and I need you to have my back. I'm sure one of the guys who sat around this table will tell Sal that I shot Vinnie."

"Okay, I got your back, now and always." Giuseppe made up his mind not to leave Victor out in the cold. He knew he was in for life, and he'd better forget about leaving.

Chapter 21

Chris was working in his office when his phone buzzed. "Someone's here to see you," Robin announced. "He says he doesn't have an appointment."

"Who is it?"

"Stu's cousin, Amos."

"Let him in! I've been waiting for this."

"I have your ring, Mr. Yacenda," Amos said, entering Chris' office.

"Fantastic! Can't wait to see it." Chris opened the box and stared at the beautiful, sparkling ring. He shook Amos' hand. "You did a great job! I love it."

"Thank you. It was my pleasure to help you."

Chris kept staring at the ring, elated by Amos' ability to make exactly what he had in mind. "Are we all squared up with the money I owe you?"

"Yes, we charged the balance to your card."

Chris put the ring on his desk and reached into his pocket for a tip, but he didn't have enough cash. He went to his safe and grabbed four thousand dollars in hundred-dollar bills.

"No, no, no," Amos protested. "You do not owe me anything more."

"This is for your outstanding craftsmanship. Please, I want you to have it."

"Okay, and thank you, Mr. Yacenda."

"Please, call me Chris. We'll be doing more business together, I'm sure. Once Nicole sees this ring, she'll want me to get all her jewelry from you."

Robin was watching, and as soon as Amos left, she ran into Chris' office. "Is that what I think it is?"

Chris handed her the ring box. She almost fell to the floor when she opened it. "Oh my God, it's beautiful!"

"Thanks, I love it myself, and I can't wait for Nic to have it on her finger."

"You're going to make me cry, stop it."

Chris tried to get back to work, but all he could think about was his plan to ask Nicole to marry him. He'd tell her they were meeting Tony and Lisa in the city for dinner. The new restaurant would be ready, but still not open to the public, so they'd have it to themselves. Tara, the event planner, would decorate the place with Nicole's favorite flowers and set a single table in the middle of the dining room. Luke Combs would sing "Beautiful Crazy" as they walked through the door. Tony would show them to the table. As Nicole sat down, Chris would get down on one knee and propose, then Luke would play "Forever After All."

He'd hired him to play for only an hour because he wanted to have Nicole all to himself. Tony would hire a professional to videotape the event. It was all falling into place.

He picked up the phone. "Tony, it's a go for Valentine's Day! I got the ring today and it's beautiful."

"I am truly happy for you. I'll have everything set up and ready to roll, but let's talk before the actual day."

"Yeah, of course. And don't forget, Luke Combs could cause a bit of a mess."

"I'll handle it."

Tara was excited to hear the news and told him she had it all covered. Since he wasn't getting anything done at work, he decided to leave early and put the ring in the safe at his house.

***

Gee wanted to see Lisa. He had so many things spinning in his head, but what would he say? He couldn't tell her what had happened between Vinnie and Victor, or what happened with the kid and his father, but he really wanted to see her. He called her but got no answer, so he left her a message to call him back. He was doing what Victor told him to do: tell Mario he was sick and avoid work for a few days.

He felt like a caged animal. He had to get out of his apartment, so he decided to go to Victor's office. When he got there, the garage door was open, which was very unusual, and Victor's car was there. He walked in slowly carrying his gun.

"Yo, Victor, you in here?" No reply. He tapped on the office door. No one was there. When Victor stepped out of the bathroom, they both raised their guns.

"Damn, boy, you almost gave me a heart attack! You know I'm on edge!"

"Sorry, I yelled out when I was coming in, but no one answered me. I was thinking I'd find you dead in your chair!" They both laughed hard from the stress.

"What are you doing here?"

"I'm going nuts in my apartment, so I thought I'd see what was happening around here. I can't stop thinking about that kid I trained."

"I got an idea about that situation."

"Please fill me in, because I'm going crazy thinking I'm going to jail."

"Okay. What we used to do, back in the day, when we knew someone had to go away, we got someone in the lower ranks to take the hit. In return, we took care of this person's family while they were in. Once the individual came out, he would be given a beautiful new house and lots of money. Then he would be placed higher in the organization."

"But how is that going to work in this case. The boy knows who I am!"

"We'll have to convince him how much better he'll be if he goes along with us. Maybe we can throw in, get him to the best doctors to fix his back. I feel bad he's paralyzed right now."

"If someone told me I could walk again, I'd do it in a minute."

"Well, let's hope he has your same thinking."

"Can we do this now?"

Victor laughed. "Yes, Gee, I'm going to get the plan started. Now that I'm the boss, we won't be doing that kind of stuff. You stay far away from this kid and his family. I'll have someone convince him. You hear me?"

"Loud and clear."

Victor picked up the phone and explained what he needed to a lieutenant. He didn't like doing it over the phone, but he wasn't leaving his office much because he was afraid Sal might be after him. He told the lieutenant to do it as quickly as possible and not to hurt anyone in the process.

Giuseppe was sitting in the office watching TV when Lisa called. "Hey, you!" They made plans for dinner that evening. He knew he had to get out of the area, so decided to take her to a fun sports bar in Morristown. He was heading home when he remembered he hadn't taken any pills since all the shit started with Vinnie and felt proud of himself.

A package was by his door. He wasn't expecting anything, so he was suspicious. He looked around and picked it up carefully, put it on the table, and noticed there was no postage on it. He called Victor.

"Yeah, Gee, I think it's okay," Victor said. "Open it, and I'll wait on the phone." Victor remembered that Mario had agreed to give Gee cash without letting him find out who it was from.

"Holy shit, it's filled with hundred-dollar bills!"

"Now go buy yourself a new car."

"Is this money from you?"

As much as he wished he could take credit for the money, he said, "No, but it's from a friend who did you wrong."

Gee had no idea what he was talking about but started counting the bills: fifty thousand dollars. He began to think this business might not be so bad after all. He decided to buy himself a Chevy Camaro. He didn't have all the money, but he could finance the rest.

When the sales associate saw him walk into the dealership, he came up to him.

"Hey, Giuseppe, Corvette treating you okay?"

"I wish I could tell you it was great because it was. But I had a little accident with it. Now I'm looking to buy a Camaro."

"I can definitely help you with that."

Gee got exactly what he wanted, a fully loaded blue Camaro. He couldn't wait to show Lisa. Victor had given him the keys to his house, so when he returned Victor's car, he went inside to leave the key. He'd never been inside before and looked around a bit, peeking into Victor's bedroom and the other bedrooms, which were no longer being used. In the corner of one of the rooms, he saw a huge safe and wondered what was in there. Guns? Money?

A few hours later, he pulled into Lisa's driveway and honked the horn playfully. He saw someone look out the window, then Lisa ran out the door. "Is this your new ride?"

"Yes it is, you like it?"

"I love the color!"

"You ready to go?"

"Let me just grab my purse."

As she ran up the steps, he watched her, thinking she was one hot lady.

Gee was happy that the sports bar wasn't crowded. Lisa told him about her week, then said, "Again, I'm doing all the talking. Tell me about *your* week."

There was no way he could tell her what he'd been through. "Same old stuff, except today I got a new car."

As they were leaving, a guy purposely bumped into Giuseppe. "Yo, man, watch where you're going."

"Tell Victor to watch his back, his days are numbered."

"I'm watching Victor's back, so if you got something going down with him, you got something going down with me. Do you want to take care of this little problem right here, right now?" Gee opened his jacket to display the gun he wore at his waist, and the guy left.

Lisa gasped and stared at Giuseppe, unable to say a word.

"You okay?"

"Why do you have a gun on you? I know you're not a cop."

"Can we go outside, and I'll explain?"

He threw some money on the table and grabbed her arm, gently guiding her to his car. He had no idea how he was going to get out of this one.

"Okay, let me explain. I've taken a new security job, and I have to wear a gun."

Lisa finally looked at him.

"I was hired by a really rich dude named Victor, and I got a carry permit. I forgot to take the gun off before I came to get you. I'm sorry. I should have told you."

"Ya think?"

"I'm really sorry. I should have left it home."

"And when where you going to tell me you had a new job? I always do all the talking when we're together. You know everything about me, but I don't know anything about you. You need to fill me in a little more if this is going to work."

"Again, I'm sorry, and I should have told you." She was buying his bullshit, so he added a little sympathy. "I didn't want you to think I was some sort of loser who had to get a second job in order to buy a car."

"Gee, I don't think you're a loser. I like you a lot, but I'm not going to be with someone who doesn't tell me everything or lies to me."

If she knew how much he was lying!

"Who was that guy in the bar?"

"I honestly have no idea, but he threatened my boss, so I needed to tell him he was barking up the wrong tree."

"Where does this Victor live?"

"In Livingston, in one of those huge mansions."

Lisa was getting answers that made sense. She invited him to hang out and watch TV back at her place, and he loved the sound of that. He thought maybe he'd get a chance to see those breasts of hers.

They sat on the couch, and Gee put his arm around her shoulders. He wanted to touch her so badly, so he kissed the top of her head. She looked up and they started to kiss. His hands brushed over her breast and he felt her nipples get hard. Then he tried to unhook her bra, but she said, "No."

He stopped, afraid to do anything else. She stood up, took his hand, and led him to her bedroom. "Sorry, but my sister will definitely come in," she said.

No sooner had they shut the bedroom door when they heard the front door open. "See what I mean? I think I made a big mistake having her as a roommate."

Gee started to kiss her again and unhooked her bra. He took her shirt and bra off, then unbuttoned his pants and guided her to her bed. She lay down and pulled him toward her. He kissed her stomach and, at last, caught sight of her beautiful breasts, which were perfectly round and soft. He wasn't sure how far she would let him go, but he had no intention of stopping before she said so. He kissed her tenderly all over, and her hand roamed to his groin as she spread her legs, and he wandered between them.

She reached down and started to unhook her pants, but Gee stopped her, because he wanted to do it himself, and he lifted her out of them. There she was, with only her panties on. He had been waiting for this moment and didn't want to rush it. He roamed her body with his hands and kissed her all over. She looked into his eyes and that got him even more excited. He needed to taste her, so he pulled down her panties and got out of his clothes, went to the foot of the bed, and crawled up her legs, kissing and licking her, then slid two fingers inside her as she moved her hips, moaning.

She pulled him up to her mouth and he got on top of her, holding his body above hers. Lisa wrapped her arms around his shoulders. He spread her legs with one leg and entered her very slowly but as deeply as he could. She grabbed his ass and rocked to his rhythm. She couldn't hold back and let out a soft moan. Gee didn't stop; he moved in and out of her until she came, and seconds later he did too.

Chapter 22

"**M**r. Yacenda, this is Detective Franco. I'm calling to update you on your building fire case. I wish I had better news. The case has gotten very complicated. Your security guard was recently killed at his house, and we believe his death is related to the fire. His son was shot in the back and is paralyzed. At first, the son gave us good information, but as of today, he keeps changing his story and we're not sure why. First the men were white, then he changed that to black. There were two men, then he changed that to three. One man was old, the other younger. Now he is saying they were both in their twenties. The boy no longer wants to cooperate with us. He asked us to stop calling him and allow his mother to grieve in peace. I'm sorry to tell you this, Mr. Yacenda, but we have no evidence, and since the boy was our only witness, we're at a dead end. We'll keep your case open and help you with whatever you need for insurance purposes, but otherwise, we're at a halt."

"*Really*? Would it help if I told you who did it? *My* fucking cousin did this!"

"Do you have any evidence to back that up?"

"No evidence, but I know it was him!"

"I can't charge him without corroborating evidence."

"I understand that, but you don't have *anything*?"

"No, sir, we don't. Something happened to make the boy stop talking."

"Yeah, my cousin Vinnie happened."

"Is your cousin Vinnie Yacenda?"

"Yes! Tell me you didn't know that." Chris was getting madder and madder.

"No, I did not realize you were related. As I said, we are not closing this case, but we have no concrete evidence at this time."

Chris could hear his heart pounding in his ears. Vinnie must have someone from the police department on his payroll, most likely the asshole on the phone. "If you investigate my cousin and find something, call me. Until then, I'll have my insurance people and attorneys call you." He slammed the phone down.

Robin looked up, but decided to stay where she was. Chris rarely lost his temper, so she knew it had to be bad.

Chris called Nicole. "Well, isn't this a nice surprise."

"Nic, I am so pissed off right now. I just got a call from the police about the fire. They have *no evidence*. Can you believe that? They have *nothing*!"

"How can they have nothing? Don't they have the camera footage?"

"Oh yeah, they have it, but they tell me it's an arm turning the cameras away from the scene."

"Come on, how is that possible?"

"Exactly! How could that be possible? My cousin Vinnie is how that's possible. I think he's paying someone off in the department. They explained that the case got *complicated*. The guard's son was talking, but all of a sudden he started changing his story. He told the cops to stop calling him. Come on, tell me this isn't Vinnie using his power."

"Definitely sounds that way."

"I'm asking for your legal thoughts on this."

"Let me go talk this over with my boss, and I'll call you right back."

"Thanks."

Five minutes later, she called. "My boss said he could put a little pressure on the police, but he also said it wasn't looking good if they told you they didn't have any evidence."

Chris was silent for a moment, digesting this.

"But, Chris, look how fast you're rebuilding. It's amazing," she said, trying to make him feel a little better.

"You always try to see the bright side, don't you?"

"No, I speak the truth, and you're doing an amazing job with what you got handed."

He decided to talk with Alex and Dan and drove to the job site. As he pulled into the lot, he saw both their cars. The hammers and saws were going non-stop. Alex was sitting behind his desk in the office.

"Yo, the big man came to visit us," Alex said jokingly at Chris.

"Yeah, yeah, yeah. Where's Dan?" Chris was in no mood for joking today.

"Must be in the building somewhere. I'll call him on his radio." There was no answer, so he called again. Still no response.

"That's alright, I'll take a walk over to the building and find him."

"I'll come with you."

As they walked around the building, Chris was surprised by how much had been rebuilt. When he asked one of the workers if he'd seen Dan, the guy pointed to a closed door. They opened it to find Dan on top of Alex's secretary, Andi.

"***WHAT THE FUCK?!***" Chris yelled. Dan jumped up and was trying to get his pants on when Chris kneed him in the groin. It was more than Chris could take. He punched Dan in the face, kneed him in the groin again, and kept beating him until Alex pulled him away. Dan was bent over, holding his balls. His mouth was bleeding, and one eye was beginning to swell.

"Let me go, Alex," Chris demanded.

Alex released him and he went for Dan, but Alex grabbed him again, and one of the workers came over.

"Help me get him out of here," Alex said.

Outside, Chris began screaming. "What the fuck is my sister going to do with this? You think what I just did to him was bad, wait until Suze finds out! They just got married. Oh my God, my dad is going to kill him!"

Alex had no idea this had been going on. "Boss, let's get you back to the office and calm you down."

Andi was buttoning up her shirt, while Dan leaned against a table holding a rag on his face, trying to stop the blood.

In the office, Chris was pacing.

"What can I do for you?" Alex asked.

"I don't know! Dan is like a brother to me! Another brother who stabs me in the heart! What am I going to do with this one? Go out there and tell him he's fired and ***never*** to set foot on any of my properties? Then tell him to go to his house and clear his shit out because my sister will absolutely destroy him?"

"Okay, boss. Stay here!"

"Yeah, I gotta call my dad."

His father started cursing in Italian. Chris could hear his mother in the background asking what happened and his dad answer her in Italian, but Chris' Italian failed him when his father started asking questions. He was talking way too fast. "Dad, English, please."

"What are we going to do with this? Your sister... Oh, my poor little girl. How can this be true? They just got married."

"I saw them with my own two eyes, Dad. It's true."

"Okay, we need to tell her as a family."

"I agree with that. I'll meet you in the parking lot of my office." As he left, he saw Alex and the worker helping Dan out of the building and yelled, "Don't help that son of a bitch! Get your ass off my property on your own, you piece of shit!"

As soon as he got in his car, he called Nicole, who was in shock and offered to be with the family when they told Suze.

When he got to the parking lot, he found his mother crying and his father pacing and Nicole getting out of her car.

When she saw that her whole family was there, Suze got off the phone fast. "What's going on? Why are you all here? This can't be good."

"No, it's not," Chris said. "I gotta tell you what happened when I went over to the Jersey City site."

Marie walked around Suze's desk and took her hand.

"I walked into a room and found Dan screwing the secretary."

Suze jumped out of her seat. "*WHAT DID YOU JUST SAY?*"

"I beat the shit out of him and fired him."

"Wait, you actually caught him in the act?"

"Yup."

"No way this is true! We just **fucking** got *married*! How can he be screwing around on me? He loves me," she shouted, tears streaming down her face. "No way... No way is this true."

Nicole was rubbing her back while Marie held her hand tightly, but she broke free and began pacing around her office, sobbing. Then she fell into Chris' arms and beat his chest. "Tell me this is a joke. This can't be true. He wouldn't do that to me. He loves me."

"I'm sorry, Suze, but it's true. I wouldn't have believed it either."

Suze collapsed into a puddle of tears, and the whole family got down onto the floor and hugged her.

"I told him to get his shit out of your house before you got home," Chris said. "I don't want you to ever see his face again."

"But I love him, Chris."

"I know, Suze, I know. Stay at my house for a while until you figure things out."

"Can we go to Mom and Dad's place so I can be in my old bed?"

Giuseppe was feeling awesome. He had a new car, a new girlfriend, and a new position within the organization. He no longer craved his pills or thought much about his mother and father and Chris. He was beginning to live for himself, not worrying about the other side of the family. When he walked into the office, Victor was looking at the ledgers as usual, making sure everyone was doing what they were supposed to do.

"I'm thinking about quitting Mario's Gym."

Victor looked up.

"I think I could be more useful here."

Victor had a big smile on his face. "My boy is growing up! I think that's a great idea. This way you can be here more, and I can give you things to do besides watching me work."

"I'm your security, remember?"

Gee called Mario and gave him two weeks' notice. Mario was relieved to get rid of him and all his drama. He told Gee he didn't need to come back. He didn't want another visit from Victor.

Gee told Victor about his date with Lisa, leaving out the part about making love to her for the first time. When he told him about the guy who bumped into him at the sports bar, Victor brushed it off, saying he knew he'd have a lot of enemies. He'd already sent his wife, daughter, and son-in-law to his house in Florida for their protection.

The phone rang, and Gee heard, "Uh-huh, yeah, uh-huh, okay, and who's taking the hit? Good, very good work. Come see me with that information today and I'll take care of you."

He hung up and looked at Gee, smiling. "You can sleep easy. Our problem with the kid is taken care of. He's not talking to the cops anymore."

"Oh my God! That's the *best* news I've heard so far! But how?"

"Don't you worry about that, it's done!"

Gee got out of his chair and gave Victor a bear hug from behind.

"Knew that would make you happy."

"Oh, you have no idea! Victor, let me ask you something, how do you keep your wife out of all this stuff?"

"I tell her just enough. She knows what I do now, and I'm sure she had a very good idea back in the day. I'd let her know if I was going to be late, or tell her about some of the meetings, making it sound a little more business-oriented than it actually was. Why are you asking me this?"

"It's Lisa. She's not a dumb chick. She can figure things out."

"Sounds like she's got you, huh, Gee?"

"Yeah, I think she does. I haven't had this type of relationship in a very long time. Just not sure how to handle some of this. She saw I had a gun on my waist the other day and was a little freaked out. But I covered by saying I was your security guard and you're paying me very well."

"Speaking of pay, for now, I'll be increasing you to two thousand a week."

"What? Really? In cash?"

Victor laughed. "Yes, Gee, in cash, and it will go up as soon as I get the structure of this organization to my liking."

"Holy shit! This is awesome! Thank you, Victor. Whatever you need me to do."

"Watch that word 'whatever.' Something's going down today I want you to know about. I don't want to be looking over my shoulder much longer, so I'm putting a hit out on Sal. It should be going down any minute."

"How did I not know about this?"

"I have to bring you to more meetings. I'm not used to having a bodyguard, but that will change."

Victor answered his phone and Gee went back to watching his TV. Breaking news interrupted his show.

"Salvatore Yacenda was shot and killed while getting a haircut. The well-known mob godfather was in the barber's chair when he was riddled with at least twenty bullets. No one else was injured."

Gee pointed to the TV and Victor gave him a thumbs-up, which made him wonder how this man, who had been close to Uncle Sal, didn't care that he'd had him killed.

***

Chris took Valentine's Day off to make sure everything was in place. He was nervous, but so excited. He called Tara and Tony to be sure they were all set, then went to his parents to tell them he was planning to propose that night. For a moment, he forgot Suze was still living with them. From her bedroom, she could hear them talking and yelled, "Don't do it! Don't get married! It ruins everything!"

She came downstairs looking like she hadn't showered in days. Chris knew she'd been struggling, but he didn't realize how badly. "Suze, we're talking about Nic, not Dan."

"Yeah, that fucker had us all fooled."

"Watch your mouth," Marie scolded her.

Chris said, "I think it's time you start getting yourself together, don't you? You need to reach out to my attorney and ask him to recommend a good divorce lawyer—"

"This is not work, Chris. I am not taking orders from you on how to handle this."

Chris sat back in his chair. He realized he was barking orders like a boss. "You're right, you're right. I'm sorry. I'm just trying to help you."

Suze started to cry. She was a mess, and he had to help her. Their parents had been leaving her alone, letting her go through the motions, but he wanted her to move on. She told them Dan had tried to call her at least a thousand times, so she'd blocked his number. Chris said he'd have someone call her about starting divorce proceedings.

"Now can we talk about me?" he asked jokingly. A small smile came to Suze's face when he showed them the ring.

He'd arranged for a car to drive to take them to the city, as he often did when they got together with Tony and Lisa.

Tony and Lisa were standing at the front door to greet them as they got out of the car.

"Ready to see your new place?" Tony asked.

Chris took Nicole's hand and led her inside. She was so distracted by the beautiful décor of the bar area, she didn't even notice that there was only one table in the dining room. Then she noticed her favorite flowers in huge vases, and right on cue, Luke Combs' band began to play, and she stopped dead in her tracks.

Chris got down on one knee and asked, "Nicole, where do I begin?" And she began to cry. "I love you more than I could put into words, but I'm going to try. From the moment I met you, I knew there was something different about you. You are so caring and loving. You have the same family values as I do. You are always there for me. And you're the most beautiful woman I've ever laid my eyes on. You are the best of the best, and I can't imagine my life without you being by my side through good and bad times. Will you do me the honor of becoming my wife?"

Nicole's hands were shaking, and tears were rolling down her face as Chris put the ring on her finger. "Yes, Chris, yes."

He stood up and kissed her, tears running down his face as well. Then he held her tightly and they danced to Luke's singing.

"How in the world did you get Luke Combs here?" she asked.

He put a big smile on his face and said, "Anything for you, babe."

Tony handed them each a glass of champagne. "To the rest of your life."

Tara came out from the corner where she'd been watching. She was shedding tears down her face as she ran up to Nicole and gave her a joyful hug, both of them weeping as they admired the ring.

***

Victor gave raises to all the underbosses. Things were going well, and they were respectful and obedient. He ran the organization the way Sal ran it back in the day, and he brought his family back to New Jersey.

Giuseppe loved making so much money, knowing even more was coming his way. He no longer made deliveries with Victor, so he was being paid more for doing less. And he no longer craved his pills. He had a girlfriend now to care for his needs, and she was beginning to like his "bad boy" side, especially since he could buy her jewelry now and then.

Chapter 23

Chris and Nicole were having dinner at a steak restaurant, enjoying each other's company, when he interrupted her.

"Do I hear Gee's voice?"

They both looked around. Giuseppe was at the bar with his arm around Lisa, drinking his usual Jack and Coke.

Chris turned red. "What should I do, Nic?"

"Let's just ignore him. Hopefully he'll be an adult and ignore us too."

Chris wanted to try to talk with his cousin, but Nicole convinced him it was neither the time nor place, which made him want to get out of the restaurant. As they were leaving, two short stocky guys hurried in, almost knocking Chris and Nicole over, and headed straight to Gee. One of them pulled out a gun and Chris yelled, "Gee, hit the floor, hit the floor!"

He instinctively protected his cousin, and Gee instinctively listened. He grabbed Lisa with both hands and pulled her onto the floor. Gunshots flew over their heads and into the bar. Before Gee could return fire, the two guys had run to their car.

When Chris helped Gee get back to his feet, he saw the look on his face. He was shocked that they'd been shot at, and even more shocked that Chris had saved him and Lisa. He stood there staring at Chris, then bear hugged him.

"Dude, you just saved our lives," he whispered. "Where the fuck did you come from?"

"Nic and I were leaving when we saw what was happening. I just did what we always did—save each other's asses."

A pair of cops showed up with their guns drawn and said the perpetrators were gone. The other diners were milling around, wondering what was happening. No one was hurt, but everyone was scared.

"You want to go somewhere for a drink?" Chris asked.

"Yeah, I think I could use a drink," Gee said.

They walked to a nearby bar, found a round table, and ordered. Then they were silent. Chris rubbed his hands together, searching for something to say.

Nic rescued him. "Gee, don't you want to introduce us to your girl?"

"Oh shit, I'm sorry. Lisa, this is my cousin Chris and his girlfriend Nicole. Guys, this is Lisa."

"Nice to finally meet someone from his family," Lisa said.

Then they were silent again. Chris wasn't sure if he wanted to punch Gee in the face or hug him again. Gee squirmed as though his chair was on fire. When the drinks arrived, Chris nodded to Gee, and they took their glasses to the bar where they could talk privately. Nicole told Lisa that the guys hadn't seen each other in a while and needed to sort through a few things.

They stood at the bar looking at each other, fidgeting. Chris said, "First, thank God I saw that guy coming for you with a gun."

"Right, thank God you were there to save me again, right, Chris?"

"No, I didn't mean that. I meant thank God you're alive. Do you think you can just stop, *please*? Lose the attitude for five fucking minutes?"

"Sorry, man, it's just that we have a pretty shitty history."

"Yeah, but regardless, I hate that we don't talk anymore."

"Me too, but I'm not sure we can go back to where we were."

"I don't care that we don't go back to where we were. I want you back in my life, Gee. This is crazy and stupid."

"A lot has happened in the past year. I've changed."

"Are you saying you don't want to be in my life? Not now, not ever?" Chris asked.

"No, I'm not saying that. I just don't know how our two lives will connect anymore. I'm not the same person. I work for the other side now, and I'm moving up the line. I like it."

"I know you're working for Vinnie. I've known that for a while. But I don't know if that means we can't be friends."

"But I do *things* now."

"I know, I don't think I really want to know exactly what you do. But are you ever going to tell me what you *did*?"

"You know I can't do that." He took a big gulp of his drink. "Let's just say you really don't want to know what I've been doing."

"Okay, I don't need to know. But I do want you back in my life, Gee."

"Me too. Where do we begin?"

"Well, Nic and I are engaged."

"No shit? The guy who said he'd never get married is engaged."

"Let's go back to the girls and include them in the conversation. Maybe they can help us get through this."

Back at the table, Nicole kissed Chris and whispered, "I'm so proud of you." He winked at her.

Gee said, "Lisa and I have been dating for about eight months now. I think things are going pretty well, but after tonight that might have changed."

Lisa said, "No, I'm tougher than I look."

"You'd better be if you're hanging with this guy," Chris said jokingly.

They kept the conversation light. Nicole and Lisa exchanged phone numbers, and they went their separate ways. It was a beginning. Chris felt good about seeing Gee again, but questions raced through his mind. He wanted to know whether Gee had anything to do with setting his building on fire. He wanted to know if he was off drugs. He wanted Gee to talk with his parents so his aunt would stop worrying every second of the day. He wanted to help him get away from Vinnie. Then he realized this had been the first step, and that he had to stop trying to help his cousin. He'd have to let Gee live his own life, make his own mistakes or successes. He knew they had a long road ahead but was happy to have talked to him.

Chapter 24

Suze had gone through the shocked stage, then the sad stage. Now she was onto the angry stage. She'd do anything she could to make Dan and the secretary's lives a living hell. She posted all kinds of derogatory comments on social media, accusing Andi of being a home wrecker and a whore who hooked up with anything that could walk. She had a better plan for Dan. She still had his credit card, and she went shopping. She planned to max it out with clothing, dinners, gifts for her parents. She had crawled under his truck, loosened the oil plug, then followed him until he broke down in the middle of a highway and drove by while he was trying to push it out of traffic, honking her horn and giving him the middle finger. Revenge was fun. She wasn't killing anyone, so what harm could there be in a little payback?

Chris tried to keep her busy with work. Now that the Jersey City apartments were almost rebuilt, he was ready to focus on the Blairstown complex. Dan had been his site manager there, so he needed a replacement. When he walked into Suze's office, she was setting up a team of carpenters, electricians, and plumbers. Chris sat in the chair listening to her do her thing. She was impressive, on the phone with two contractors and a third on speaker. She gave him a look like she was going to kill somebody.

"Alright, so when can we get this started? The property has already been leveled but nothing's happening up there! Chris is on my ass to get this going, and I don't even have a fucking date!"

Chris pointed at himself. He didn't want anyone to know that he was in her office, so he couldn't say anything but tried to communicate with facial expressions. He loved his sister and appreciated how hard she worked for him. He was paying her a fortune, but she was worth every penny.

Tom, the head electrician, was on speaker phone. "Maybe you should hire a new project manager now that we don't have Dan," he said.

Chris knew that would hit a nerve. Her face turned red, and she called Tom every name in the book.

Chris decided to speak up. "Okay, gentlemen and Suze, let's bring this down a few levels. Suze, take a breath. We're in the process of getting a new project manager, but it takes time to find someone with the right organizational skills."

"I didn't know you were in the meeting, Mr. Yacenda," Tom said.

"I wasn't until I heard screaming coming from my sister's office. It doesn't matter if I'm in this meeting or not. Never talk down to Suze. She's your boss and deserves your respect."

"I apologize for my comment. I know it's a sensitive area, but if we had a project manager, we could get all our eggs in one basket."

"That's exactly what I am trying to do here," Suze said, "get us all on the same fucking track. For the time being, I'm the project manager."

All three department heads said, "Yes, ma'am."

"Okay, now that we got that settled, when are the roads are going in?"

Chris headed back to his office. Robin buzzed him to say that an applicant for the position for project manager was standing in front of her desk. Chris greeted him at the door with a strong handshake.

"Good afternoon, Mr. Yacenda."

"Have a seat, Michael."

Michael was a tall, well-built, very athletic-looking guy in his early thirties who had the experience Chris was looking for. He explained what he'd done on his last job, which had recently been completed.

"Does that mean you can start right away?"

"Yes, sir."

Chris went over his application and saw that they'd both graduated from Montclair State College, and that Michael had played football, baseball, and wrestling. He said he'd be in touch by the end of the week. When Michael left, Chris gave Robin the thumbs-up.

As Michael was waiting for the elevator, Suze walked past him and straight into Chris' office. "Do you believe that fucking prick telling *me* to hire someone to replace Dan? Who the fuck does he think he is?"

"Close the door if you need to vent," Chris said calmly.

She kept talking as she closed it. "I am so sick of hearing that man's name."

"I know, but—"

Suze started to cry, so he got up and gave her a hug. "I got some good news after all this."

"What, you heard Dan fell off the face of the Earth?"

"Well, not exactly, but I think I found a replacement for that man you want to fall off the Earth." He was afraid to even say Dan's name.

"You did?"

"I just had a good interview with a guy who meets all the requirements, plus he went to Montclair. You probably walked right past him at the elevator."

"I didn't notice anyone by the elevator, but I wasn't looking. When does he start?"

"I didn't tell him he had the job yet. I need to look over the other applicants one more time. I'll make my decision tomorrow at the latest."

Robin looked at Chris as Suze was leaving, as if to ask if she could do anything to help her. Chris shook his head no. They were used to communicating without saying a word.

***

Victor had an office built for Gee next to his. Although Sal and Vinnie were both dead, he knew he still had to watch his back and preferred to keep his bodyguard close. He put Gee in charge of all the pick-up and delivery crews, and made him responsible for keeping track of the money coming in and the inventory going out. Gee liked having more responsibility, although Victor told him exactly what to do.

Things were running smoothly for him, both at work and at home. After seeing Chris, he decided to call his mother. He tried to explain that he was fine and enjoying his life, but couldn't be the son he once was because he was no longer that person. He said he was enjoying "the other side of the family," without mentioning that he'd dumped his cousin Vinnie's body in Newark Bay or that he knew his Uncle Sal was dead.

His mother couldn't understand his decisions and asked him to come home, but he told her that wasn't going to happen. He tried to tell her about Lisa, but she just kept begging him to stop what he was doing and come home. He knew he was breaking his mother's heart, and he felt terrible, but when you work for the mob, there's no getting out. He told her he'd call every now and then, maybe even stop by, but that was all he could give her.

Victor called from his office, "Gee, get in here!" Gee was there in seconds. "Frankie just got busted. I need you to go down to the station and bail him out. I'll call Marco and get him to work on this. It's not too bad. Frankie beat a few people up because they were mouthing off while he was collecting the money." Marco was their go-to attorney. Victor opened the safe and handed Gee several rolls of hundred-dollar bills. "I'm not sure what the bail is, so just take this and bring me back the receipt and the remaining money."

"Okay, Victor, I'm on it. Where was he arrested?"

"Newark Second Precinct on Lincoln Avenue."

Frankie had a big smile on his face as Gee walked him out of the precinct past the cops who busted him. Gee had learned by now that no one should be cocky or showy in their line of business. He said, "Wipe that fucking smile off your face before I kick your ass right here." Frankie knew he couldn't mess with Gee, so he stopped smiling and got into Gee's new Camaro.

Back at the office, Victor calmly asked Frankie, "Is there anything I should know about what happened?"

"No, sir. I went to Branch Brook Park to meet my regular customer, and he started mouthing off about the increase we're putting on our supplies. He was disrespecting me, and I hit him with a baseball bat. Someone from the park called the cops, and the rest you know."

"Okay, Marco will be in touch. Listen to every word he says, got it?"

"Yes, sir."

"Now get out of here."

Not long after Frankie left, Gee heard Victor yell, "What the fuck is going on? This is the second time today we're bailing someone out. Maybe we need to remind those cops that if they leave *us* alone, we'll leave *them* alone. Crackdown? Really? Fuck 'em! I'll show them a crackdown."

He sent Gee back to the Second Precinct to bail out another guy. In the car on the way back, Louie told him that the Newark cops had been ordered to get the drug dealers out of Branch Brook Park. Back at the office, Gee told Victor the cops were talking about a new female prosecutor.

Victor made a call to his contact at the precinct. "Yo, Coca-Cola, what the fuck is happening in Branch Brook? Two of my guys got popped today."

"We got orders to clean up the park."

"Really? And who gave these orders?"

"I'm not sure yet, I was just told that a female prosecutor over on West Market is trying to stir things up."

"When you find out who this female prosecutor is, let me know."

"Okay, Victor. I will."

Victor hung up the phone and turned to Gee. "Some chick is trying to make a name for herself at the prosecutor's office and decided to start with our territory. If she knows what's best for her, she'll find somewhere else to make a name."

"Who is it, do you know?"

"No idea, but we'll find her. Do me a favor and round up three guys to throw a couple of Molotov cocktails into the lobby of the Second Precinct. Get it done today."

Within an hour, Gee had three guys standing in his office while he told them what to do. It made him feel powerful, almost as high as the drugs had made him. He missed that feeling, but he knew Victor would shoot him if he ever touched another pill.

Two hours later, Gee told Victor to turn on his TV, and they watched the Newark Fire Department put out the blaze at the Second Precinct. It was just enough damage to get Victor's point across.

Chapter 25

Chris had plans to meet Tony at his restaurant, while Nicole had dinner with her girlfriends. He always drank a lot when he was around Tony, so he had his driver take him into the city. He brought along the top five applications for project manager to study on the way in. Robin had made notes in the margins after she checked out all the references, all of them excellent. Only Michael had a degree from Montclair State. Chris circled Michael's name. He had the new project manager for the Blairstown site.

They hit a lot of traffic, so he used the time to check in with his parents. He'd already heard that Gee had called his aunt Annette, but for some reason, his mother told him again, which made him worry she was forgetting things, and he hated the thought that she was getting older. Then he asked if his sister was there, and she got on the line.

"Of course I'm here, where else would I be since my *newly* married husband cheated on me, and I'm back living with Mom and Dad?"

"You don't have to stay at Mom and Dad's place. You make enough money to live anywhere you want."

She laughed. She was staying there because she needed her parents. "Maybe I'll build a big house somewhere like you did."

"You could, you know? You could do anything! I just wanted to tell you that I figured out our new project manager for Blairstown. It's Michael Della Piazza, the last guy I interviewed today."

"Boy, that's some last name. I see we're back to hiring Italian boys."

"I didn't hire him because he's Italian. He's qualified and he went to Montclair."

"Oh, I get it, he's a Red Hawk." That was the Monclair College mascot.

"Wow, that brought back a ton of memories. Speaking of memories, I'm heading in to see Tony, and we just pulled up, so I'll see you tomorrow."

Tony was waiting for Chris at the bar. They moved to a comfortable booth and didn't stop talking. He told Chris that the restaurant was doing so well, they had a waiting list for reservations, even on weekdays.

The next morning, Nicole was in the shower when Chris woke up, so he joined her. "Get out of here!" she said laughing.

"Nope." He pushed her against the shower wall and kissed her back as the warm water ran over their bodies. He lathered her up, then slid his fingers inside her, and she lifted her leg onto the shower seat. He held her in his arms, and she wrapped her legs around his waist as he entered her. She had no control until he put her down, pulled out, and let loose on the stone wall.

Nicole watched Chris rinse the soap from his body. She was so in love and knew she was lucky to have him.

At her office, Nicole saw that her directive to clean up Branch Brook Park had resulted in two arrests. The neighborhood had once enjoyed the park, but drug dealers, gangs, and the homeless had taken over, and now everyone else was afraid to go there. She was glad the cops had started listening to her. As she was looking over her court schedule, her boss called her into his office.

"I just got off the phone with the chief from the Second Precinct."

Nicole thought he was going to congratulate her.

"He said his rookie cops arrested two people in the park yesterday, and somebody threw Molotov candles into the precinct a few hours later. Luckily, no one got hurt, but it was a message from the mob."

"Oh shit! How bad was it? I guess we ruffled a few feathers."

"Yeah, I would say *you* did!"

"I was trying to help."

"I know, Nicole, but maybe you should stick to prosecuting criminals who've already been charged. Don't you think you have enough on your plate?"

"Drug dealers and gangs do their business at that park. Where is it safe for the people of Newark? The police need to clean it up."

Skip looked at her over his reading glasses. "The police know what they need to do. You should stay out of it."

"But all I said—"

Skip held up his hand, then waved her out of his office.

Nicole left his office, but now she was mad. She was only trying to help the people of Newark, not get the police station burnt down.

***

Suze was leaning against her car in front of Dan's house, waiting for him to step outside. She'd made a pile of all the belongings he'd left at their house and poured lighter fluid over it. She was already late for work and losing patience, so she decided the hell with it, and banged on the door.

Andi answered wearing a baby-doll night gown. "What the fuck do you want? Get the fuck out of here, you cunt."

Suze hadn't expected to see her. She'd imagined that Dan was suffering from the breakup as much as she was. She never thought he was still with Andi. Her mind was going in a million directions.

She grabbed Andi's hair and pulled her out of the house, but before she could punch her, Dan stepped out, lifted her off the ground, and carried her to her car.

"Get out of here, Suze!"

She didn't move.

"Suze, get out of here, and don't ever come back or I'll call the police." She spun her car around, leaving a circle on the blacktop, then remembered she hadn't set fire to Dan's stuff, so she slammed on her brakes, and put the car in reverse. Dan was still standing outside. She lit a cigarette and tossed it on the pile, then peeled away as the flames shot up.

Suze walked into Chris' office and slammed the door behind her. She told him Dan was still screwing Andi and that they were shacked up. She said that Andi had called her a cunt and Dan told her he'd call the cops if she came back.

Chris knew she'd crossed the line.

"Why did you go to his house? You're better than that. Stay away from him, Suze! Fuck him! You don't need him."

"I need payback, Chris! He hurt me!"

"I know, but for your own good, you need to stay away from him. The longer you don't see him, the stronger you'll get. We're better off knowing who he is now than finding out years down the road."

Suze sat quietly for a few minutes. "I dumped his stuff at his front door and set it on fire."

Chris stared at her, then he cracked up, and they both laughed until tears ran down their cheeks.

"Well, I think you got your payback. Now get the hell over it!"

That night, Chris was in the mood for Portuguese food. He told Nicole he'd pick her up at her office and take her to one of the restaurants in Newark. Over lobsters and sangria, she told him about the Second Precinct and Branch Brook Park. She was still angry that her boss had told her to lay off. Chris told her about the new project manager and what Suze had done at Dan's house.

"You don't want to mess with a pissed-off Yacenda."

"Well, you'll be a Yacenda soon. Maybe you should try a little pushback on your boss."

They decided to take a walk along the Passaic River. Chris liked to look at the housing complexes that lined the waterfront. The moon was big and bright, but when it got chilly, they headed back to the car.

"See, this is what I'm talking about," Nicole said. "We just took a nice walk in Newark without being bothered by gangs or drug dealers. We could never have done that at Branch Brook Park. I'm not giving up my fight."

"Good for you. If something bothers you that much, you gotta do what you think is right."

"Yeah, because I'm a future Yacenda."

"I didn't mean you didn't have it in you before."

"I know what you meant. It was cute."

***

Gee was watching TV at Lisa's house while she finished up her notes from the day at the hospital. Just as he was starting to fall asleep, she jumped over the couch and onto him.

"Don't you think you should let me meet your parents sometime soon?"

He wasn't ready for that conversation. "Lisa, I haven't even seen my parents since we started to date. I don't talk to them anymore. We're no longer close, and I don't need their approval for anything."

Lisa knew his family was a sore subject, but she wanted to meet them. "Okay, then how about meeting mine? Don't you think it's time?"

"I know your sister. Not well, but I met her a few times."

"Come on, you know what I'm saying."

"So set it up. I'd love to meet your parents, your aunts, your uncles."

"Okay, now you're getting sarcastic."

"Me?"

"I'm going to find out if my parents are around this Saturday. Maybe we can take them out to dinner."

"That works for me. Just let me know. I promise to be on my best behavior." He kissed her and put a hand on her breast. She took off her bra and threw it over her computer, unhooked his belt, and began to unzip his jeans, but he stopped her, stood up, and put his gun on the coffee table. Lisa rolled her eyes at him, then slipped her hand into his fly and massaged him through his boxer shorts. Gee leaned back as she started to jerk him off. He hadn't been expecting this, but he was enjoying himself. She took out his dick and worked her magic, making circles on the tip. He slowly pushed her head down and she knelt in front of him, licking his hard dick and flicking her tongue on the tip. He didn't want to cum all over her, so as was about to explode, he brought her up to his lips, pulled her underwear off, and got on top of her, moving slowly. He pulled out and pushed back in slowly. Lisa grabbed his ass as he entered her, each time a bit deeper. Then he picked up his pace and she climaxed. He hadn't bothered to put on a condom. They'd been too into each other.

Lisa snuggled up to him, her bare butt peeking out from under the blanket. They heard someone unlocking the door—Lisa's sister coming home from a date—grabbed their clothes, and ran to the bedroom like schoolkids getting caught. Lisa's sister saw them and laughed. "Aha, I caught you!" Then she noticed Gee's gun.

In the morning, as Gee was getting his stuff together, he realized he'd left his gun on the coffee table.

"Oh shit, Lisa, I left my gun on the coffee table overnight. Do you think your sister saw it?"

"Most likely! She doesn't miss a trick, that one!"

"Fuck! What should I do?"

"Nothing, I'll handle it."

Lisa was making coffee when Dana came into the kitchen. "Do you want to tell me why you're dating someone who carries a gun and isn't a cop? Are you crazy?"

"Dana, he carries a gun because he works for an armed security place."

"Yeah, and I just hit the lottery. He doesn't work for a security company. He's in the freaking mob!"

Lisa knew he protected a rich guy named Victor, and she thought about the time Chris saved their lives at the bar. It was starting to make sense. She'd never wanted to know. She was falling in love with him and knew he didn't want to share much about that life. He had a way of scooting around the questions she asked.

"You may be right," she said. "He said he was guarding a rich guy who paid him very well."

"So, what are you going to do?"

"I don't know. I'm in love with him."

Dana took her coffee back to her room, leaving Lisa to ponder what it would mean to be a mobster's girlfriend. How much danger was she in? She needed to talk to Gee, the sooner the better, so she called him.

"I need to talk to you. It's kind of important."

"You want me to come over now?"

"Can you?"

"I'll be right there."

He told Victor he had to run out for a few minutes. Lisa was waiting for him on her front steps.

"You know I'm not stupid, right?"

"Oh shit, what did I do?" Gee asked.

"Nothing. The problem is what ***you do***."

Gee felt his body get hot. He knew she was breaking up with him.

"Tell me the truth. Do you work for the mob?"

He didn't even know what to say.

"Gee, answer me."

"I'm not sure how to answer that question, or even if I'm allowed to answer it."

"Well, I have my answer, don't I?"

"What do you want me to say?"

"Right now, I'm just asking for the truth."

"Yes. The truth is, yes."

Lisa's eyes filled with tears. "I don't know what to do with that information. What does that mean for me? How much danger am I in? Hell, we were already shot at in a restaurant! Should I be looking over my shoulder all the time? What about my family, are they in danger too?"

Gee sat beside her and put his arm around her. "Lisa, I'm in love with you. I'm new at this relationship thing. I would do anything to keep it going. I would also do anything to keep you and your family safe. Sure, my work can be dangerous, but let's take Victor, for example. He's married and has a family, and they've never been in danger." He didn't mention that Victor had sent his whole family to Florida to keep them out of danger. "I love you, and I want us to have a future if you still want that."

"I love you too, but I need to think about this, and I need some space."

"Okay, whatever you need. I'll be here waiting for you. I'll do whatever I can to reassure you."

"Give me a week. I don't want to hear from you at all."

"Okay, I'll do my best not to text you, but I'll miss you more than you know."

She laughed a little as tears flowed down her face, then she went into the house. Gee sat there for a few minutes with a lump in his throat and a pain in the pit of his stomach.

He went into Victor's office, closed the door, and sat on the other side of the desk with a tear running down his face. Victor got up and sat on the corner of his desk.

"What the fuck, Gee?"

"Lisa just asked me if I worked for the mob. I didn't know how to answer it. I wasn't even sure I could answer it without getting in trouble. I think I lost her."

"Gee, I know where you are right now. Years ago, I had the same conversation with my wife. Yes, you have to be honest with them, and no, you are not in trouble with me. It's a hard balancing act. We don't want to involve our loved ones, but they figure it out. My wife knows because I needed someone I can talk to, but she doesn't know the details. I have to be honest with her to keep her. I also give her everything she wants—houses, jewelry, money. Whatever she asks for, she gets. I don't fool around like some guys. She's my one and only and I want to keep it that way. I love my family and would do anything to keep them away from all this. We need someone in our lives to talk with, and for me it's my wife."

"Lisa said she needs space to think about things."

"Give her that space, Gee. She'll come around."

"I hope so. I haven't felt this way about a woman in a very long time."

Lisa was in her bedroom with the blinds closed and the door shut. Dana came home at lunch, knowing her sister was in a bad place. She tapped on her door. "Can I come in?"

"Yeah."

"I think I can tell how the talk went. Are you okay?"

"No! He was honest with me and told me he did work for the mob. I just don't know if that's the life I want. He treats me so well. I'm like a princess when I'm with him."

"Well, mobster wives get whatever they want."

"What movie are you watching?"

"No, really, they do." She mentioned a few women they'd grown up with. Lisa had never put it together that some of her friends had fathers who were "connected."

"How do you know these things?"

"I'm just more observant than you are."

"What do you think I should do?"

"Give it some time. Think about Gee, not his job. That's what I'd do. I really think you could handle it. You don't find many guys who treat you like he does. I can tell he really loves you. I think he's a keeper, but it's your decision. Meanwhile, stop this undercover routine. It's your day off. Go do something."

***

On Monday morning when Suze drove the new site manager to the Blairstown project, it looked like a deserted lot. The trees had been cleared, and the ground had been graded, but it was overgrown with weeds, and the entrance was blocked with a heavy padlocked chain.

"Looks like I got my work cut out for me," Mike said.

"I'm sorry it's in such bad shape. We had a massive fire at one of our sites in Jersey City and Chris had to pull all his workers to rebuild it."

She handed him the key to unlock the chain, and as they drove the dirt trails, she explained what had to be done to build the luxury townhouse development. Back at the office, she ordered more trailers for the site. Mike would need to set up a mobile office, and she wanted the project out of her hands as soon as possible.

Nicole went to the Second Precinct to inspect the fire damage. She knew she couldn't get the park cleaned up without help from the cops, so she asked to speak to the chief.

His greeting was less than friendly. "Do you have any idea what you started here?"

"I'm just trying to help the residents get their park back. I hate to see drug dealers and gangs taking over, don't you?"

"I advise you to go back to the prosecutor's office and do your job before I lose my patience."

"Excuse me, this *is* my job. You arrest and I convict, and as a team, we'll clean up the park. What's the problem?"

"Didn't you get told to stand down?"

"Not exactly, Chief. I came here for a friendly talk, but it's not going that way. I'll talk to your boss, if you'd like that better."

"Go right ahead. Do what you have to do. But you're not making any friends here, missy."

She called Chris from her car. "I need your advice."

He heard the hurt in her voice. "You got this, Nic. Just because some asshole closed his door doesn't mean there aren't more you can open. Why isn't your boss giving you more support? He should have your back. Don't you think it's a bit weird he told you to leave the park alone?"

"Yeah, he usually backs me up, so I'm not sure what's going on with this one."

"Maybe your next step is to find out. Maybe someone got to him."

"No way! He's the county's highest law enforcement officer. I don't think he could be bought."

"Nic, *everyone* can be bought. Just be careful. He's not going to back you on cleaning up the park if the mob is paying him to stop you."

Nicole peeked into her boss' office. "Skip, you got a minute to talk?"

"Not really, but what's up?"

"I went down to the Second Precinct and the chief basically threw me out of his office."

"Jesus, Nicole, why can't you just leave this one alone? I told you to move on to something else. Why can't you do that?"

"Skip, what's happening here? Talk to me. Something's up, and I don't like what I'm seeing."

"You're not seeing anything, because there's nothing to see. If you don't have enough work, I can find a lot more for you."

"Have you been down to Branch Brook Park lately? It's become a war zone. Drug dealers and gangs have taken over. It used to be a beautiful place where people could hang out, play, exercise, whatever. Isn't it our jobs to help that?"

"Leave it alone, Nic. I won't tell you again. Now get out of my office."

She went back to her desk feeling defeated and stared at her computer, not knowing what to do.

Chapter 26

Gee gave Lisa three days, then decided to send flowers. The entire nursing staff was excited when the arrangement arrived at their station, and they gave her the encouragement she needed to let Gee off the hook. She texted him that she wanted to talk, and he texted back suggesting dinner, then ran into Victor's office to tell him.

"Good," Victor said, "maybe you'll stop walking around like your life was over. Now go down to Branch Brook. Make sure nobody else is getting arrested."

As he pulled into the park, he saw three unmarked police cars, and when he approached one of his dealers, one of the cops started walking in their direction.

"Good afternoon, Officer," Gee said from his car window. The officer kept walking, and the dealer laughed.

"Any problems down here today?" Gee asked.

"Not today, man, not today."

"Good. Call me if anything starts up."

That night as he drove to Lisa's place, Gee's heart was in his throat. She opened the door before he knocked.

"Wanna talk here before we go to dinner?"

He thought that was a good sign. "Yeah, whatever you want."

She silently went to her bar and came back with drinks. Gee was sweating. In complete control, Lisa motioned to the couch, and he sat beside her, careful not to sit too close.

"Where do we start, Gee? I spoke to Dana about us, so she knows what you do. Actually, she'd already guessed. I just didn't want to see it. She convinced me to look at you as a person, not at what you do. What you do scares me in so many ways. For you, for me, for my family. What kind of danger am I putting my family and friends in?"

Gee looked up from the floor. "I can't answer that because I don't know. I've been doing this work for a short time, and so far, there hasn't been much to worry about. Do we do things that may be illegal? Yes, but we're not killing people like in the movies."

"What *do* you do, Gee?"

"I do a lot of counting money for Victor. I do whatever he needs me to do."

"What about when we got shot at? That wasn't cool! What was that all about?"

"Lisa, that stuff does not normally happen, and I am so sorry you were with me for that. I will do everything and anything I have to do to protect you from any of that happening ever again. We were going through some reorganization. I didn't know about it because I am so new to the business. Victor is teaching me as I go."

"Well, I'd better not have to go to your funeral because Victor didn't teach you something."

"Does that mean you'll take me back?" he asked with a big smile.

"You never lost me. I just needed a little space to think. I love you, Gee, but I can't put my family or my friends in danger because of you."

"Victor tells me his family is never involved with any of his problems. They only do that stuff in the movies. But I'm not going to lie to you. When we were going through that rough reorganization, he sent his entire family to Florida for a couple months just to be safe. It was a very scary time in the organization. I won't be able to tell you everything, but I promise to keep you more informed than I have in the past. I love you like I've never loved a woman before."

"I don't want to know everything, just don't lie and tell me you work for a security company when you actually work for the mob."

Gee thought he'd said all the right things and could breathe again. He wasn't used to feeling this way about a girl.

***

When Chris got home, Nicole was on the deck, bundled up in her winter coat with a bottle of wine beside her.

"What's wrong with this picture?"

"I'm just having a day I want to forget."

"Wanna talk about it?"

"Yeah, but I may need another bottle of wine," she said sarcastically. "I hate my job! I hate the politics and I hate that it prevents me from doing what needs to be done."

"Is this about the park?"

"Again, Skip told me to mind my own business and stop trying to clean it up. Isn't **that** my business? Isn't that part of why I'm working for the prosecutor's office? What am I doing so wrong here?"

Chris let her talk without interrupting, hoping he could come up with something to help her.

"I feel like I'm being punished like a child for doing something wrong. In all my years at this job, I've never been treated so poorly. I'm trying to help the people get back to normal lives not war-ridden by gangs and drug dealers. What is wrong with that?" She took another big gulp of her wine.

Chris took her hand and held it for a minute. "I hate to tell you this, but everything about your job is political. You've been lucky to stay out of that shit for all this time. You just didn't see what was going on because you care about the victims, and there aren't many like you. Somebody above you is always pulling the so-called string of justice, but which way is that justice flowing? Who does it benefit?

"I come across this problem when I'm starting a new complex. Who has their hands out for money to look the other way? It's the same in your office. Someone's pulling the strings, and you're in the middle, doing the right thing, trying to help people. But sometimes it's bigger than that. And this looks to me like a very big string."

"I want to cut that string, Chris!"

"Oh no you don't! You could lose this fight and get hurt."

She knew he was right. Someone was getting payback. She didn't think it was Skip, but maybe someone above him. She knew she had to let it go. Whoever had the nerve to set the police precinct on fire could do something terrible to her.

"I got an idea," Chris said. "Why don't you come work for my company? I could use an attorney who cares."

"Thanks, but no thanks. I don't have any experience in that kind of law."

"Doesn't mean you can't learn it."

"True, but—"

"But nothing! Just think about it for a couple days. No pressure, but I'd love to get you out of the prosecutor's office. They're all corrupt!"

"I'm not corrupt, and neither are my colleagues. That was a nasty comment, Chris!"
She got up and went into the house.

Chris felt terrible, but in his eyes, most of the people in the prosecutor's office were corrupt. He gave it a few minutes, then went inside to find her.

"Nic, I'm sorry. I didn't mean to insult you. You're such a great lawyer. Come work for me. I need more people like you on my team."

"No, I'm not coming to work for you because someone hurt my feelings. I think I'm better than that."

"I didn't mean you weren't. I'm—"

"I'm going to my place for the night. I need to get my head together, and I don't want to take it out on you. I know you're trying to help me, but right now, it's not working."

Chris felt his heart drop, but let her go. He didn't know what else to do. He called Suze and told her about their fight. She advised him to let Nicole have space. "You call that a fight? You two really gotta have more disagreements. This is nothing! She had a hard day at the office, and you can't help her. Leave it alone! You can't fix everything and everyone, Chris."

"I'm not trying to fix everyone, just trying to help Nic feel better, and I made it worse!"

"No, she just didn't like what you said. She doesn't always have to agree with you."

"God damn it! You women are driving me crazy! I never said she always had to agree with me."

"Call me anytime, brother. I'm here for you," she said, taunting him.

Chris hung up, made himself a drink, and sat down to watch TV. He was done with everyone.

Nicole decided that since her boss told her to forget about her crusade to make the parks safe, she'd reach out to the media. She had a few contacts with the local television stations, and they were all interested in doing a story. She gave them the information she had and pointed out that the drug dealers were connected to the mob. She'd get the word out without being directly involved.

Skip walked into her office and closed the door. "Turn the TV on." The first story about the parks was live. They watched as the presenter explained that the mob was preventing the police from cleaning up the parks.

"Tell me you had nothing to do with this."

"I did not have anything to do with this."

"Can you see why I don't believe you? Is it just a coincidence that you started to stir the pot, and now the TV news is all over it? You know I don't believe in coincidences. Do you know how much danger you put yourself in? We've worked together too long for me not to know you had something to do with this. Now I have to worry about your safety."

"Skip, I don't need your protection."

"Yes, you do." He held his head in his hands. "You have no idea what you did, Nicole, and I'm worried for you. First, you're not going to court today. I'll get your cases postponed."

"No, don't do that."

Not listening to her, he said, "Second, we need to get you some sort of security."

"Don't you think you're blowing this out of proportion?"

"Hell no I'm not! You don't know who you're messing with! I told you to leave it alone because I was afraid of the people who were telling *me* to leave it alone! Do you understand? This is no joke! You stepped on the wrong toes. If I don't protect you and something happens, I'd never be able to live with myself."

Nicole began to understand that he really was afraid for her. Maybe she did step on the wrong toes. "Okay, I'll skip court today. How about if I go home and lay low for a few days?"

"Now you're starting to make sense. I'm not messing around, Nic, you're messing with the wrong people, and they know you're behind the news story."

Nicole said very quietly, "There may be more news stories."

"Oh, for Christ's sake! My Lord, Nic, who did you tell?"

"I have contacts with all three networks, and they're all starting to work on this story."

"Go home and lock your doors *now*! I'll get you security!"

Angry at her for disobeying him and afraid for himself, Skip went back to his own office and called the Essex County sheriff, who assured him he'd station an officer outside Nicole's house. Then he called Chris to let him know what was going on and told him that the sheriff would provide her with twenty-four-hour security until he felt she no longer needed it.

Chris couldn't believe what he was hearing. He knew Nic's job always involved an element of danger, but not to this degree.

"Skip, I'll hire my own security to make sure she's safe. I don't want to interfere, but this is my Nicole we're speaking about, and I can't allow anything to happen to her."

"I get it, Chris. Just let me know what you need. I wanted to make sure you knew what was going on. Have you watched the news today, by any chance?"

"No, and don't tell me it's on the news."

"There's a story about how drug dealers are taking over the parks. Guess where they got that. I tried to tell her to stay out of it, but you know Nic. If she thinks she can help someone, she'll do whatever it takes."

"She told me a little last night, but I never thought she'd get the media involved."

Chris called the foreman at the Jersey City site and asked what kind of security he could get to protect Nicole. Then he called Suze, who immediately went to Nicole's place to persuade her to stay at Chris' house, which had an alarm.

Within an hour, five guys that were so big they made Giuseppe look like a tiny guy were in Chris' office, all of them dressed in black suits and wearing earpieces. Chris told them what he knew. He wasn't sure who was threatening Nicole, but he didn't want anyone near her, not even Essex County sheriff personnel.

"We got this, boss. No one will get close to her."

"I'm assuming you guys are licensed to carry."

"Of course."

When they left, he realized he'd been so focused on her security, he hadn't spoken to Nicole since he'd gotten the call from Skip.

"Hey, Nic, where are you? I heard from Skip what's going on."

Nic was trying so hard to hold back tears, she couldn't talk.

"You'll be okay. Suze is heading over to bring you to my place. I'll meet you there. I love you, and I got you. You'll be okay, I promise."

"Thank you, Chris. I'm really scared this time."

"I know. I'll be with you in less than an hour."

Chris told Robin what was going on and asked her not to bother him unless there was an emergency.

When he got to his house, he looked around for an Essex County sheriff's car, but didn't see one. He grabbed Nicole and held her while the security guys checked out the garage. Then he introduced her to the five men and told her the one called Jeff was in charge. She gave them each a hug in gratitude.

Chris went outside to call Skip. "I am at my home with Nicole. Where's the security you set up? Didn't you say the Essex County sheriff was sending somebody? Something is wrong with this picture, and I'll find out who's after Nicole for doing her fucking job. I got my own security, so you can tell the sheriff we don't need his help."

Chapter 27

Gee was in a great mood. He'd worked out his problem with Lisa and would introduce her to his parents. His mother couldn't believe her ears.

"Yes, of course! I'll make a big dinner. Oh, Giuseppe, I'm so happy, and I'll make sure your father is on his best behavior."

"Yeah, good luck with that, Mom." And for the first time in years, they laughed together. His father had been right. He'd needed to grow up, and he felt he had, but he knew his father didn't want him working for the mob, and doubted he'd ever come around.

He wouldn't let that bother him today. Lisa was working, so he texted her about having dinner with his parents, then went to Victor's office and waited for him to get off the phone. He didn't like the look on Victor's face. He was writing things down and kept repeating "Okay" to whoever he was talking to.

"We got a problem."

"Now what?"

"Your cousin strikes again! Actually, not your cousin—his freaking girlfriend, the prosecutor. Somebody wants her dead and they want us to do it."

"Wait... Nicole? She's the nicest person you'll ever meet."

"Yeah, well, she stepped on somebody's toes, and she's in very big trouble."

"Come on, Victor, we can't do that. She's—"

"Are you telling me what we can and cannot do?"

"No, sir, I'm just saying she's a cool person. What did she do?"

"She's trying to clean up Branch Brook Park, and one of the cops down there doesn't like it. He's making quite a bit of money keeping that park the way it is. It's the same guy who asked us to burn the Second Precinct. We have to keep peace with him. He's our main guy down there."

Gee didn't say a word, but he was thinking this was going to kill Chris. If he got involved in it, he'd be in a real predicament with everyone, including Lisa. "Victor, I'm begging you, please keep me out of this one. I want nothing to do with it."

"Kid, we don't get to pick and choose our jobs around here. I get why you don't want to be involved, but if you're my right-hand man, you will be involved. You understand me? You do what I tell you, now and always."

Gee knew Victor wasn't messing around. He went back to his office to think, then realized he was too on edge and needed something to do, so he went to work collecting and supplying. As he was driving around, he decided to swing past Chris' house to see if there was any activity going on. Three black Chevy Suburbans with the windows blacked out were in the driveway. A guy sitting in one of them saw Gee's car and walked up to him. Gee didn't need to let anyone know he'd been there and sped down the road with his heart in his throat.

That night at Lisa's house, he was very quiet.

"Okay," she said. "What's going on with you?"

"What...? Nothin'."

"Come on, Gee, something's up with you. You are not yourself, and you're not talking to me."

"I got a lot on my mind."

"Can you share, or is this something I don't need to know?"

"Oh, trust me on this one, you do not want to know."

"Are you in danger?"

"No, it's not me in danger this time. And please, that's all I can say for now. I'm trying to be open with you, but as I told you, some things I can't talk about."

"Okay, just know I'm here if you need me to listen."

He leaned over and kissed her. He needed to contact Chris without Victor finding out. He'd have to cross the line between what was right and what he was ordered to do. Victor had lower-end guys in the business all over the place, and Gee wasn't sure who they all were. He had to be very careful. Lisa was already back to reading the book she'd started.

"Hey, you got your phone on you?"

"Y-e-s, why?"

"I need to make a call with it."

"Why don't you use your own?"

"Come on, if I could, I would. Can I just use it for one minute?"

"Sure."

She watched him pace the room. "Suze, it's me, Gee."

"What a fucking weird day! Why the fuck are you calling me?"

"Suze, I know we have some crap to work out, but I don't have time for that right now. Just listen. Is Chris near you?"

"I'm not fucking telling you anything." And she hung up.

He screamed at the phone, "Motherfucker!"

He called her again. "Suze, don't fucking hang up. Listen to me." She hung up again.

Chris and Nicole had been sitting beside her.

"Gee's telling me to listen to him. I'm not listening to a word that asshole has to say! We're in the middle of a crisis here and I don't need him to complicate things."

"Wait," Chris said. "Giuseppe is reaching out to you now?"

"Yes, that's who keeps calling me."

Chris grabbed the phone out of her hand and looked at the number. It wasn't Gee's. The phone rang again, and he answered. "Gee?"

"Yes, it's me. We need to talk."

"Now is not a good time. I got something going down here that needs my full attention."

"I know all about what you're dealing with, which is why I'm telling you we need to talk. We need to go where we played every Sunday when we were kids. Do you understand me? Do not say where, just know I'll be there tomorrow morning at six." He hung up and deleted Suze's number from the phone memory.

Every Sunday, Chris, Suze, and their parents had gone to Gee's parents' house for lunch. Then they'd watch football or go swimming. Chris and Gee always played in the basement, while Suze helped in the kitchen. Chris knew he had to go to his uncle and aunt's house to meet Gee. He told Suze and Nicole, and they agreed that Gee must know something.

That morning, Chris felt better when he looked out the window and saw Suburbans parked all over his property and a guy was sitting on a lawn chair by the back door. He told Jeff he wanted an escort when he went to meet Gee.

He knew how to get into his uncle's basement without going through the house. The bodyguard followed him.

Gee was sitting on a stool by the work bench. "What the fuck...? You brought security?"

"Yup! I have no idea what you're up to, and as I said on the phone, I got a lot of shit going on."

"I'm not talking to you with your bodyguard here."

Chris told the guy to wait outside.

"Okay," Gee said, "what I'm about to tell you could get me killed, so that's why I have to be secretive. I hear Nicole is in trouble."

"Yeah."

"Victor got instructions to wipe her out. When I told him we couldn't do that, he was all over me about picking and choosing my jobs. I tried to explain the type of person she is, and he didn't care at all. Someone in the police department is making the order, and he could not refuse whoever this cop is."

"What the fuck! Nic is scared out of her mind. See this bodyguard I have with me? There are four others at my house with her. She feels like a prisoner! She didn't do anything but her fucking job. This is insane!"

"I know, but she pushed someone's buttons down there, and they want her gone. I mean, like dead gone! We have to figure out a plan to stop this from happening."

"Like you and me together?"

"Yeah, like you and me together, like we always did. We can figure out the other shit later. Deal?"

"I agree. What's the plan?"

"I'm not sure yet. I want to find out more so we can all three stay alive. Give me a day or two and we'll speak again."

"Okay." Chris gave Gee a hug before he left.

When Chris got back, Suze and Nic were drinking coffee at the kitchen table. "What did the asshole have to say?"

"You gotta stop that, Suze. He's helping us. Forget the other shit for right now."

Nicole asked, "What did he say?"

"He said someone from the Newark police department has ordered a hit on you. Someone there is very connected with Victor, and when Gee said he couldn't do it, Victor went off on him. Gee's trying to get more information so we can come up with a plan to keep you safe."

"Oh my God! A cop ordered me dead?! I thought that only happened in the movies."

Suze grabbed her. "Don't worry, Chris won't let anything happen to you."

"That's right, you're safe. We just have to make sure you stay that way. You need to lay low for a bit."

"Okay, I'm not moving from this house unless you're with me."

Suze said she'd stay with Nicole while Chris went to work.

When Robin saw him step off the elevator, she ran up to him. "Is she okay?"

"Not really, she's scared out of her mind and so am I."

He decided to reach out to the detective who had helped him with the investigation into his building fire. They agreed to meet at a place called Top's Diner.

Detective Franco still felt bad that he hadn't been able to get more evidence about the fire, so he was glad to help.

Chris said, "This is a very sticky situation."

"O-K-A-Y..."

"My fiancée's life is being threatened, and the threat is coming from someone in your department."

"That's an extreme accusation. Why do you think so?"

"I'm going to be completely straight with you, and I pray this doesn't bite me in the ass. I got this information from my cousin, who's connected to the mob. A cop in your division ordered my cousin's boss to have her killed."

"You mean one of the detectives?"

"I'm not sure, but this individual works in the Second Precinct."

"It's hard for me to believe someone in my precinct would do that. Why do you believe your cousin?"

"Because he's putting his own life on the line by telling me everything he knows. He's trying to get more information, and when he does, I want to have my contacts lined up. Is it okay with you that I consider you on my side?"

Franco said he couldn't believe Chris' story, but he agreed to help. He watched Chris leave and saw his security guy open the door and walk him to a blacked-out Suburban, which made him take Chris' story seriously. Chris was never a showy type of guy and would never have security with him unless he was in danger. Now he doubted all his co-workers. He'd gone through the police academy with a bunch of them, but he wasn't especially close to anyone except his wife, Mayte, who was a lieutenant in the department.

He went straight to her office and closed the door. She looked up from her computer. "Oh, this must be big."

"I got a story for you." He told her he hadn't thought much of Chris' story until he saw him with a bodyguard. He believed something big was going on, and he trusted no one until he figured out what it was.

"Holy shit, this is crazy!" she said. "You'd better be careful. We know everyone in the precinct isn't on the up-and-up. I could think of a few people who could be connected to the mob or taking paybacks."

They narrowed it down to three cops they thought were most likely to have mob connections. Franco went down to see one of his buddies in the evidence storage department, where every piece of evidence was kept under lock and key.

"Hey, Paul, how's it going down here in the dungeon?"

"Pretty good, Franco. How's things by you?"

"Can't complain! Hey, I need the evidence we have on the arson fire of that new building I was working on."

"Sure, no problem. Do you know the case file number by any chance?"

"I do."

When Paul gave him the box, he opened it, then looked up. "Where's the rest?"

"What do you mean? That's all we have."

"No, I logged in more stuff myself. Has anyone signed this case out?"

Paul checked his computer. "Looks like Bio took it out December 13th last year."

Lieutenant Alfredo Bio's brother was an attorney who represented a number of mob families. Franco couldn't believe how obvious it was. He signed out the box and went to his office, where he pulled everything out and laid it on a long table. Half of the evidence he'd logged in was missing.

He had to tell someone he could trust higher up the ranks. Lieutenant Detective Brian Stevens was a friend, so he called and asked him to come over to his office. He told him Chris' story and showed him that the evidence was missing.

Lieutenant Stevens called Chris and told him they'd help. They knew who was involved from the precinct but couldn't tell him yet. "All I want you to do, Mr. Yacenda, is to keep Nicole safe. Tomorrow, I'll contact you again to tell you the plan."

"I hired my own security for Nicole. She's doing okay for now."

"Great. I'll be in touch tomorrow."

***

Gee was in his office counting the money from the drug dealers when he heard Victor on the phone. "Okay, well where is she? Okay, when you find out where she is, let me know and I'll take care of it."

Gee knew that if Victor found out he'd talked to Chris, he'd be as good as dead. He had to play it cool and go along with whatever Victor said. He took the money he'd just counted into Victor's office and handed it to him along with the ledger. Victor put the money into his safe as he did every day, then sat down.

"Is there anything you need me to do today?"

"Not yet. I know you don't want anything to do with your cousin's fiancée situation, but I hope you know that sometimes we have to do things we don't want to."

"Victor, you know I'm not the killing type. I have no problem keeping guys in line for you, but killing is not something I can do."

Victor got up and slammed his door shut. "Did I fucking ask you to kill anyone, Gee?"

"No, Victor, I—"

"So shut the fuck up about killing people! You never know who's listening."

"Okay, you're right, I'm sorry."

"As long as I'm in charge, I won't ask you to kill anyone. You're my right-hand man, and we don't do that. We have other people do it."

"Oh, okay, boss."

"The person we need to take care of is in hiding somewhere and we don't know where. The cop who ordered the hit has people looking for her, and as soon as they find her, I'll have to order it."

"Okay, boss. Who is this guy ordering the hit?"

"It's Bio."

"Bio, as in the attorney we go to for everything?"

"His brother, Alfredo, the cop, has been making a lot of money with some of the dealers in Branch Brook, and he doesn't want anyone messing that up, including us."

"Since when do we take orders from him? That was our area before I even started working with you."

"This guy keeps us out of a lot of trouble, so we owe him. He's the one who destroyed the evidence on the fire we lit. He warns us about different things going down on the police side and keeps us out of a lot of shit. He's got our backs, so we have to take care of him. And if he needs someone out of the picture, we take them out, no questions asked."

Gee had planned to take Lisa out to dinner that night, but when he pulled up at her place, her car wasn't there, and when he called her cell phone, it went to voicemail. Then he noticed that he'd missed a call from her. She'd left a message apologizing. She had to cover for a nurse who called in sick and wouldn't be free until the next day. He texted her not to worry.

He needed to get in touch with Chris, but he couldn't use his phone, so he drove to a store and picked up a couple burner phones.

"Chris, can you talk?"

"Yeah."

"I got more information. The cop's name for the hit order is Alfredo Bio. His brother is the lawyer we use for everything."

"That makes sense." Chris was on the couch and Nicole was lying across his lap, asleep. She woke up when she heard his voice. "I gotta tell you something too. I reached out to one of the cops who I trust, Detective Franco. He's going to contact me again tomorrow with what he can find out at the precinct."

"Chris, you went to the *cops*? What the fuck is wrong with you? What did we agree to this morning? We, and only we, are going to come up with a plan. I'm in as much danger as Nicole, and if anyone figures out I'm talking to you, I'm a fucking dead man."

"I know, Gee, but I trust this guy, and I think we may need to include someone in law enforcement. No offense, but I don't completely trust you since we stopped talking over a year ago. You work for the guys looking to kill Nicole. I need someone else involved. I'm sorry if that pisses you off, but I don't give a shit because this is Nicole's life I'm talking about. You would do the same thing if someone was trying to kill someone you loved and you didn't work for the fucking mob."

"Chris, I'm risking my life, you can trust me on this one."

"I do, but I needed reassurance, so I called Franco."

"Okay, I get it. Let me know what he says about Bio. You'll see I am not fucking around here. I'm trying to help you and Nicole."

"Okay, I'll call you tomorrow."

"No, I'll call you when I'm somewhere safe."

When Chris told Nicole that Bio put the hit out on her, she said, "I knew it! I kept wondering who down there could hate me that much. He's up to something no good in Branch Brook, Chris. I knew it was him."

"Well, now that we know, we need to keep it between just us. I'm pretty sure Franco is a good cop, but I'll find out what he has to say tomorrow."

Suze rolled around the corner rubbing her eyes from a nap. "What are we keeping to ourselves?"

"We found out which cop put the hit out."

"Who is it?"

"It's a lieutenant named Alfredo Bio," Nicole said, "and he is such a scumbag."

"Maybe we should just kill him."

"What is wrong with you, Suze? We do not kill anyone."

"Just kidding... Not really."

Chapter 28

Chris woke up to find Nicole staring at the ceiling, so he rolled over and asked her if she'd slept at all. She said she had, but he knew she was lying. Then he headed out with one of the bodyguards to meet Detective Franco.

"What did you find out?"

"I am not at liberty to share that information with you yet."

Chris looked him in the eye, stood up, and started to walk out.

"Okay, wait, come back here."

"I'm not fucking around, Detective. I told you my cousin was connected, which should have been enough to prove that I'm not worried about anyone but Nicole."

"Okay, it's one of the lieutenants."

Chris got up and started to walk out again.

"Okay, wait, I'll tell you. It's Lieutenant Alfredo Bio."

"Yeah, that's the name I got, so I guess we are all on the same page. What are we going to do now? What's the plan?"

"I talked to two other cops whom I trust with my life. One is my wife, and the other is the godfather to my first born. We're thinking of using my wife as a decoy to look like Nicole and take them down. We just have to figure out a way to make sure Bio is there so we can take him down too."

"I like that plan. That could work."

"We know what Nicole looks like, and my wife has the same body shape, but she has brown hair, so she'll have to wear a wig. We think if Nicole's boss lets everyone know she's coming back to work on a certain day, that will get the ball rolling on their side, and we'll be ready for the hit to take place in front of the Essex County prosecutor's offices in the Veteran's Building. I'm sure if Bio hears she's coming out of hiding and going back to clean up the park, he'll be so pissed, he'll come watch the hit go down. We'll take the mob hitman and Bio down at the same time."

"I like this plan a lot. Nicole will be locked up at my house with the bodyguards while you all do what you do to get this prick."

"Tell Nicole to call Skip today and let him know she's coming back to the office on Thursday, the day after tomorrow. That gives him time to spread the news that she's still on her Branch Brook crusade."

"Okay, I'm on it. When will we talk again?"

"My wife will have to stay at your house for a night so she can leave from there that morning. She's done this a few times, so she knows what she's doing. She'll give you a call tonight to confirm everything. The lieutenant and I are putting together a team of people we trust. We'll all be at your house tomorrow night to go over everything."

"Okay, and thank you, Detective Franco. I knew I could trust you."

"Please stop calling me Detective, call me Frank."

"Okay, Frank, I'll see you tomorrow night at my house."

Chris left feeling positive. On the way home, he called Skip and told him he needed to see him, and they made a date for later that night. Now he had to wait for Gee to call so he could fill him in. Back at the house, he told Suze and Nicole what was happening, and Nicole took her first deep breath in days.

"Skip's coming over tonight. We need him to spread the word that you'll be back in the office and that you're still working on the Branch Brook clean up. They want that asshole Bio to show up to watch the hit go down so they can arrest him on the spot. They have a lot of evidence against him already."

Nicole jumped into Chris' arms and kissed his face all over. "What would I do without you?"

"You'll never find out. I love you, and this is almost over."

"You did good, my brother," Suze said. "You did really good."

"Hey, let's wait for this to be done. Then we can celebrate."

Chris went outside to tell Jeff to let Skip into the house when he arrived. When his phone went off, he knew it was Gee, who was relieved when he heard the plan, especially because it didn't involve him.

Nicole greeted Skip at the door and started to cry, thinking how angry she'd been at him for trying to protect her.

When Skip left, Chris led Nicole to the bedroom, removed her clothes, spread a towel over the bed, and asked her to lie face down. He wanted to give her a relaxing massage, and as she was falling asleep, he whispered in her ear, "If anything ever happened to you, I don't know if I could live anymore." But she was sound asleep.

Chris went to work the next day while Nicole stayed in with all the blinds closed and security guys patrolling outside. She knew if she called her parents, they'd be so worried they might interfere with the plan, so she tried to keep busy at her computer.

Meanwhile, Skip told everyone in the office that Nicole would be back the next day and pretended to be angry that she insisted on pursuing her Branch Brook Park crusade.

Then Lieutenant Alfredo Bio called him. "Yes, Lieutenant, what can I do for you?"

"What's this shit about our girl coming back to work tomorrow?"

"I tried to get her to stop her damn crusade, but so far, she won't listen."

"She's making a very unhealthy decision."

"Lieutenant, I swear I tried, but the woman has a strong will."

"Aren't you her fucking boss?"

"I am, but I can't do any more than I have."

"That's too bad for her." He slammed the phone down.

At the Second Precinct, Franco kept an eye on Bio and put a tap on his desk phone, so he heard the conversation with Skip.

Now that they knew Bio was the dirty cop, they needed to get their chief in the loop. When Brian told him what they knew and what they were planning, he was totally on board.

"Victor, it's Bio."

"Yeah, what's up?"

"I got word that our girl is coming back to work tomorrow."

"Okay, we'll take care of this tomorrow morning as she goes to work."

"Perfect, my friend. I was thinking of putting that bullet into her head myself."

"Do you really want to do that?"

"Yeah, I think I do."

"That could get very tricky for all of us."

"I don't give a fuck! I want that bitch and her rich fucking boyfriend to know who they're dealing with!"

"Okay, Bio. Be at my office at the port tomorrow morning at eight, and I'll have one of my guys drive you to the Veteran's Building."

Listening to Bio's conversation with Victor, Franco thought the plan was falling into place nicely. He knew Bio was stupid enough to kill Nicole himself and took the recording to the chief.

Chris was too nervous to accomplish anything at his office, so he headed home around noon. Just as he was pulling into his driveway, his phone rang from a number he didn't recognize, but he answered it, knowing it was Gee.

"I just heard Victor call one of the captains from the other side of Newark, and about fifteen minutes before that, I heard him talking to Bio. It sounds like Bio wants to do the hit himself."

"What? Really? That's crazy!"

"No, that's stupid! So many things can go wrong, and he'll be square in the middle of it."

"Good, that fucking prick should rot in jail."

"He just might, brother." It had been a long time since Gee had called Chris "brother," and it felt great. "You're not involved with this, right?"

"No, I already told Victor I couldn't do it, and if he didn't like that, too fucking bad." Gee would never have talked to Victor like that, but he wanted Chris to think he had some control over what he did.

"Okay, I'll talk to you sometime tomorrow."

"Cool, and stay safe, bro."

"You too, Gee."

When Chris got home, the security guys were still in place, and Nicole was in the kitchen, baking. "What the heck are you doing?"

"I'm trying to keep busy so I don't go nuts!"

"Too late for that," he joked with her.

She threw a handful of cookie dough at him, and as they cleaned it off the floor, he filled her in. Franco's wife, Mayte, arrived with an overnight bag, and when Chris let her in, he caught Franco flashing a thumbs-up sign as he drove off.

"Damn, dude, this is some house," she said.

"Thank you! If you keep Nicole safe, you can come here anytime you want."

"That sounds like a deal."

"Nicole is making cookies, so I'll show you to your room. Come down once you settle in."

Chapter 29

That night, Chris and Nicole barely slept. Mayte was up early and talking on the phone downstairs. She wore a blonde wig and a bulletproof vest under a long dress coat. When Nicole came down and saw her, she laughed.

"I just have to look similar to you," Mayte said, "not an exact duplicate. Which I think is impossible since you are so beautiful."

"Oh, stop. You look great! I just don't think I'll be wearing a wig any time soon!"

"We're all set. I'll leave at 8:45 to go to your office. Skip has made it known to everyone you were coming back to work today. This will keep all your colleague upstairs in your office."

"Mayte, how do I ever thank you for doing this?"

"No thanks needed. I'm doing my job, and I want Bio out of our precinct as soon as possible." She poured herself another cup of coffee and ate a few more of Nicole's cookies.

Meanwhile, Victor's captain was ready to drive to the Essex County prosecutor's office, but Bio was late, and Victor was getting pissed. He finally arrived in his Porsche and slammed on the brakes.

"For God's sake, Bio, why don't you just hang a fucking flag out and tell everyone what you're about to do! You're a fucking idiot."

Bio laughed and got into the captain's car.

At 8:45, Mayte called Franco for the third time that morning. She'd drive Nicole's car, then Brian would pick up her trail and follow her to the office. The chief already had five undercover cops from another precinct outside the Veteran's Building, dressed in business suits. One was drinking coffee at the corner. Two were pretending to discuss a case, and the other two were at a food truck with Franco.

As he drove to the building, the mob captain didn't say a word. He didn't trust cops, good or bad. He pulled into the first spot he could find. "Get me closer," Bio barked.

The captain didn't like being told what to do by a cop. "Get out here! I'll meet you in front of the building, and you'll get in after you take care of this hit. Then we'll calmly drive away."

"You're a fucking prick, you know that?" Bio said as he got out of the car.

"Fuck you, cop." The captain drove toward the front of the building, then decided to leave the cop there for calling him a prick and headed back to Victor's office.

Franco saw Bio and told the food truck guy to blow his horn, signaling the other undercover cops. Mayte pulled up to a spot in front of the building marked for Nicole. Brian drove past her and parked next to Nicole's car. Mayte nodded as he got out of his car, then went around to the trunk and pretended to be searching for something.

Bio saw what he thought was Nicole and started walking in her direction. Mayte saw his gun pointed straight at her from the side of the building, waited a few seconds, and then dove into the back seat as Bio let off a shot. Franco was already out of the food truck yelling at Bio not to move. He and the other cops formed a line beside Franco, all their guns pointing at Bio.

"Bio, throw your gun down! Don't be stupid. Put your gun down!" Franco ordered.

Bio thought he could make a run for it, but the captain's car was nowhere in sight. He spun around so his gun pointed straight out, and the line of cops moved closer. Franco yelled, "It's over, Bio. Put your gun down now!"

Bio turned the gun on himself. Mayte crouched by the car and pointed her gun at him, yelling, "Bio, you don't have the guts to shoot yourself, so put your gun down!"

Bio recognized her voice and realized she wasn't Nicole. Now he knew he was screwed, so he tried to talk his way out of it. "You fucking assholes, can't you see I'm on the job? I'm protecting one of the judges. I'm not putting my gun down until you do, and that's an order."

"Like fuck you are!" Mayte yelled. "This is your last chance, Bio. Put your gun down."

Franco lowered his gun to make Bio look at him, and the other cops wrestled Bio to the ground, took his gun, and handcuffed him.

"It's all over, Bio," Franco said. "I'm reading you your Miranda rights, so listen up."

Mayte flipped off the wig. "Maybe you should keep that for later," Franco said, grinning.

On the way back to the precinct, he called Chris and Nicole. Chris asked about the guy who drove Bio, but Franco told him no one from the mob showed up, which meant Gee was completely out of it.

He hung up the phone and held Nicole, both of them sobbing with relief.

"Thank God this is over," Suze said. "Can we please *not* do this again? Let's stick to construction."

"I agree totally! You know who we have to thank for giving us the heads-up on this? Gee. He came through for us."

"Yeah, I guess I'll have to give him a little more slack."

"Okay, now we need to let your parents know what happened."

Nicole was in no hurry, but she knew she needed to call them. As she headed up the stairs to make the call, Suze grabbed Chris by the arm and told him he had to get her to quit her job. It was way too dangerous. Any one of the criminals she put behind bars could get out and come after her.

"I agree," he said, "but I can't force her to do anything. I already asked her to work for us, but she was pissed I even suggested it."

"I'm going to suggest it again, now that all this shit's over with," Suze said.

Chris turned on the TV. It was all over the news. Luckily, it was described as a shoot-out involving a bad cop, and Nicole was never mentioned. He owed Franco and Mayte for that, but first, he wanted to thank Gee, so he texted him on his regular phone: "Hey, can we meet in that same spot tonight at seven?"

Ten minutes later, Gee answered: "Yeah, see you then."

He turned to Suze, who was beside him on the couch, and asked, "What do you think I could give Franco and Mayte as a thank you?"

"Expensive booze?" she suggested. "Don't all cops like to drink?"

Chris just shook his head. "Where do you come up with these ideas?"

Nicole came downstairs and handed her cell phone to Chris. "My parents want to hear from you that I'm okay."

He took the phone to the kitchen. "She's fine. I promised I'd never let anything happen to her, and I meant it. Nothing will happen to her if I can help it. She's tired, but she's not afraid to walk out the door."

"They want me to quit my job," Nicole said sadly.

"I have to agree with them, Nic," Suze said. "Let's just think about this for a minute. If one of those criminals got out of jail and decided to hurt you because you put them away, we wouldn't have any warning. Your name isn't a secret, and they could find you."

Chris thought Suze was making so much sense, he didn't have to say a word.

"This has me thinking the same thing," Nicole said. "My parents are really worried about me."

"I think we know someone who can find a spot in his company for a good attorney."

Chris said, "I need someone I can trust. I have a great group now, but I can use more, especially somebody as good-looking as you."

"It's not about looks, brother. It's about how much she can help us."

"I didn't mean—"

"I know exactly what you meant," Nicole said and kissed him passionately.

"Looks like it's my time to leave," Suze said.

This time, Gee wasn't waiting for Chris in his parents' basement, but at their kitchen table. Chris thanked him and hugged him, and for the first time since Atlantic City, they felt truly reconciled. They made plans to have Thanksgiving dinner with the whole family at Aunt Annette's and Uncle Mike's.

***

Michael, the new manager for the Blairstown complex, began dating Suze, and by the time Thanksgiving rolled around, he was invited to join the family for the traditional endless meal. Before they were all called to the table, Chris and Nicole watched the Westminster Dog Show on TV and tried to decide on a breed to add to their family. Gee was in the kitchen picking at the food, until his mother yelled, "Wait for it at the table!"

When they sat down, Uncle Mike was at the head of the table, as always, and John at the other end. They began with a traditional antipasto of cheeses, cured meats, roasted peppers, olives, stuffed peppers, and artichoke hearts.

"Hey, Gee," Chris teased. "Leave a little for the rest of us!"

"I didn't even start yet!"

"Don't you dare eat without saying grace," Maria warned.

The two moms sat down, made the sign of the cross, and thanked God for everyone sitting at the table, their good fortune, and the food they were about to devour.

Next came chicken soup with escarole and beans. "I'm full already!" Nicole said. "How can you people eat so much food?"

"It takes years of practice," John said. "We take breaks. This is an all-day meal."

Gee and Chris got up from the table and spread across the couches to watch football, both rooting for the Giants to win.

"You got any money on this game?" Gee asked Chris.

"Hell no. I work too hard for my money, unlike you!"

Gee threw a pillow at his cousin, but missed and knocked a picture off the wall.

"Knock it off, you two!" yelled Uncle Mike from the table.

"You two are like two little boys," Nicole said to them. Suze ran into the room and jumped onto Chris. "Oh my God, it runs in the family!"

An hour later, they were summoned back to the table for a third course of stuffed shells with meatballs and sausage and pork bones, and spaghetti *cacio e pepe*.

Then they retreated to the sofas again, while Uncle Mike carved the turkey. Annette was complaining her stuffing didn't turn out exactly how she wanted. Marie convinced her it was perfect. Lisa stood beside Gee with a drink in one hand, holding his with the other, amazed at all the food. Suze and Michael were sharing a kiss in front of Annette's already-decorated Christmas tree. Nicole was sound asleep on the couch, her head on Chris' shoulder. Then Annette called them back to the table. Chris pulled her up as she protested that she couldn't eat another thing.

They were together again as though Atlantic City had never happened, joking, drinking, and eating. The kids were adults now, paired off with significant others, their parents still yelling at them for being kids. Chris asked Gee to be in his wedding and Nicole asked Suze to be her maid of honor.

Plans were moving right along for the biggest event of their lives. Chris' complexes were up and making tons of money for himself and his investors. Gee was happy doing what he was doing, and with his life with Lisa. He'd learned to balance what he told her. Suze heard that Andi left Dan for another guy and that made her day. She was happy with Michael.

Annette and Mike, John and Marie played cards and talked quietly while the others slept on the couches. John picked up his glass. "To family," he said, and the others replied, "To family. *Salute.*"